"Nick..." Dacy hesitated, then threw caution to the winds. "Would you marry me now?"

She waited, hoping as only a fool would hope, knowing what he would say, but craving the tiny window of possibility the waiting opened to her.

"No." His whisper closed the window.

She cupped his cheek in her hand and smiled sadly up at him. Rising on tiptoe, she placed a gentle kiss on his lips. "Good night, Nick," she breathed against his mouth. "Thank you for the walk. Don't dream about me."

She left him standing on the rolling prairie, with the moon rising behind him in the east. Of one thing she was certain. Whether they were in love or not, she and Nick were connected *now*, not just in the past. Time alone would tell how strong those ties were....

Dear Reader,

Weddings, wives, fathers—and, of course, Moms—are in store this May from Silhouette Special Edition!

As popular author Susan Mallery demonstrates, Jill Bradford may be a *Part-Time Wife*, but she's also May's THAT SPECIAL WOMAN! She has quite a job ahead of her trying to tame a HOMETOWN HEARTBREAKER.

Also this month Leanne Banks tells a wonderful tale of an *Expectant Father*. In fact, this hero's instant fatherhood is anything but expected—as is finding his true love! Two new miniseries get under way this month. First up is the new series by Andrea Edwards, GREAT EXPECTATIONS. Three sisters and three promises of love—and it begins this month with *On Mother's Day*. Sweet Hope is the name of the town, and bells are ringing for some SWEET HOPE WEDDINGS in this new series by Amy Frazier. Don't miss book one, *New Bride in Town*. Rounding out the month is *Rainsinger* by Ruth Wind and Allison Hayes's debut book for Special Edition, *Marry Me, Now!*

I know you won't want to miss a minute of the month of May from Silhouette Special Edition. It's sure to put a spring in your step this springtime!

Sincerely,

Tara Gavin
Senior Editor

Please address questions and book requests to:
Silhouette Reader Service
U.S.: 3010 Walden Ave., P.O. Box 1325, Buffalo, NY 14269
Canadian: P.O. Box 609, Fort Erie, Ont. L2A 5X3

ALLISON HAYES

MARRY ME, NOW!

Published by Silhouette Books
America's Publisher of Contemporary Romance

With heartfelt thanks to my critique group—Nancy, Sonia, Barbara, Lucy and Lynn—for your generous help and support, given with patience, grace, humor and intelligence.

SILHOUETTE BOOKS

ISBN 0-373-24032-5

MARRY ME, NOW!

This edition published by arrangement with Harlequin Books S.A.

Printed in U.S.A.

ALLISON HAYES

writes romance novels as part of an elaborate procrastination scheme to avoid finishing her doctoral dissertation. She currently lives in Berkeley, California, with her husband and far too many books, romance and otherwise.

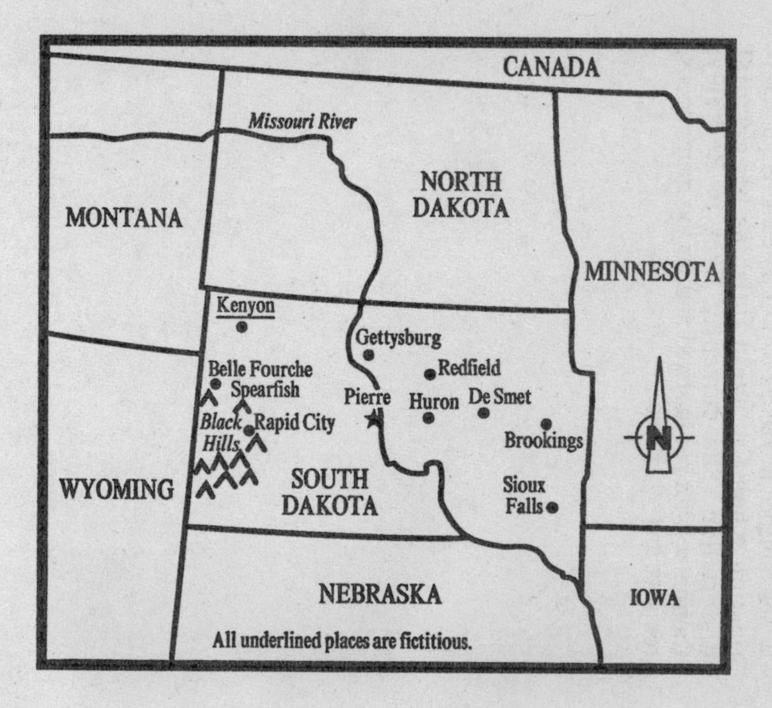
CANADA
Missouri River
MONTANA
NORTH
DAKOTA
MINNESOTA
Kenyon
Gettysburg
Redfield
Belle Fourche
Spearfish
Pierre
Huron
De Smet
Black
Hills
Rapid City
Brookings
N
WYOMING
SOUTH
DAKOTA
Sioux
Falls
NEBRASKA
IOWA
All underlined places are fictitious.

Chapter One

The sun slipped over the prairie's edge into a red-and-amber twilight as Dacy Fallon swung her feet out of the car. Her tennis shoes sank just a little into the damp ground. Stiff from four days on the road and drained by grief, she arched her back and took a deep breath. Soft, cool air, barely touched by the scent of spring earth and new grass, rushed into her lungs, deep, full and clean.

She held that breath against the tightness in her chest and the prickling threat of tears. At least this time the tears were of relief. Things would be okay, she told herself. She was home.

She was finally home again, where the lilacs would be blooming soon, white, deep purple and pale lavender. The passage of time hadn't diminished Dacy's knowledge of the rhythms of her grandmother's garden and her grandfather's fields. Now they would cast the tempo for her own life.

She walked through the lilac hedge that shielded the driveway from the old, two-story ranch house and stopped to look at the place. Gran had died eight years ago and the ranch had been sold. The house had been inhabited only intermittently since. Despite the evening shadows she could see that the shutters and porch sagged; the once-white paint had weathered to gray, and several shingles were missing from the roof. Yes, it was home, but it didn't look like it had when Dacy was a girl. It was too quiet, too still, and so dark.

And then, suddenly, it wasn't.

A burst of yellow light and the blast of an earsplitting electric guitar shot into the night. Dacy stared at the uncurtained dining room window; it took a moment for her to compose what she saw into a coherent picture. Riveted, she watched a young girl leap through the kitchen door and launch into an energetic dance routine, accompanied by a rock song that was probably audible in Belle Fourche, fifty miles to the south. Backlit by the light from the kitchen, the girl zipped back and forth across the empty room, stopping in between at an imaginary microphone to sing along.

Dacy smiled as she headed for the door.

Knowing she wouldn't be heard, she knocked, anyway. Then she lifted the old milk can beside the door. Sure enough, the key was still there, just as Jeff had said it would be. It wasn't necessary, though. The door was unlocked.

Inside, the music reverberated through the empty rooms. The floor shook with each bass note and Dacy's nerves didn't miss a single screaming guitar lick. She stepped from the entry into the dining room archway. The girl strutted in front of the fireplace, tossing her head from side to side, her whole body moving with the rapid beat. As she spun around, she caught sight of Dacy and came to an abrupt halt. Her mouth made an O. Recovering quickly, the girl skipped across the room and came to a stop in front of Dacy.

"Hi!" she shouted. Her sandy hair was caught up in a ponytail that bounced with every wiggle as she resumed bobbing to the music. She had an irresistible, open grin.

"Hi," Dacy hollered back.

"Who're you?"

"Dacy Fallon." The child couldn't possibly have heard her.

"I can't hear you!" She placed a hand on Dacy's arm and guided her back across the entryway and toward the living room.

"I'm Dacy Fallon," Dacy repeated. Loudly. "Who are you?"

"Jess. I live here now." She gave the empty, dusty room a disparaging glance.

Dacy paused uncertainly. She'd spoken to Jeff Reynolds, one of the brothers who now owned the old Fallon place, a few days ago. Unless she'd misunderstood, no one was supposed to be living here. What was more, Jeff had assured her that he and his brother would be more than pleased to take her money for the tumbledown house. Dacy had taken him at his word.

"Have you got a parent here with you?" Dacy finally shouted at Jess.

"Yeah, my dad's in the kitchen. Do you want to talk to him?"

"Yes, I would. And can you turn down that music?" Her throat was beginning to feel raw.

"Sure. Follow me!"

A few seconds later Jess hit the knob of the good-size portable stereo sitting on the floor by the kitchen door and the music volume dropped by seventy-five decibels. It was instantly replaced by a man's voice, every bit as loud.

"Jessica! I said to turn that damn thing down!"

A tall man moved rapidly through the doorway. One hand raked his hair and he glared down at Jess, not so much as glancing into the shadows where Dacy stood. He didn't flinch, either, even though he'd just bellowed loud enough for the cows across the state line in Montana to hear him.

It was just as well he didn't see her. Dacy's heart did a little flip-flop when she caught sight of the long black hair curling over his collar and recognized Jess's father. Nick Reynolds had grown up on the neighboring ranch and she'd spent every summer of her youth wishing he'd notice her—until he finally had. Dacy hadn't seen him since that memorable summer.

"But that's my song!" Jess shot back. "It has to be loud!"

"Not tonight, all right? The noise is upsetting the calves."

"And you! You're a grouch lately."

"You got that right," he grumbled, raking his hair again and looking back into the kitchen. "Amy! Get off the counter!"

Another child's voice answered. "I'm just looking for something besides cereal. I don't want cereal for dinner again. There has to be something else here."

"There isn't. I didn't have time to get into town today."

"I'm *sick* of cereal! This is the third day in a row! Oops!" There was a loud clatter, followed by a crash, a thump and a bleat of sorts.

Nick scrambled back into the kitchen. "Amy, I told you to get down! Now!"

Dacy followed Jess into the kitchen and saw a younger girl dressed in jeans and a blue sweatshirt vault down from the countertop. She glanced first at Jess and then Nick, who was now crouched on the floor beside a cardboard box that had been turned on its side and filled with blanket scraps.

"Did I hurt him, Dad?" Amy asked quietly. "I didn't mean to knock the pan over."

Nick sat and pulled a wriggling newborn calf into his lap. "He's not hurt. You just scared him a little, honey." His voice was soft now as he soothed the white-faced black calf. "Amy, please don't climb on anything in this house. I don't know what's solid and what's not."

Both girls went to their knees beside their father and petted the animal gently. Dacy watched them in silence. It had been more than fifteen years since she'd seen Nick, but she had no trouble recognizing him. She would have known that long black hair and those stormy gray eyes anywhere.

The years had wrought changes, though. He was bigger than she remembered, taller and broader through the shoulders, and there were lines in his face that he hadn't had at seventeen. If anything, he was better looking as a man than he had been in his youth, and that was saying a lot. At seventeen, Dacy couldn't have imagined anything nicer to look at than Nick Reynolds. But now, dressed in dusty jeans and a forest green corduroy shirt with the tails out, in his stocking feet with a struggling calf in his lap, he looked good. As tired as she was, Dacy was surprised she noticed. And she definitely noticed.

But then, with Nick, she always had.

After a bit, the calf settled down and Jess spoke. "His heart's not beating so fast now. He'll be okay. Hey, Dad. We have company." She bounded back to her feet and crossed the kitchen to Dacy's side. "This is Dacy Fallon. That's my dad, Nick."

"Dacy?" His eyes widened and he looked confused.

"Hi, Nick." She smiled tentatively. Once or twice on the drive out from New York she'd wondered how she'd feel seeing him again. Did he remember those July nights when they were seventeen? All of a sudden, she remembered them more vividly than she'd thought she ever could.

"Do you guys know each other?" Jess looked from one to another, waiting for an answer from either one.

Nick's mouth moved once but he didn't say anything. It was Dacy who finally spoke.

"We knew each other when we were kids," Dacy told them, pleased with the easy tone she affected. "This is my grandparents' house. I spent a lot of time here in the summers."

Nick found his tongue finally. "It's not your grandparents' house now," he said quietly, lifting the calf and placing it in the nest of blanket scraps in the box.

Dacy grew wary when he said that. "No," she agreed without emotion. "It isn't."

Nick rose and put a hand on Amy's shoulder. "I take it Jessica introduced herself. This is my second daughter, Amy."

"Hi." Amy walked forward and inspected Dacy carefully. She zeroed in on her ears. "My mom would like those earrings. Half a karat each, right? I thought so," she said when Dacy nodded. "My mother's really into diamonds. Did you know they're the hardest natural crystals on the earth?"

Dacy was a little disconcerted by this, but Nick saved her from replying. "Amy, please. The last thing I need now is to hear about Tammy's diamonds and your geology."

"Tammy's your wife?" Dacy couldn't help asking.

"Ex-wife." Nick draped an arm over Jessica's shoulder and pulled the girls toward him. "But that's ancient history. Haven't you kept up with gossip from the home front?"

She shook her head and gave him a small smile of apology.

"Too bad. That puts me at an advantage. I know all about you. Your aunts alternately worry and brag vocally about any and all Fallon kin." Nick's grin was tired, but knowing.

"Who are your aunts?" Jess wanted to know.

"There's a lot of them. Don't ask," Nick warned.

"Well, there aren't all that many of them that you probably know. There's my Aunt Reena and my Aunt Edna around here," Dacy said.

"That'd be Mrs. Berglund and Mrs. Colombe," Nick clarified for the girls.

"Oh, they're old," Amy said, leaning into her father, who frowned down at her. Then her eyes brightened and she looked back at Dacy with new interest. "Mrs. Colombe is Dani's mom. We like Dani a lot. Is she your cousin? She's teaching Jess to barrel race. But boy, you're right, Dad. Edna talks a lot about people we don't know."

Nick and Dacy both laughed. "Well, Dacy's one of those people she talks about. She's from New York, where she's an investment banker. She works too much, she's never married and she has a beautiful apartment she's too exhausted to enjoy. Oh, and she doesn't write enough letters and she loves Aunt Edna's blond brownies."

Dacy was impressed and a little scared by this recitation.

"And she also looks about as tired as I feel. I'd offer you a chair, but we don't have one, so I'll offer you the floor and the wall for your back."

"And you can have Cheerios for supper with us." Amy rolled her eyes, making clear her views on the menu.

"Right." Nick grimaced, releasing the girls and sliding to the floor. "Is there any pop left?" Jessica went to look in a paper bag on the floor by the back room door. Nick leaned back against a sagging cupboard door. "Please, Dacy, sit down. I don't mean to be rude, but I'm so beat I can't stand up another minute. What are you doing here after all these years?"

Dacy sat cross-legged on the floor, and Amy settled next to her. "Didn't Jeff tell you?"

"My brother Jeff?"

Dacy nodded.

"He hasn't mentioned you recently."

"I called your place last week and spoke to him. You were outside, but he said it was okay for me to come."

Both of Nick's hands raked into the already disheveled hair at his temples and he sighed loudly.

"Uncle Jeff was the last one in the house last Thursday," Jessica said, handing Dacy a cola.

"Yep," Nick agreed with another sigh. "He sure was. And Thursday evening the house burned."

Their house had burned. Now they were living in her grandparents' old house. That explained a few things.

"Oh, dear. What happened?" Inside, though, all Dacy could think was, *I have to have this house.* Dismayed by her selfish reaction, she remembered to ask, "Was anyone hurt?"

"We left some chili on the stove while we were out at the corral. The fire marshal said the wind must have blown the curtains down onto the stove. We were looking at a new horse Jeff got while we were gone. Nobody was in the house—" Nick began.

"Except Snap," Jess reminded him.

"He's our cat," Amy explained.

"But Snap's okay. He got out," Jess interrupted. "Nobody was hurt."

It was Amy's turn again. "We lost everything but the clothes in our overnight bags. They were in the truck because we just got back from Billings. Dad gave a seminar there."

"We lost everything else," Jess concluded with a big sigh.

Dacy looked at Nick, who had leaned his head back and was staring at the ceiling. "Everything?"

He brought his gaze back to hers and nodded slowly. "Everything."

"You're a long ways from a fire department," Dacy observed.

Three heads nodded in solemn agreement.

"At least the fire didn't spread farther than the house. Even the trees are still there. But the house is gone. Jeff moved into the bunkhouse," Nick said.

"So did Snap," Amy added.

"Since there wasn't room for the girls, we're camped here." Nick waved his arm toward the family room and Dacy leaned to look past him. Two camp beds with rumpled sleeping bags occupied one corner of the room along with two small suitcases and a couple of backpacks. A third sleeping bag lay heaped against the wall; next to it sat a pair of worn cowboy boots. "The neighbors have been good about supplying us with the basics. The church has collected clothes for all of us, too, when I can get to town to pick them up."

"Uncle Jeff must have forgot to tell you about Dacy calling," Amy said.

"Yep." Nick looked helplessly at Dacy. "What brings you back here after so long?"

Dacy glanced at the two girls, suddenly feeling as if she were going to cry again. It wasn't going to work—all her dreams had gone up in smoke with the Reynoldses' ranch house.

Nick didn't seem to notice her distress. "Unfortunately, it's kind of a bad time to stop by to check out the old homestead. We're not prepared for guests and it's nearly dark and there's a storm forecast. I wish you'd called first."

"We don't have a phone here, Dad," Amy reminded him.

"I *did* call. Last week." The words came out all in a rush. "Jeff told me where the key was and he told me to bring camping gear because he wasn't sure if there was any electricity or gas. He also said you guys would be relieved to have me take this place off your hands. I'm sorry, I had no idea about the fire. I wouldn't have come if—" She stopped. Thoughts of coming here had been all that had kept her going since Charlie had died. What else would she have done?

Nick frowned and leaned back against the counter, crossing his arms over his chest. "Wait a minute. You're saying you wanted to stay here?"

"Yes."

"For a week or two?"

"Well, no, actually." She paused. "I want to buy the house back and live here."

"Uh-oh," Jessica said. "Where are we going to live, Dad?"

"We're going to live right here, girls. Dacy, I'm sorry you came all the way out here to find this out, but this place isn't for sale."

"Jeff said it was. He said you needed to raise some cash."

Nick slammed his hand flat on the floor so abruptly that Dacy jumped. When he spoke his voice was tight, but controlled. "Girls, would you take that calf into the back room with the others? The bottles are warming on the stove and they need to be fed."

"Sure, Dad." Looking unconcerned by Nick's sudden burst of temper, Jessica pulled Amy up with her. Nick was silent while his daughters collected the calf and the bottles and maneuvered everything into the room off the kitchen that had held everything from a thirty-year-old deep freeze to deer antlers and old pop bottles when Dacy had been a girl.

Dacy watched Nick carefully. She remembered that he'd had an awful temper as a kid, and he obviously hadn't lost it. He was scowling like a bulldog now. The last thing she wanted was an argument.

The door banged shut behind Jessica and Amy. Nick looked Dacy in the eye. "I don't know what Jeff told you, and I'm sorry if he misled you. We've had some bad luck, not the least of which was our house burning last week, but we're managing. My family needs a home, and this is what we've got right here, run-down and dilapidated as it is. We need it. It's not for sale, even to a Fallon. Not even for you, Dacy." It was his first acknowledgment of the past. "I'm sorry."

She couldn't accept this. "Aren't you going to rebuild your own place?"

Nick's fingers zoomed through his hair again. "I don't know how long that'll take."

"Probably it could be done before next winter, and then you won't need this place anymore."

"Dacy, it's not that simple. There's a problem." He paused but didn't elaborate. "It could take longer than that. A lot longer. It might not even get done."

"Why not? It doesn't make any sense for you to live here. All your barns and corrals are at your place. There's nothing here but Grandpa's old shed. You tore all the outbuildings down years ago. This place is three miles farther from the highway than yours, and—" Her voice was taking on a sharp pitch and she stopped herself.

"Look, Dacy, I'm exhausted. I've been chasing down calves since before sunup and talking to insurance people since noon. There's a late-winter storm forecast for tonight and my daughters don't have enough clothes to get them through the week unless I can get time to go into town. This hasn't been the best week of my life, all right?" He looked straight at her and she saw a wild edge to his fatigue that checked her impulse to interrupt him. "This is a bad time to try talking me into selling you this dump."

She bristled when he called the house a dump, but she didn't say anything.

"Maybe you should go back to your job in New York." He used a gentler tone than she expected.

"I quit last week. On Friday. After I talked to Jeff."

"Damn." Nick reached to pick up the pan Amy had knocked to the floor earlier. He stood and tossed it into the sink where it landed with a clatter. "Well, I'm sorry, but you can't stay here. We need the house."

"I can't go back." She spoke almost in a whisper. She hadn't meant for him to hear the desperation in her voice, but it was too late.

Nick pivoted and stared at her for a long moment. Whatever he saw made him walk over and hunker down before her. When she didn't look any higher than his ankles, he tipped her chin up and searched her eyes. "What happened, Dace?"

She tried to get the words out, but they knotted up in her and nothing came—except the tears.

Nick looked away from her, but curved his hand under her jaw. The simple gesture was more than Dacy could take. She closed her eyes and the tears spilled.

"That bad, huh?" His sigh made his voice gravelly.

All she could do was nod. Nick released her chin and took her hand, sliding next to her against the wall. He held her hand, their forearms locked together and resting against his thigh. Dacy felt his solid warmth and the tears fell unchecked.

In the space of a few minutes her world had been thrown back into chaos. Coming home had been the center that had held her since Charlie's death, and now... she didn't think she could let it slide away so easily.

It was a while before she cried out the lump in her throat and could form any words. She wanted Nick to know why she needed to be here. If he knew, if she could make him understand why she needed this house, he might still sell it to her. "A friend of mine died," she whispered. "Three weeks ago. He had a heart attack while he was playing basketball and—" Her voice quit on her again and more tears slid down her cheeks.

Nick gripped her hand harder. "Shhh, it's all right," he said, and they sat awhile longer. But it wasn't all right, not for either of them, and they knew it.

Dacy stared up at the bare light bulb hanging from a frayed cord in the center of the room and tried to calm herself down by focusing on better times. Nick was right, the house was in bad shape now, but she remembered this room filled with people and good food and laughter. Fragments of memories flashed through her mind: Gran sitting on a stool beside the sink shelling peas while she listened to Dacy tell about the latest place her father had been stationed and her adventures in San Antonio or Cheyenne or Germany; her cousins Margie and Michelle racing in with the news that Jeff and Nicky Reynolds were mowing in the creek bottom alfalfa field, begging Gran for a jug of lemonade to take to them. And, once, when she was only seven or eight, she and Gran had made watermelon pickles in a crock that sat on the counter beside the flour tin. Every morning they had poured the thick golden pickling syrup into a saucepan and heated it until the vinegary fumes caught in Dacy's throat, making it hard to breathe. Then they'd poured the hot syrup back over the pickles in the crock and covered it with a towel. After two weeks, their ritual had yielded the sweetest, crunchiest watermelon pickles ever, and the memory of it had fed Dacy long after the pickles had made their last appearance on Gran's table.

Now the countertops were empty, cracked and peeling. Most of the cupboard doors hung crooked, and there was exposed wiring on the ceiling and running down the walls. All the paint on the walls, cupboards and ceilings was chipped and dirty. The vinyl flooring had buckled in front of the sink, evidence of water damage, and it was worn thin in other places. There was no telling how much damage years of neglect had wrought throughout the house.

How could she want to live here? It would take months to get it in shape, and it would cost a fortune, far more than the house itself would ever be worth. Yet she wanted to be here; she had to be here. She wanted to see this kitchen filled with family, friends and laughter again. In August, there should be watermelon pickles in a crock of vinegary syrup sitting next to a big canister of flour. If not this year, then the next. Maybe Nick and his daughters needed the house now, but she needed it for the rest of her life.

Somehow, she had to make him understand that.

Chapter Two

Nick sat quietly with Dacy for a few more minutes, waiting for her to tell him about her friend before the girls came back. When she didn't say anything for a long time he stole a look at her. Her eyes were closed again, so his look lingered. This close to her he could see tiny lines around her eyes that hadn't been there when she was seventeen and he'd been even closer.

She looked so pretty to him, just as she had then. Her features were nearly classic, though her eyes were a little too big and her mouth a little too small. He'd never minded and he didn't now, but he'd liked her hair better when they were kids. Then it had hung to the middle of her back, a thick auburn curtain that had glowed like dark fire in the sun. Now it was cut in a smooth, sophisticated shoulder-length style that turned under a little at the ends. It reminded him where she came from now.

She opened her eyes suddenly and caught him looking. She looked startled, almost flustered.

"Was it your boyfriend who had the heart attack?" he asked.

Dacy nodded and looked back at the floor. "Yes. Charlie was my best friend. When I first moved to New York we lived in the same building. He'd started his first job out of law school two weeks before I arrived, so he showed me the ropes. Sort of. More often, we figured things out together." She smiled at her memories and Nick felt as if he'd missed something he never knew he'd wanted. "We learned how to get promotions, impress our bosses and where to find the fastest Chinese delivery at two o'clock in the morning. We were such good friends. Then, a few years ago, something more happened. One night he kissed me, and then it was different between us. Now I miss him so much I don't even have words for what I feel."

"I'm sorry, Dace."

She met his gaze. "I need to be here now, Nick. At home."

He looked back at her, but didn't say anything. He didn't see how she could stay. He didn't think she understood what it would be like. Besides, he and the girls needed the house.

The door to the back room creaked open and Jess and Amy came back in, carrying the empty bottles. The calves stayed behind.

"What's wrong?" Jess asked immediately, taking in Dacy's tearstained face. "Dad?" She looked to Nick for reassurance.

"A close friend of Dacy's died recently."

Both girls made suitable remarks of condolence. Nick was proud of their manners. No one could tell that they were growing up in a household of boorish ranchers and cowboys without the benefit of a mother's instruction.

Then Amy got right to the heart of the matter and asked Dacy, "Are you going to stay here?"

Dacy glanced at Nick. He felt his mouth tighten in response to the determination in her eyes.

"Do you have a sleeping bag?" Jessica asked, ignoring his obvious disapproval.

"Yes. And a foam pad. Along with a lot of other camping gear. Jeff told me to be prepared to rough it," Dacy explained, shooting another glance at Nick.

He wasn't at all sure she should stay for even one night. "I suppose it's too late to go back to town tonight, but—"

Amy cut him off. "Did you bring any food?"

Damn! He could tell from the gleam in Dacy's eyes that she thought she'd won. For tonight.

"Yes," she answered, smiling. "A lot. Including chocolate-chip cookies, ice cream and pretzels. And a propane stove to cook the healthier stuff."

"All right! Can you cook better than my dad?" Amy's grin lit her small face.

"Anybody can cook better than Dad," Jessica said with tolerant disregard. "He can't even make microwave popcorn very well. Are you a good cook?"

Dacy smiled. "Pretty good. Cooking's one of my hobbies."

Nick frowned. "I suppose you've taken vacations to France and Italy to study with master chefs." It sounded like an indictment.

"Once or twice," she acceded.

He lifted his eyebrows in evident doubt about the merits of such behavior. "That's what I figured. You know, cooking for your friends in Manhattan isn't like cooking for ranch folks in South Dakota. We don't have adventuresome palates. Jessica hates onions and Amy won't touch anything with tomatoes in it. I hate herbs, especially tarragon and that Chinese parsley stuff. That's just the beginning of how picky we can be. There's a lot more stuff we don't like."

Dacy grinned at him. "Don't forget that my grandma taught me how to cook in this very kitchen. I may have dabbled in truffles and arugula, but I can still overcook a roast with the best of the ranch crowd. Do you girls like beef stew?"

Nick knew then that Dacy intended to stay even if she had to make hamburgers and hot dogs with potato chips, beans and Kool-Aid into eternity.

"Yeah," Jessica said. "As long as there's no onions."

"Or tomatoes," Amy said. "I'll help bring stuff in from your car. Is it open?"

"Hold on a minute." Nick was losing control of the situation. "Just bring in enough for tonight. There's no sense unloading everything."

But nobody was listening. Dacy and the girls were already on their way out the door. Nick reluctantly pulled on his boots and followed them, intent on making sure they didn't unload every bit of Dacy's gear. It wouldn't do to have her get too settled. The last thing he needed now was to have to worry about dislodging a determined-to-stay city woman, Dacy Fallon or not.

It was best to be clear from the beginning that he didn't have room in his house for city women who would stay for a while and then get bored, or tired of ranch life, and leave. The girls' mother, Tammy, had done just that. And given that he and Dacy were single, healthy and had a history together, he'd only be fooling himself if he thought they wouldn't eventually get more involved than was smart. He didn't need any more disasters in his life. She couldn't stay, and that was all there was to it.

Supper was definitely better than cereal. Dacy had crammed her brand-new four-wheel drive with dishes, silverware and more camping gear than a troop of Scouts could use in a month. Dacy even made a separate little pan of stew without onions for Jessica. As they ate, the girls chattered constantly to Dacy, telling her about school, 4-H and all the things they had lost in the fire. It made Nick sick to listen to the litany of their destroyed possessions. He didn't know how he was ever going to replace even a fraction of it if he couldn't get the insurance fracas sorted out. Thinking about his discussion that afternoon with Roy Holloway, the claims adjustor from his insurance company, made him so angry he knew he needed to work off a little steam before he started shouting again.

Dropping his bowl in the sink, Nick excused himself. "I'm going out for a smoke. You girls help Dacy clean up."

"Dad." Jessica's voice held a reprimand. "You aren't supposed to smoke. You'll leave us orphans if you do."

"Tough." He reached for a well-worn black felt Stetson and crammed it down around his ears, then grabbed a heavy denim jacket lined with fleece.

"But you went through all that work to quit," Amy pleaded. "Don't start again, Daddy, please. We don't want you to die."

Nick growled and stomped out the door, rattling the glass when he pulled it shut behind him.

He headed for the shed, the only outbuilding on the place. The wind had shifted to due north and it was already ten degrees colder than it had been when they'd unloaded Dacy's car. Half the night sky was dark with clouds and in the remaining half the stars glittered cold with the promised return of winter. Nick hoped the storm wouldn't be too bad. They'd already had higher than normal stock losses because of the late, cold spring, and they were fast reaching the point where he and Jeff were going to have to be visiting Marv Petersen at the bank to talk about a loan. Since Nick had a pretty good idea how that conversation would end up, he wasn't looking forward to it.

When he reached the shed he pulled the door open against the wind and flipped on the single light bulb. His fingers wrapped around the pack of cigarettes he kept in his coat pocket for emergencies and in scant seconds, he had a match cupped to his face. The smell of sulfur from the match made him smile, but when he inhaled the first drag it didn't taste as good as he thought it should. He took a couple more drags, then tossed the cigarette to the earthen floor and ground it out with his toe. Stupid kids. Someone should have taught them to respect their elders better, he thought morosely.

Eyeing the pile of wood and the ax he'd had one of his hands drop off earlier in the day, Nick stripped off his coat and picked up the ax. It would be cold tonight, and the only heat in the house was the old wood stove in the kitchen. He might as well do something useful with his pent-up frustration.

Dacy got things cleaned up from supper, a bed organized for herself next to the girls, and Jessica and Amy settled in their makeshift beds with books and a camping lantern. Then she went looking for Nick.

The light from the shed window drew her. Once she rounded the corner and was sheltered from the wind, she could hear the rhythmic thwack of an ax biting into wood. Pulling the door open carefully, she was instantly transported to her childhood by the earthy smell of the shed. The dirt floor, decades worth of spilled engine oil, the remains of barn swallow nests and heaven only knew how many hidden mice and other creatures created a dense, dusty funk that made Dacy miss her grandpa fiercely. He had spent a lot of time puttering in this shed, and she had spent hours hovering and chattering while he worked on a tractor or pickup, or, occasionally, when he fired up the old forge and put on his heavy smithing apron to repair horseshoes.

She watched Nick for a minute, admiring the spare, fluid motion of his arms and back as he brought the ax smoothly through a thick piece of hardwood. Then she slipped inside.

"Hi," she called softly.

Nick turned and lodged the ax in the chopping block when he saw her. He didn't say anything as he wiped his face and neck with a bandanna and leaned back against an old sawhorse.

"I didn't mean to upset you so much," Dacy began, not sure how to convince him that she needed to stay here.

Nick lifted a hand to his forehead and combed the hair back. "It isn't just you, believe me. Things are a mess right now. How were those calves?"

"I think they're fine. Why are they in the house?"

"One of their mothers died, and the other two wouldn't accept the calves. It happens sometimes. Eventually we'll probably be able to match them up with cows that have lost calves, but it's too cold tonight to leave them out. Those little guys and a few that Jeff has over at the bunkhouse are the last of this year's calves. It's been a hard spring."

"It sounds like more than just the calving's been hard."

"Yeah."

Dacy had a lot of experience with short answers from ranchers so she wasn't discouraged by Nick's one-syllable reply. "And you're thinking I'm just one more thing."

"Pretty much."

That was three syllables—better. "You're wrong about that." The way he arched his eyebrows let her know he didn't agree, but she went on. "I can help you out. I can cook. I could get the house in better order. I can drive the girls where they need to go and—"

"In your brand-new, fully loaded Suburban," he said with a trace of irritation.

"Yes," she agreed. "That bothers you?"

"It's not the car," Nick conceded. "You're pretty well set financially, aren't you?"

She nodded, recognizing that somehow her financial success made him feel less of a man in the face of his own troubles. "That makes you uncomfortable."

"Yeah, it does a little. Thanks for the offer, Dacy, but I don't want any help. I need to handle things myself."

"I'm not offering to help you as my good deed for the day. I need to be here now, Nick. Here, at my grandpa and grandma's, in the house where my dad was born. I'll do whatever I can to help if you'll let me, but I have to be here."

"Staying here wouldn't be like what you think it would. Have you got any idea how much time, effort and money it'll take to get that house livable?" He gestured toward the house with his chin.

"Yes, I do, and I have enough of each to handle it. And I don't think you know what I'm thinking it will be like to live here."

Nick set his arms across his chest and scowled. "Why do you *need* to be here? It's a completely different way of living than you're used to. The climate is lousy. Your neighbors would mostly be a bunch of redneck ranchers. You'll end up bored and lonely and wishing you were back in Manhattan."

"I doubt it. I never liked Manhattan all that much."

"Then why'd you stay there for ten years?" Nick challenged.

She'd wondered herself. "Because of the job. And Charlie. I liked it at first. It was exciting and I felt powerful. After a couple of years, though, I didn't like it as much. It seemed pointless, like playing a game I didn't care about. But I didn't know what else to do."

Nick wasn't giving up. "What about your friends? You'll miss them."

Dacy stepped farther into the shed and ran her hand over the ax handle. "I don't have a lot of friends in New York. I worked too much and so did everyone else I met.

Charlie was the only close friend I had and he's gone." She tugged on the ax handle but it didn't budge. "Both of us had been talking for years about leaving, but we never seemed to get around to it. And now he's gone and it's too late for him." She glanced up at Nick. "I don't want it to be too late for me. I *want* a different kind of life. I want friends, maybe a family. I want to have a garden and walk by the creek looking for animal tracks. I want to live here. Now."

Nick's eyes were fixed on the ax handle in her hand and his voice sounded tired. "You want a vacation, Dacy. Why don't you go to one of those dude ranches in Montana or Wyoming for a month and get this back-to-your-ranch-roots thing out of your system."

"Don't condescend to me, Nick," she said quietly. "I know what I'm feeling and I know what I need. Both of us are tired now. Maybe we should talk about this in the morning."

"I don't have time in the morning, and I don't think there's anything to talk about, except what time you'll be leaving. Like I said before, I'm sorry, Dacy, but I need the house."

"It's a big house, Nick. Let me stay and I'll help any way I can. There'd be a lot I could do."

He shook his head in frustration. "No. Are you listening to me?"

"Why are you so set against my saying?"

"I don't need any distractions right now." The way his eyes roamed over her gave her to understand that he meant personal types of distraction.

"I'm a distraction?"

He moved off the sawhorse and stood close to her. Too close. Not as close as she suddenly wanted him to be. "Yeah. You could become a distraction."

Dacy's nerve endings tingled as they hadn't in years. "I don't have to be."

Nick was so tired he was reckless. He put his hands on her waist. "No?"

Her lips parted but she only shook her head.

"Do you remember how hot we were for each other when we were kids?"

Dacy nodded. That same fire was licking around the places his hands touched her now, right through her jacket.

"Do you think that's changed?" His voice was low and rough with fatigue, or maybe something else.

It hadn't for her, but she wasn't bold enough to say it. "We've changed. That was a long time ago. Seventeen years."

His hands tightened and he urged her a fraction closer. "Yes, we've changed. We've grown up. We've made very different lives for ourselves. But my body is reacting to you the way it did when I was seventeen. Part of my growing up, though, means that I think before I follow my hormones into hell."

Dacy recognized a certain wisdom in that, and a fair amount of bitterness. She didn't have anything to say about it at the moment.

Nick continued, his gray eyes never leaving hers. "I don't have time for you now but I'm still attracted to you and I think you may be to me, too. Things are tough right now, and I don't want you to get hurt. I don't want to get hurt, either. We're different people and we don't belong in the same world anymore."

Then he leaned forward and kissed her gently. Soft and full, his mouth feathered over hers and instinctively Dacy parted her lips. Nick's opened, too, and for a second she was aware of the space of his mouth, of his tongue, not yet come forth to explore hers.

The promise inherent in the light kiss sent a tremor through her, and Nick felt it. Gathering her into his arms, he dipped his tongue into her mouth and slowly, softly, thoroughly kissed her. Then he set her firmly away from him.

"Here," he said, "put your arms out."

Automatically, she did as he instructed, her whole insides spinning. Nick crouched down and began piling chopped wood into her outstretched arms. "It's a good thing you came out. Now I won't have to make two trips to get the wood in."

Dacy regained her equilibrium quickly. "This is just one more thing I can do to help. If you'll let me."

Their eyes met but he kept his expression empty. He didn't say a word as he filled her arms with wood.

A sharp crack woke Dacy out of a sound sleep. Instantly alert, she sat up in her sleeping bag. Lights were sweeping erratically across the room from the outside windows. A hard hand in the middle of her chest pushed her flat on her back.

"Everyone stay down," Nick ordered.

"That was a shotgun blast!" Dacy had gone hunting enough times with her father to recognize the noise.

"Girls, get your shoes and coats on fast and stay low." Nick was already pulling jeans and boots on over his thermals.

Dacy could hear a truck engine revving outside and the lights seemed to be running in a circle.

"What's going on?" she asked as she pulled on her jacket.

"We've got company." Nick grunted as he tugged on a boot. "Drunk company, if I don't miss my guess."

"I bet it's Cliff Tally and his buddies. He's such a creep," Jessica said. "Can we look?"

Before Nick could stop them, both Jessica and Amy raced through the back room door. Dacy heard the calves crying and the door glass rattling as it was flung open.

"Jessica! Amy! Get back here!" Nick lunged after them with Dacy on his heels. The calves were milling in front of the outside door and Nick shoved them aside to open the door. One managed to squeeze through the door after him, though Dacy slammed the door behind her before the other two could escape.

Nick swore as he tried to grab the calf, which skittered away from him and off the porch into the yard. There, a large black pickup with spotlights over the cab was circling in the grass. Two or three young men in feed caps and down vests were in the cab or hanging out of it, whooping and hollering. The cold wind and the truck engine drowned out most of what they were shouting, but there was no mistaking their belligerence.

When the calf scampered across the path of the pickup's lights, the truck braked so hard it rocked heavily. In the next instant the driver's door popped open and a young man leaned out with a rifle in hand, sighting the calf through the open window. The rifle cracked and the calf tore off into the darkness.

"It's Cliff," Jessica said as Dacy watched in horror. She didn't think he'd hit the calf, but it was too dark to tell. "What a jerk!"

As soon as he saw the man aim at the calf, Nick took off for the truck at a dead run. Cliff Tally was still peering into the darkness, his friends razzing him about being a bad shot, when the rifle was ripped out of his hands and sent flying. Before he knew what was happening, Nick had pulled Cliff bodily out of the cab and slammed him up against the side of the bed. Nick must have broken Cliff's eardrums because Dacy and the girls heard every word he said despite the wind.

"What the hell are you doing out here?" Nick slammed Cliff, who was as tall as Nick and looked heavier, into the truck again. "Haven't you got better things to do than booze up and ride around raising hell?"

"Hey! Let go of Cliffie!" The two men in the cab appeared to be trying to untangle their legs and come to Cliff's aid.

Nick ignored them and continued bellowing right in Cliff's face. "Are you having fun, Cliffie? Was it fun to wake up two little girls in the middle of the night showing what a big, tough, hotshot you are? What a man! Did you have fun shooting at a two-day-old calf?"

Cliff shouted right back at Nick. "Yeah, Reynolds, I did! And I'm going to have more fun shootin' every one of your stinking hormone-free calves raised on your friggin' environmentalist-approved ranch! What are you going to do about it?" He shoved hard against Nick, but barely budged him.

The men in the pickup had sorted themselves out and were moving toward Nick and Cliff.

"Get away from my buddy, Reynolds," one of them shouted.

"That's Kootch Koehler and Ricky Brent," Jessica told Dacy. "They usually follow Cliff's lead. Uncle Jeff says all they ever learned from raising sheep was how to act stupid."

Nick was yelling back at the younger men and seemed to have stopped them by the sheer force of his fury, but Dacy didn't like the odds in the situation. She doubted things would stop at a verbal battle. Her glance darted to Jessica and Amy, both of whom were watching wide-eyed. Jessica didn't seem scared, but Amy looked upset. "Has your dad got a shotgun or a rifle here?"

Before she'd finished speaking, Amy was running around the side of the house toward Nick's pickup. In less than a minute she was back on the porch, panting, with a .12 gauge Winchester pump and a box of shells.

Dacy reached for the shotgun and scooped up a couple of shells as she stepped off the porch. She'd never in her life been glad her dad had made her learn to handle guns, but now she sent up a brief prayer of thanks and a plea for luck. Her father's voice echoed in her head and she heard him telling her she should never pick up a weapon unless she was prepared to use it. Nonetheless, she was going for a bluff now.

The men ignored her approach, even when she stopped no more than six feet away from them. The lights from the pickup were blinding, and sleet was starting to fall in stinging darts driven by the wind.

Dacy slid the shells into their cells and pumped one into the chamber.

Chapter Three

The wind died suddenly and the ominous thunk of the pump action got everyone's attention. In the ensuing silence, Dacy shouted as loud as she could.

"All of you, stop it, now!"

Eloquent it wasn't, but backed up by the loaded shotgun, it was effective.

Nick immediately released Cliff and patted down each of the younger men, searching for weapons. When he was satisfied they weren't carrying anything dangerous, he looked into the pickup cab and pulled out a shotgun.

"You boys get on home and try not to hit anybody on your way. I'm going to be talking to the sheriff, and I'll leave your weapons at the courthouse whenever I get into town. If any of you pulls a stunt like this again, you're going to be mighty sorry."

Cliff wasn't graceful in defeat. "What are you going to do, sic your girlfriend on us?" He gave Dacy a rapid, insulting appraisal and shrugged. "Maybe next time we'll come prepared, now that we know you've got someone more interesting than those brats of yours around—"

Cliff didn't get the opportunity to finish whatever he'd been going to say because Nick's fist connected solidly with his jaw.

"Geez!" Cliff bellowed, clapping a hand to his face.

"Get out of here! Now!" Nick pushed Kootch and Ricky into the cab and was reaching for Cliff when the younger man danced away from him.

"I'm going!" He hopped into the cab and slammed the door shut. "But you're the one who's going to be sorry, Reynolds, not me. Going to the national press was sneaky, but it ain't gonna save your damn ecological butt. We got our lives at stake here and if you think we ain't gonna fight your stupid ideas about how we ought to run our ranches, you are one wrong dude." He flung something out the window that fluttered to the ground. "Once the rest of the county gets a look at that, you and your brother might as well be Davy Crockett and Jim Bowie at the Alamo. So long, sucker."

Kootch and Ricky found this hilarious and began singing the theme song from Davy Crockett at the top of their lungs as Cliff slammed the pickup into gear and bounced off across the yard.

Dacy watched them for a minute, not sure they were going to find the road. When they did, she looked back at Nick. His jaw was set so hard she could have cracked walnuts on it.

"Here." He thrust the other shotgun into her free hand, which she realized was shaking with cold and reaction. "Leave the rifle. I don't care if it gets ruined. I'm going after the calf. Put the girls back to bed." He turned and started off into the sleet and darkness.

"Nick!" He stopped and looked back at her. "Do you have gloves? Your hands will freeze."

He looked confused for a second, then dipped a hand into his pocket. "Yeah," he called over the wind.

"Put them on," Dacy shouted back, and he did. Then he disappeared into the night.

She realized that Jessica and Amy were standing beside her, their flannel nightgowns flapping beneath their coats.

"What's this?" Amy asked, stooping to pick something up off the ground.

"Cliff threw it out of the pickup," Dacy said.

"It's a magazine," Amy answered.

"Hey!" Jessica exclaimed, making a grab for it. "Look, Amy, it's the new *Newsday*. The one Dad's in." She began rapidly paging through it.

"Let me see!" Amy insisted.

The sleet was starting to dampen their hair and the wind was icy. "Let's go inside," Dacy suggested, anxious to get the girls out of the storm and to get a look at the article Nick was in. She hoped it would explain what was going on. "You can see better with a light. Come on."

Jessica and Amy needed no further urging. Together, the three of them headed back to the house.

Nick had no idea what time it was as he trudged up the porch steps with the runaway calf in his arms, but he knew he was going to have to be up again and working a lot sooner than he wanted to be. The calf had run toward the creek, half a mile from the house, and then followed the banks a good mile and a half farther before it wore itself out and collapsed. Once he'd found the frightened, exhausted animal huddled underneath a scrubby juniper, he'd had to carry it back uphill through a driving mixture of sleet and snow. Both he and the calf were half-covered with mud and they were wet through. The calf was weak and shivering and Nick's ears felt as though they'd never be warm again. Somehow in the ruckus earlier, he'd forgotten his hat.

Pushing open the outside door, he saw a faint glow of light through the glass of the door into the kitchen. He saw that the calves and their boxes had been moved out of the back room. He looked into the kitchen, calf in arms, as quietly as he could.

Dacy was sitting in the director's chair she'd brought in and placed next to the stove, reading a magazine by lantern light. In her long flannel nightgown with a green cardigan over it, she looked at home, as if she really did belong here. Dressed practically, not in some silly, silky New York negligee, he could picture her waiting up for him on other nights, when animals were sick or equipment broke and had to be fixed before morning. He could also envision her waiting up for him wearing that silky negligee—in black, maybe—and that made him swallow hard. He quickly thrust the images and the warm emotions that accompanied them from his mind. She'd be leaving in a few hours because it was for the best. It was what he wanted. He turned the knob on the door and went in.

Her green eyes lifted when she heard the door. He saw both relief and welcome in her unguarded look and it stopped him in his tracks. He couldn't help feeling better just looking at her.

She was on her feet and moving to greet him. "Thank God, you're back," she said in a low voice. "I was getting worried. Is the calf okay?"

"He's weak." He glanced into the shadows on the far side of the room and saw the other calves in their boxes on the floor next to Jess's and Amy's camp beds. Both the girls and the calves were sound asleep. It was warm in the room and there was a faintly sweet, grassy smell that reminded him of summer. "I need to clean him up and dry him off. I'll feed him and get him warm."

Dacy hovered around him as he moved toward the stove, which was radiating warmth; then somehow she guided him into the chair. "Sit down and I'll get some towels."

Before she did, though, she poured a mug of something into a cup, stirred in a generous spoonful of honey and handed it to Nick.

"I could probably use something a little stronger," he whispered, afraid he'd rouse the girls.

"This is chamomile tea. It'll soothe you."

She glided over to a pile of bedding and towels and pulled out a couple of old, faded towels and wash rags. In her long nightgown, her feet disappeared completely. Sipping his tea, Nick wondered if maybe she wasn't an angel come to soothe and deliver him from chaos. She certainly seemed capable and kind, and she was lovely. On second thought, he decided, an angel wouldn't have such dark circles under her eyes. Only humans got as tired as Dacy looked and he felt.

When she brought the towels over, he set down his mug and they each took a washcloth, dipped it into the warm water heating in a basin on the wood stove and started washing opposite ends of the calf.

"He doesn't seem to mind this," Dacy commented.

"He wouldn't have the strength left to protest if he did." Nick stopped rubbing the calf for a minute to stretch his shoulders. He hadn't even taken off his coat yet. "I'd throttle Cliff Tally in a minute if I thought it would do any good. Some kids never grow up."

"Earl's his dad?" Dacy stroked the calf's head. He closed his eyes and leaned into her hands. "Aren't they our neighbors on the north?"

Nick noted her habitual use of "our," but he only grunted assent and went back to drying. He'd like to be the calf, he thought, having Dacy rub a warm washcloth all over him, too. But that was dangerous thinking. Damn, he was so tired, he just couldn't control where his mind wandered.

"I remember Earl," she continued. "My dad always called him a punk. I seem to remember Earl's dad and

Grandpa had an ongoing dispute over Grandpa's forest service lease on the buttes and that Earl continued the feud when his dad died."

"Earl still wants that land, worse than ever, now that Jeff and I have it. My dad took over the lease when he bought your grandfather's place, and we've kept it."

"And you're trying out some of the new range management techniques and trying to restore the streamside environment along Badger Creek."

Nick smiled a little. "I see you found the magazine Cliff tossed at me."

"Amy did." She scratched the calf's ears and set the damp cloth aside before taking up a dry towel. "She and Jessica were thrilled to see that article on new ranching that featured you. They were so proud and excited I think they forgot all about Cliff and his friends. Jessica read the whole thing out loud."

"They may not be so excited when they realize how some of our neighbors will react," Nick said quietly. "The Tallys aren't the only folks around here who think Jeff and I are traitors to our heritage and a threat to everyone's livelihood."

"I don't understand what's happening at all," Dacy said. "The magazine article made it sound like you and Jeff are heroes. If you can make a living without using hormones, pesticides and herbicides, why wouldn't everyone jump on the bandwagon?"

Nick chuckled low and soft. "You've got a lot to learn about ranchers, for all that you come from a ranching family." He switched his wet cloth for a dry one and began to rub the calf more briskly. "A lot of these new ideas for different range management and farming techniques are threatening. Most folks around here have been running their farms and ranches with the same mind-set for the past hundred or more years. That mind-set has put high crop yields and animal weights as the top priority, because that's how folks made money. If pesticides, herbicides, fertilizers, growth hormones and antibiotics helped make money, a lot of folks never questioned their value. So guys like me go off to get Ivy League degrees and come back telling our parents and our neighbors that they've been doing things wrong all their lives.

"I think they sometimes feel like we're trying to tell folks who love and value the land that their grazing programs are destroying it. We tell them they should change their attitude about their relationship to their work, their homes, their livelihoods. They're mad that anybody's criticizing what they've done. Mostly, though, they're afraid they're going to lose everything they've worked for, and folks out here have worked hard. All their lives they've seen other hardworking people lose everything because of the economy, the weather or just plain bad luck. They don't want to have a thing to do with anything that seems like it might lessen their chances of survival."

"I guess I can understand that." Dacy stood, placing one hand on Nick's thigh for balance.

He felt it like a brand, the heat streaking up his leg, but he didn't take his eyes off the calf.

"It seems like you understand your neighbors pretty well," she said.

"I understand, but I don't agree with a lot of their ideas. Still, I can't force any of them to change. I just wish they'd lay off Jeff and me and let us do our ranching our way." Then he grinned. "Well, I do have to admit that I wish some of them would at least listen to us."

Dacy smiled back at him. "Oh, I almost forgot—Jessica fixed a bottle for the calf before she went to sleep." She reached past Nick to the back of the stove. Her arm brushed his shoulder, and he wondered if she was touching him in these little ways on purpose. Or was she that unaware of him? "Why don't you let me hold him now so you can take off that damp coat and get yourself dry and warm?''

He was definitely getting warm, he thought as he stared dumbly at her. She was waiting for him to get up and hand her the calf.

"The soup pot is full of warm water if you want it,'' she added helpfully.

Looking up into her pale green eyes, the words just popped out of his mouth. ''Will you help me get clean and dry like you did the calf?''

Dacy's cheeks flushed a little and her lips parted. She considered him for a moment and her pupils widened. ''If you want,'' she finally offered.

Nick stood and handed her the calf. In the process the back of his hand brushed her breast. It was so soft beneath the flannel. He closed his eyes and tilted his head back, fighting not to leave his hand where it was, trapped between her breast and the calf. Retrieving it, he sighed. ''Maybe that's not such a good idea.''

"Maybe not,'' she agreed. Then she sat and gave the calf the bottle. ''But nothing untoward is going to happen with your daughters and three calves for company.'' She smiled faintly.

"Don't underestimate my ingenuity, Dacy,'' he warned. ''Remember there's a pickup parked out in the yard.''

Her eyes met his in a startled gaze. ''We aren't kids anymore.''

''No, we sure aren't.''

''The only reason we're talking like this is because we're so tired.''

He nodded slowly. ''I believe you're right about that.'' Shrugging his jacket off finally, he draped it on a corner of her chair and gently caught her jaw in his hand. ''Why didn't you marry Charlie, Dace?''

She pulled away from him and stared down at the calf, which suddenly seemed to fascinate her. After a long moment she spoke softly. "We were friends for so long, first, you know. We were used to that. I had my apartment. He had his. We didn't need to be in each other's pockets."

"Didn't need to be or didn't want to be?" He could tell she didn't want to talk about this.

"Both."

He barely heard her. "It doesn't sound very passionate."

"I loved Charlie."

He backed off. "I know, Dace. I can hear it in your voice. I just wondered."

She sighed. "Maybe I'm not a very passionate person."

"That's not strictly true, as I recall."

She knew exactly what he was talking about. "But we were too young."

"We were old enough to know we wanted to be together."

Her expression grew sad. "Yes, we knew, but I'm not sorry my dad took me away that summer. I was furious at the time, and I missed you for years, but I'm glad I went to college. I'm glad you did. Aren't you? Aren't you glad you have Jessica and Amy? Would you have had things be different?"

"Some things, yes." When she drew her eyebrows together and frowned, he sighed. "I'm not sure which things, though. Tammy hurt me and the girls pretty bad. It took us a long time to get over it." He paused.

"What happened?"

"I'm too tired to go into it now. Call me sometime and I'll give you the gory details. But you're right about one thing. I wouldn't trade my girls for anything. Not even a profitable ranch, a nice new house and cooperative neighbors."

"I thought you said the ranch was doing okay."

His long fingers combed into the hair at his right temple, brushing it back, before he caught himself self-consciously. "We're not sunk yet, but that is mostly pride talking. Things are rough right now. We can't seem to find a steady market for our beef. We've also had high losses among our breeding herd this past year and a half. It's been a run of bad luck. Storms at the wrong times, calf scours, stuff like that. A good wet year wouldn't hurt us a bit, either, and now we've had this fire. You know, Jeff's great with the animals and I know a hell of a lot about range management, but neither of us are good businessmen. That's the bottom line in ranching, and we're hurting."

Dacy looked thoughtful for a moment and then she yawned all the way down to her toes. The calf was asleep in her arms, still sucking on the empty bottle. Nick reached down to lift it from her lap. "Come on, you two. It's way past bedtime."

"What time are you getting up?"

"What time is it?"

She followed him across the room and sat down on her bed while he put the calf in a box with one of the others. She peered at a sleek little travel alarm on the floor beside her. "Three o'clock."

Nick grimaced. "I think I might sleep in a little. I won't get up until six."

"That's sleeping in?"

"Welcome to ranch life, Dacy Fallon."

"You're going to let me stay?" She perked up a bit.

He shook his head. "I don't think you should. We'll talk about it tomorrow." He reached out and took her hand in his. It was small but surprisingly strong. It was a hand that could handle a lot of work, he thought. And that could touch a man softly and sweetly if she wanted to. God, but he'd wanted her hands on him when he'd watched her rub that calf. "Thanks for waiting up. For helping. For listening."

"It was my pleasure. I always liked you, Nick Reynolds. I think I still do."

Leaning forward, he placed a gentle kiss on her forehead. " 'Night, Dacy. I like you, too."

"Good night, Nick."

He made a point not to look back at her as he stripped off his clothes, washed in the water she'd heated for him and crawled into bed. His last thought before he sank into exhausted slumber was that he really did know some of the things he'd have had different in the past. Dacy would have made a great partner if they'd gone ahead and gotten married when they'd finished high school.

Now, though, he couldn't lie to himself. There was no way in hell she'd ever be satisfied on a struggling ranch twenty-five miles from the nearest town, and that a backwater burg of 424 souls. Not now. Not after two college degrees and ten years in Manhattan making herself and a lot of other people rich. Like he'd told her, they were different people now, from different worlds, and they didn't belong together.

It was a damn shame, though. It truly was.

Dacy lay awake for a few minutes thinking, trying not to peep at Nick through her nearly closed eyelids and trying to turn her mind off. He needed her, in more ways than one, she realized. She'd envisioned herself alone on the prairies with her grief, slowly healing and building a new life, but she saw that she might just get what she needed in the midst of a chaotic, foundering family with more irons in the fire than they seemed able to manage.

Nick needed another partner in addition to his brother, she thought. That partner was her. She didn't know diddly about cattle, range management or surly neighbors armed with shotguns, but she knew how to cook and keep a house clean and pleasant. She knew how to organize, drive and be supportive. From what she could see, all these skills would come in handy around the Reynoldses.

Most of all, though, she knew business and she had plenty of capital and experience to invest—in exchange for a piece of the action. In this case, the action she wanted was her grandparents' house, and maybe part of the old ranch. She'd never dreamed of restoring the old house in order to share it with Nick and his daughters, but the idea had definite appeal. Like she'd told Nick earlier, it was a big house. There was more than enough room for all of them. Fixing it up and helping Nick would more than fill her time, keeping her mind off Charlie's death and her own unfulfilled and vague yearnings.

Besides, she thought, a smile curving her lips as she snuggled deeper into her sleeping bag, who knew what might happen? The possibilities seemed promising.

Chapter Four

By ten o'clock the next morning Dacy was leaning against the checkout counter in Char's Gas'n'Gitit in Kenyon, the tiny town that served as the Antelope County seat, trying to hand over a dollar for the cup of coffee in her hand.

"I'm not takin' your money, Dacy," Charlene Potter said, shaking her head. Not one of her graying, tightly permed curls moved, but her oversize glasses slid down her nose. She shot Dacy a stern look over the lavender rims. "Not one other day in your life will I refuse your money. Take advantage of it." Her brown eyes snapped as she pushed her glasses back up with one bright red fingernail. Then she slid a pastry across the counter. "Have a bear claw, too, dear. You look peaked." Char's glance darted past Dacy. "Look who's here now. Edna and Dani."

Dacy's Aunt Edna swept through the door with a gust of cold wind, with her cousin Dani right behind her. Both women were tall and blond, and both had cornflower blue eyes. In their jeans and warm denim jackets, their hair clipped back in barrettes, their cheeks pink from the wind, they were a striking pair. Dacy grinned, stuffed her change back in her pocket, deposited her coffee cup on the counter and turned to greet them.

"Dacy!" Aunt Edna exclaimed, enveloping her in a hug. "You look pale, honey. I'm sorry about your friend's death." She gave Dacy another squeeze. "But I'm glad to see you here. I was so surprised when you called this morning."

"I wasn't," Dani said. "Move, Mom. Let me give Dacy a hug." Edna released Dacy into Dani's arms. "When you called after Charlie died, I figured you'd be coming."

"How did you know?" Dacy asked when Dani released her.

Dani smiled. "I lived in New York, too. And when I was hurting, I came home. I knew you would."

"Family's a comfort during tough times," Char added. "You did the right thing coming here."

"Are you sure you won't come stay with us?" Edna asked. "We'd love to have you."

Dacy had explained on the phone where she was staying and why. "Thanks, Edna, but I want to stay at Grandma and Grandpa's place."

Edna gave her a careful smile and glanced at the copies of *Newsday* prominently displayed beside the counter. "Are you sure that's wise? It is Nick's place now, honey. Isn't being there a little awkward?"

"It is, a little. But I think it will work out." Dacy hoped she sounded more confident than she felt. Nick had asked her to leave again that morning, but when she'd volunteered to take the girls to school and pick up the clothes the church had gathered for them, he'd been hard-pressed to refuse her help. She had her foot in the door, and she was ready to thrust a shoulder in after it. "Nick needs some help after the fire, and I don't have anything else to do. Besides, I think he'll sell me the house."

"Was that your car I saw in front of the co-op half an hour ago? Brand new, big and red?" Dani asked, helping herself to a cup of coffee from the self-serve stand.

"Yeah. I asked the guys at the co-op to fill the propane tank. They'll be out this afternoon. Do any of you know someone who could come take a look at the furnace for me?" Dacy pulled a list out of her pocket and glanced at it.

"Chip Stiller, over at the implement shop," Char suggested.

"Great," Dacy said, scribbling down the name.

Dani chuckled. "What else have you been up to this morning?"

"I called the phone company to get some new lines installed. They have a truck up here today, so I lucked out. By tonight we should have gas and a phone. I need a plumber, too. I called Sears and ordered a washer, dryer, refrigerator and stove. They should be here tomorrow. And the electric co-op is sending someone out to check the wiring."

"Wow." Dani sipped her coffee. "You don't waste any time. Are you planning to renovate the whole house?"

"I'd like to," Dacy said. "I'd like to see it looking like it did when we were kids."

"Or better," Edna said dryly. "I imagine Nick has no idea what he's in for, does he?"

Dacy flashed her aunt a nervous smile. "He knows me."

"He *knew* you, dear."

"What you need is a general contractor," Char interrupted.

Dacy jumped on Char's comment. "You're right, I do. Do you know one?" Her pencil was poised over her list.

"Harley Widner. He does good work, he's reliable and he's my nephew," Char told her. "He's working down at the Boodle ranch this morning, about twenty miles south of town. You girls could drive out there and catch him before noon. He could use a big job that'll last through the summer, seeing how Donna's pregnant again."

"Harley Widner," Dacy repeated, jotting down the name. "What's his phone number, in case I miss him?"

Edna wouldn't let her alone. "You and Nick have already talked about this?"

Dacy grinned, but she also had the good grace to blush. "Nick doesn't know."

Three pairs of eyebrows rose in unison, and three chins inclined, silently questioning the wisdom of her actions.

"It'll be okay," Dacy assured them, picking up her coffee and taking a sip. "I made a career out of taking risks, and a pretty successful one at that. This is going to work out. Nick will sell me the house. I know he will."

"Either that, or you'll have sunk thousands of dollars into someone else's property," Char noted with a little shake of her head. "Not many folks can afford to do that."

"Dacy can. Financially, at least," Dani answered. Her eyes narrowed speculatively. "What do you think of Nick after all these years?" she asked a little too casually.

"Well, he seems stressed," Dacy replied, knowing that wasn't what Dani was asking about.

"He's a hunk," Char stated firmly. "And he was in love with you at one time. Is there any spark left?"

Dacy's cheeks warmed. "That was a long time ago. We were just kids. Everything's different now. I didn't even think of him . . . that way." It was a bald-faced lie, and she suspected the other women knew it.

"Mmm-hmm." Char's tone was indulgent. "Well, he could use a wife. Those girls of his need a mother, and a man as handsome as Nick Reynolds shouldn't go to waste." Char's gaze swung to Dani. "Neither should his brother, Jeff. No, siree. It's too bad those boys have scared everyone off with all their preaching about the environment. Two fine men like that remaining single all this time isn't natural, but it's their own fault. They're isolating themselves from their neighbors, and that isn't right."

Dani's mouth tightened a little. She looked as if she was going to make a comment, but the moment passed. Instead, she grinned at Dacy. "Come on, let's go see if we can find Harley Widner." She handed Char the money for her coffee and a couple of copies of *Newsday* and started for the door. "Do you have any other errands?"

"Oh, yes," Dacy answered, waving her list and following. She waved to her aunt and Char, ignoring the knowing look that passed between them. "'Bye. See you soon."

The wind had swept the parking lot clean of last night's snow, and the clouds were gone, leaving a clear, cool morning that felt more like winter than spring. Dacy had to hustle to keep up with her cousin's long-legged stride.

Dani slowed to hand her a *Newsday*. "I saw you looking at them."

"I already read it."

"It's good to have an extra copy around."

"Sure." Dacy accepted the magazine. "I can give it to Nick for the girls."

Dani's laughter was cut short when a black pickup pulled into Char's lot, going too fast and turning sharply into a parking space.

"Uh-oh." Dacy recognized the truck.

Cliff Tally launched himself out of the pickup. He took one look at them and squared his shoulders.

"Damn, he's going to come over." Dacy didn't want to talk to Cliff. She'd dropped his guns off at the courthouse right after she'd let Jessica and Amy off at school, and she didn't have a thing she wanted to say to him.

Cliff moved toward them with a fierce scowl on his ruddy face.

"Cliff!" A gruff male voice halted Cliff in his tracks. "Not now, son. Go get us some coffee." An older man, tall and ruddy-faced like Cliff, handed him a couple of big, insulated refill mugs. It was Earl Tally.

"Come on, Dad! That bitch pulled a shotgun on me!"

"Mind your manners, Cliff. Go on in." Earl spoke like an officer in an old war movie, all grit and nerve. An undisciplined kid like Cliff didn't stand a chance. He swore as he gave in, stalking over to the door and flinging it wide.

Earl watched him, shaking his head. Then he looked at Dacy.

He smiled at her. It was a smile that made the hair stand up on the back of Dacy's neck.

"What's going on?" Dani whispered.

"In a minute," Dacy whispered back.

Earl ambled across the parking lot toward them, taking his time. He was a big man, more than six feet tall, with a barrel chest and a steel gray crew cut. He wore the standard rancher's uniform of jeans, jacket, boots and feed cap, and an amiable expression as he approached. In fact, he looked almost conciliatory. That made Dacy wary.

"Howdy, girls." He nodded at Dani. "Your folks in town today?"

"My mother's inside," Dani responded. She was polite, but cool.

Earl turned his pale blue eyes on Dacy. "You must be one of Ed and Arlene's girls," he said. "I recognize your mother's red hair. Is it Dacy or Denise?"

"Dacy." It always amazed her that people here remembered her name—even people like Earl.

"Dacy," Earl repeated. "The one from New York?" He named the bank she'd worked for.

She nodded. Earl was fishing. She didn't tell him she'd quit.

Undeterred, he pressed on. "You were out at your grandparents' place last night with Nick Reynolds?"

The question was polite, but there was the slightest suggestion of impropriety in it. It wasn't, however, enough that she could call him on it without sounding as if she was guilty of something. Dacy began to appreciate that Earl wasn't the bull in the china shop his son was.

"I was there. The result of a misunderstanding." It was all she would give him.

"Ah," Earl said, nodding. "A misunderstanding. Well, at any rate, I'm sorry you were there when Cliff showed up. I apologize for any inconvenience he may have caused you."

"He showed up drunk, tearing around in that truck and firing weapons. There were children there, Mr. Tally. Cliff will be lucky if Nick doesn't press charges."

Earl chuckled. "Oh, there's no need to get riled. Cliff's young. He's kind of a hothead. Nick understands. He won't press charges."

Dacy was furious, but she controlled her tone. "It wasn't funny."

"I'm sure it wasn't, but it wasn't serious, either. In a couple of days, after he cools down, I'll send Cliff out to apologize. Sorry for the hassle." He turned to go.

Dacy reached out and caught his arm. "Mr. Tally, what Cliff did was illegal. He was driving while he was drunk. He was trespassing. He recklessly fired a weapon, nearly killing a calf and endangering people, including two little girls. He threatened Nick, and he threatened his property. I, for one, will not forget that. I suggest you get Cliff into alcohol treatment at the very least, and I would recommend a good course of therapy to help him deal with his aggression, as well."

Dani gave her a sharp elbow in the ribs.

Earl laughed again. "Would you now?" He slowly pulled out of her grasp. "Well, that's interesting." He laughed again. Then he took a step closer and got very quiet. When he spoke, his voice was tight. "This isn't New York, Dacy. You don't know how things work out here. Since we're making suggestions, *I* suggest *you* don't go sticking your nose into matters that aren't any of your concern. I would also suggest that you stay clear of those Reynolds boys. They're nothing but trouble. I don't know what you're doing out here, but I'll give you a little free advice. Don't set sail on a burning ship. You'll only end up going under with the rest of the crew. Now if you'll excuse me, I have business to attend to. Good day, ladies." Earl Tally wagged the bill of his cap at them and walked away.

"What the hell was that all about?" Dani asked as Earl retreated.

"Come on, let's get out of here." Dacy practically ran to the Suburban. "I'll tell you in the car."

On the road, Dacy explained what had happened the night before.

Dani shook her head when she was finished. "That doesn't sound good at all. If I were Nick, I'd press charges."

"He didn't even mention it," Dacy said.

"He's got a lot on his mind right now. You know, I've heard grumbling about Nick and Jeff, but nothing threatening. Not like what Earl was talking about."

"Last night was no joke," Dacy said. "And I think Earl means what he says. I've dealt with his type before."

"He's not going to like it at all when he finds out you want Nick to sell you the house. That would give Nick and Jeff some money. Earl's been waiting for years for them to bail out so he can get those leases and Badger Gulch. If you buy the house back, they may make it."

"Only if they'll sell it to me." Dacy was growing more hopeful that they would. "Listen, Dani. How do you think they'd react to a partnership offer? What if I offered to help them out now in exchange for the house later? Here's what I was thinking." She outlined the plan she'd concocted that morning.

Dani listened thoughtfully until Dacy was finished. "It would be to their advantage to take you up on it. Jeff will want to. He's pragmatic, and nothing could make him leave that ranch." Dacy thought she heard a certain frustration in her cousin's voice. "Nick will hate the idea."

"But will he accept it?"

"Probably. But, Dacy?" Dani's look was piercing. "Why are you doing this? It's crazy."

Dacy drove a few moments in silence. "I'm not sure. I feel like I have to be there. At Grandma and Grandpa's. It is crazy, but it feels like this is my last chance for—" She broke off and the tears started to well up again.

"For what?" Dani prodded gently.

"For the life I want." The tears flowed freely over her cheeks. "But I'm not even sure what I want."

Dani handed her a tissue from the box on the seat between them. "Here. You'd better pull over and let me drive if you're going to cry."

Dacy nodded and pulled onto the shoulder of the highway, scrubbing at her tears as she and Dani traded places.

The day had warmed considerably by late afternoon. The sun was out, last night's snow had melted and meadowlarks were trilling in the pastures. Nick was so exhausted that he slumped down in the pickup seat and tipped his Stetson forward over his face. Even if he couldn't sleep, it felt good to close his eyes for a minute. He let the jouncing ride over the rough gravel sway him as he listened to Jess and Amy chatter with his brother, Jeff, who was driving. He tried to hope Dacy Fallon would be long gone by the time they reached the house, but instead he felt a niggling anticipation at seeing her again. He frowned over his ambivalence.

"Thinking about that meeting with Roy?" Jeff asked. They had met with Roy Holloway, their insurance agent, again this morning, and the news had been bad. Very bad.

"Nope," Nick replied without opening his eyes. "Not until you mentioned it." A tight, churning knot in his solar plexus turned his frown into a grimace. "I was sure I paid that premium."

"It's not your fault," Jeff said, his tone easy. "We may not be the best businessmen in the world, but we pay our bills. It's got to be a computer glitch."

"We aren't going to get a new house, are we?" Jessica interrupted, leaning forward from the back seats.

"I don't know." Nick sighed. "Not right away."

"We can fix up the Fallon place, can't we?" Amy put one small hand on his shoulder, and he immediately raised his own hand to cover it reassuringly.

"We sure will, Tiger. Money's tight right now, but we'll do the best we can."

"I'll bet Dacy would us help out. I think she's rich, and she wants to fix up the house," Jess added. "It belonged to her grandparents. Did you know her dad was born there?"

"I know, Jess, but Dacy won't be here long. We'll fix the place up ourselves." His stomach dipped as they crested a hill and dropped quickly down the other side. The house would be in sight now, but he didn't open his eyes.

Jeff whistled a long, warning note. "I don't think you're going to get the chance."

Amy jerked her hand away from Nick and bounced against the back of the seat. "Wow," she breathed.

"Cool," Jess said. "We're getting a phone."

Nick opened his eyes and looked out from beneath the brim of his hat. The sight that greeted his gaze brought him ramrod straight in his seat.

In the gravel driveway and surrounding the house were an assortment of utility trucks and other vehicles. Smack in the middle of them sat Dacy's red Suburban. As Jeff turned into the drive, they passed Eddie Hicken, dressed in blue coveralls and a feed cap, filling the propane tank. Eddie waved laconically.

"Hi, Eddie," Amy called out the open window.

"That's Chip Stiller's black truck," Jeff noted cheerfully. "Looks like your furnace will be running soon."

Nick shot him a quelling glance. "What's she doing? This isn't her house!"

"In a way it is, Dad. Why are you so mad?" Jessica sounded irritated. "We *need* a phone."

Amy inventoried the rest of the trucks with maddening logic. "And propane, and the wiring looks dangerous, you told us that yourself. And lots of things need fixing. Harley can fix them."

Nick stared at the old blue pickup with Harley Widner, General Contractor, Kenyon, South Dakota stenciled in white letters on the door. Jeff pulled to a stop beside it. At that moment, Dacy stepped through the kitchen door, with Harley on her heels. She gestured toward the slumping back porch, and Harley busily jotted something in a notebook before reaching for the measuring tape at his belt.

Jeff reached across the seat and tried to grab his arm, but Nick was out the door before the engine had died.

Chapter Five

Dacy looked up when she heard the pickup door slam. Nick stalked across the yard toward her, anger radiating from him like a heat shimmer off the highway on an August afternoon. Adrenaline surged into her system, and she summoned the confident smile that had carried her through dicey negotiations in the world of high-stakes investment. This time, though, so much more than money was on the line.

"What the hell is going on here?" Nick bellowed. He came to a halt less than two feet from her, forcing her to tilt her head back to look at him.

For an instant, she wavered. Then she pushed herself past the moment of doubt. "Hello, Nick. You know Harley, don't you?" Her tone was relaxed and friendly, completely ignoring Nick's question and his anger.

Harley, a short, wiry man with laughing blue eyes, stuck out a hand. Nick took it by force of habit. "Hey, Nick."

Harley nodded to Dacy, explaining, "We went to school together. We're old pals."

"Harley, what are you doing here?" Nick wasn't going to be sidetracked.

"Dacy asked me to put in a bid on renovating this place. She said you and the girls are going to be living here now."

Nick turned to Dacy. "Why are you doing this?"

She was saved from answering when a tall, angular man with dusty brown hair and a warm smile joined them. "Hello, Dacy. It's been a while." He offered his hand and she took it gratefully.

"Hi, Jeff. It's good to see you again." Something in Jeff's gray eyes told her she had an ally. Dani had been right.

"Dacy, why are you still here?" Nick's eyes never left her.

Again, she didn't answer him directly. "Nick, I have a business proposition to make you."

"We don't have any business to discuss. I asked you to leave today." Nick raised a hand to rake through his hair and encountered the brim of his hat, instead. It went tumbling back over his shoulder, and he spun around to catch it.

Jeff caught the hat and Nick's attention. "I want to hear what she has in mind. This ranch is my business, too."

Two pairs of flinty eyes clashed for a long moment. Then Nick took a deep breath and released it slowly. "All right. I'll listen to what she has to say." He spoke to Jeff, then turned back to Dacy. "Here's your chance. Shoot."

Dacy was ready. "You know I want the house eventually, but I know you need a home for the girls now. Harley and the other guys tell me this place isn't safe. The wiring is dangerous. The pipes are held together with duct tape where they aren't broken. The floors in the kitchen and bathrooms are rotted through. That's only part of the damage. It will cost tens of thousands of dollars to renovate this house. It would be cheaper for you to rebuild over at your place."

"We can't do that," Nick said tersely.

"Why not?" Dacy looked between him and Jeff.

"Roy Holloway, our insurance man, says we aren't covered. He never received the last premium." Nick held her gaze.

"Did you pay it?" Dacy asked quietly.

Nick nodded, clearly annoyed that she asked. "Yes. But my financial records were lost in the fire. And the bank says the check was never cashed."

"All the more reason for you to accept my offer," Dacy stated firmly. "You two need a business partner. You need someone who knows enough to keep records in a fire-proof safe, and to keep multiple copies."

"What's your offer, Dacy?" Jeff prodded. "Spell it out."

"I want to invest in your ranch. In addition to the usual returns, I want you to sell me the house and two hundred acres around it. And I want an active role in the business end of your operation to ensure that my investment is worthwhile."

"No." Nick's voice was firm.

"Hang on a minute, Nick," Jeff said. He turned to Dacy. "You want this place bad cnough to invest in a failing ranch?"

"We're not failing," Nick corrected.

Dacy ignored him and nodded. "It was my grandparents' place. It doesn't feel right not having it in the family. And I want to live here. I need to be here, now."

Jeff nodded slightly. "Dani told me about your boyfriend. I'm sorry for your loss."

"Thanks, Jeff." Dacy couldn't afford the emotions that bubbled suddenly to the surface. Not now.

Luckily, Nick was so consumed with his own feelings, he bulled right ahead, not stopping for a second. "You don't know anything about ranching," he insisted.

"I know business," she countered. "I can learn ranching business. You two know ranching, but you told me yourself that neither of you are good businessmen. We can help each other."

"What kind of investment are we talking about?" Jeff asked.

"I'll cover all loan and interest payments for the next two years and justifiable equipment and new stock purchases. You would be responsible for other general operating expenses. I'll also pay for the renovations on this place and I'll pay you fair market value for the house and the land at the end of the contract. I'll also want a one-third share of any profits the ranch makes during the two years and a dividend after that."

"Dacy, that's nuts. You could end up paying hundreds of thousands of dollars for this old ruin that isn't worth a tenth of that." Jeff was incredulous. "You might never see any return on the other money. Can you afford to throw away that kind of money?"

"I can," she answered steadily, "but I don't think I'll be throwing it away. I've got a knack for being able to spot profits where other people see disaster."

"I said no and I meant no," Nick interjected. "Dacy, please. Let it alone and go stay with your aunt."

"Nick, we're not turning this offer down out of hand," Jeff announced. "When do you want an answer, Dacy?"

She looked at Nick. "When do you want a safe home for your daughters, Nick? As soon as possible. Tomorrow."

Nick glared at her fiercely, but she didn't break his gaze. She felt his frustration and his anger, and she knew his pride was at war with his need to provide for and protect his children. She tried to make it a little easier for him.

"Nick, please. I know you want to handle matters on your own, but I need this place. This is a way for both of us to get what we need, even if it isn't exactly what we want. It isn't perfect, but please, think about it."

"Where would you live now?" he asked.

"Here."

"What about us?"

"There's plenty of room for you and Jessica and Amy, and me, too." It might prove a little awkward at times, but she'd handle it.

"People would talk," Nick objected.

"Tell them I'm your housekeeper."

"Nobody's going to buy that," he scoffed.

"Then don't worry about it. This is the nineties, Nick."

"I don't like it. Besides, things will be all torn up if you start renovations."

"I'll put up with the inconvenience in exchange for being here," she insisted.

Harley had been watching them silently, but now he grinned and his eyes twinkled. "You two wouldn't by chance still be carrying a torch for each other, would you?"

Nick and Dacy both stared at him, too startled to reply. Jeff chuckled softly.

"If you were, there'd be a real easy solution to all this." Their silence invited him to continue. "Nick, if you and Dacy got married, you'd both be set."

Dacy blushed scarlet and stared at Harley with her mouth open. It took her a few seconds to realize he was teasing them. When she did, she was aware of a tiny disappointment, as if perhaps marrying Nick *would* be a solution to a number of problems. There was something comforting in the notion—and something alluring, as well.

But it was just a joke. She gave a little laugh and glanced cautiously at Nick.

He had gone still the way a cougar does before it springs upon its prey. Where before his anger had been a heated, moving force, now it was a cold, ruthless energy, only barely contained. Dacy's heart sank with dread when he started to speak.

"Harley, I'm not a suitable husband for Dacy. Look at her," Nick began. His voice was deceptively gentle. "Look at her clothes. Those boots probably cost as much as you spend on heat for the whole winter. One trip across my pasture would ruin them. The earrings she's wearing would pay off your mortgage, and if one of them fell into a cow pie, she'd buy another one before she'd fish that one out. Her damned haircut probably cost a hundred dollars. You couldn't spend that much on a haircut within four hundred miles of this ranch. Harley, there's no way I could keep a woman like Dacy happy out here. I tried it once, and I'm not going to repeat the mistake."

Dacy was shaking by the time he finished. Her throat was tight and her mouth had gone completely dry. Tears welled in her eyes, and she willed them to stop, not to spill and humiliate her further.

Both Jeff and Harley had narrowed their eyes and were directing venomous glares at Nick.

"That was a joke, Nick." Jeff spoke through clenched teeth.

"It's not a joke to me." Nick looked at Dacy. She struggled to hold back her tears.

"I am not your ex-wife," she told him, enunciating each word carefully. "I am not here to hurt you."

"That doesn't mean you might not, anyway," Nick said flatly.

Dacy's anger overcame her humiliation. "I'm not here to be hurt by you, either. My offer stands. I need the house. You have it. You need financial help. I have capital and experience. It's a business proposition, *not* a personal one. Try to remember that." She turned to Harley and shook his hand. "Thanks for coming out, Harley. I'd like to see that bid as soon as it's ready, no matter what Nick and Jeff decide. Now if you'll excuse me, I want to tell Jessica and Amy that I picked up the clothes at the church this morning."

She felt the men's eyes on her back as she rounded the house. Out of the corner of her eye, she saw Jeff cuff Nick hard on the shoulder and she heard him utter one word, soft, but clear.

"Jerk."

Amen to that, she thought.

Nick shrugged off the blow to his shoulder and strode off toward the creek. Jeff and Harley let him go, which was just as well. He'd made a prime fool of himself, and he was still so mad he was shaking like a rattler ready to strike. He'd already struck once. That was more than enough.

When he reached the creek, Nick paced up and down the bank, thinking about Dacy and her blasted determination to reclaim her grandparents' house. She had some nerve, getting all those utilities hooked up and Harley out to make a bid on renovating a house she didn't even own. It was crazy. The Dacy he'd known when they were in high school wouldn't have done something like that, not unless she was desperate.

Desperate. The word slowly sank in. Dacy *was* desperate. Something had snapped in her when her boyfriend died, something that had probably been building for years. She was desperate to be here, to live in her grandparents' house. Why? What did she think she would find here that was worth a hundred thousand dollars or more?

Nick didn't know, but he felt desperate, too. His life was unraveling. After years of juggling to keep everything together, the balance had shifted irretrievably off center. He couldn't hold his life together. He couldn't give Jess and Amy the home they needed—at least not without help.

Out of desperation, Dacy was offering help. Out of desperation, he might have to take it.

Yet every time he thought of her staying there, of living in the same house with her, his desperation turned to panic. It wouldn't work. He liked her too much. He had loved her in the past. He needed a woman in his life too badly. She'd take on that role too easily in her desire to stay here. He wouldn't be able to stop it. Later, when it would kill him to let her go, she'd want to leave. He couldn't accept her help because it would lead straight to the disappointment that had emptied his soul when Tammy had left him and the girls. Never would he put the girls through that again, and never would he set himself up for that kind of pain again.

There was pain in losing the ranch, though, too. His family had been ranching on Badger Creek for more than a hundred years. This was the only home Jess and Amy remembered and he loved it here. Losing the ranch would hurt the girls; it would hurt Jeff, and it would hurt him. There weren't any easy choices.

Nick finally stopped pacing and sat down on a fallen cottonwood trunk. Pacing made him feel like a windup toy cranked to the breaking point. Sitting still made him feel like someone had their fingers clamped on the key; he was motionless, but wound too tight.

Resigned to settling between bad options, Nick forced himself to relax. Each breath he drew went deeper into his lungs, the cool air clearing his turbulent emotions. By the time the light had turned rosy and the sun was touching the horizon's edge, he had control of himself again.

He heard familiar footsteps approaching. Jeff walked up and sat down next to Nick, bracing his hands on his thighs. "We have to accept Dacy's offer," he said without preamble.

Nick couldn't answer. He had to hear Jeff spell it all out.

"We have a twelve-thousand-dollar loan payment due in three weeks and we're close to broke," Jeff continued. "Three of our buyers have canceled orders in the last six months. We keep losing breeder bull calves. Our house burned down and we can't replace it. I could go on, but what's the point? No bank in the state is going to bail us out of this one. Dacy's offer is a godsend, Nick."

"Feels to me more like it came straight from hell." Nick sighed.

"Why?"

Nick shrugged.

Jeff wouldn't let it alone. "Why are you so set against her? If you haven't gotten past what Tammy did to you, then it's time you did. Dacy is a different woman."

"I'm not a different man, though." The words were bleak.

Jeff shot him a glance. "Meaning you still care about Dacy." It wasn't a question.

"I could," Nick conceded. "If she was around. There's a spark between us."

"And meaning you put your whole heart into any woman you care about," Jeff concluded.

"Yeah. Probably."

"It's been so long since you cared about a woman, I don't know how you can tell anymore." Jeff sounded irritated.

Nick watched the sun slip beneath the horizon. "I can tell."

"Then fine, don't fall in love with Dacy. But we're accepting her offer of help, and we're both going to learn something about business from her." Jeff spoke with uncharacteristic force. "We have a partnership between us, but you're only thinking of yourself if you won't accept Dacy's help. Think about the girls. Think about me. I'm not going to let your pride or your fears about caring for a woman make us lose the ranch." Jeff tossed a rock into the creek and stood, looking down at Nick. "You'd better get used to having a new partner because we've got one."

Nick stared at the receding ripples in the water where the rock had fallen. Jeff stepped around him and headed back toward the house.

"Don't stay out here all night," his brother called. "The health insurance has lapsed, too, so you can't afford to get sick."

Nick picked up a rock of his own and threw it as hard as he could in the direction of the creek. It sailed clean over the water and hit an oak tree with a loud crack, rousing a startled crow. The bird flapped and cawed, protesting volubly.

"I'll stay out here as long as I want!" Nick hollered at Jeff, at the crow and at Dacy if she could hear him.

It was well after dark and Nick hadn't returned to the house. Dacy was finishing the after-dinner cleanup while Jeff listened to Amy read from a geology book. Jessica moved restlessly around the room after helping Dacy with the dishes.

"I wish Dad would come back," she said quietly, to no one in particular.

Cold rushed into the room suddenly, sending a shiver of air across the back of Dacy's neck.

Nick stepped into the doorway but didn't enter. Amy stopped reading and all eyes turned to him. Nick looked at each of the girls and smiled wanly before nodding shortly to Jeff. Then he looked at Dacy. He didn't mask his conflicts or his pain.

"C'mon, you two," Jeff said, rising from the floor and helping Amy up. "Jupiter and Venus are setting alongside a crescent moon. Get your coats and let's go take a look."

A minute later, they were gone. Dacy stood with her back to the counter, waiting for Nick to speak. Deliberately, he walked across the buckled flooring until he stood as close to her as he had outside, forcing her to look up to hold his gaze. Uncertain emotion flashed across his face, only to be quickly veiled.

"I'm sorry about the way I talked to you earlier."

She nodded stiffly, accepting his apology, but letting him know it wasn't okay.

"Are you still mad at me, Dacy?"

"I'm more hurt than angry," she said, leaning back into the counter to put more distance between them.

"Yeah, I figured that. Dacy, Jeff and I are going to accept your offer." He opened his mouth as if to say something else, but he was silent. Instead, his eyes dropped to her mouth and he licked his lips.

Instinctively, so did she. Nick took a deep breath.

"This is the hardest thing I've ever done. I don't want you to be here, Dacy, and I don't want to take your money. I want to be able to take care of my family on my own."

"I understand that," Dacy said, edging farther away. The counter dug into her back, stopping her retreat.

Nick moved closer and braced his hands on either side of her. She could feel warmth radiating from his arms at her waist; it summoned a deep throb in her belly and a lightness in her chest. Frowning, she wished she wasn't responding to him this way. It was fruitless.

"Outside," he said, "I was harsh because of this." He didn't have to explain. She knew what he meant. "We want each other. We like each other. We loved each other a long time ago. Both of us have been through a hard time recently. It would be real easy to get involved for the wrong reasons."

"You made your feelings on that matter quite clear," Dacy told him, hating this conversation. She wanted to kiss him. She wanted to push him away. She didn't want him to push her away.

"Yeah." He leaned a little closer, and she wasn't sure if he did it on purpose or not.

"I'm sorry Tammy hurt you so badly." Dacy looked up from his mouth, only inches from her.

"This isn't about her, or about the past. It's about what I want now. I want to stay here. I want to raise my daughters here. I'm tied to this land. In my heart."

"I know," Dacy whispered, closing her eyes against a surge of emotion. "So am I. I keep trying to tell you that."

He cupped her chin with his knuckles then, running his thumb over her cheek. "I'm not sure it's the same, Dacy. If it was, you wouldn't have been able to survive in New York for so long."

"I came back, didn't I?"

"But how long will you stay?"

Chapter Six

In her heart, she heard a response she couldn't voice. *I will stay as long as you want me to, as long as you'll hold me, as long as you'll love me.* Frightened by her thoughts, she didn't answer. They were a reaction to her grief, she was sure. She put her hands on Nick's chest and pushed him back a little.

He looked disappointed as he brought his hands up to cover hers, trapping them against him. She wanted to get away from him, and from all the things she felt when she was near him.

"We have a lot to discuss about the house," she began, turning instinctively to a concrete project. "And about your finances."

Nick ignored her comment. "Since you're going to stay, we need to have some ground rules. I'm going to kiss you now, because I want to so badly I can't stop myself, but after this, we're not going to touch each other."

Every nerve in Dacy's body leapt to life when he said he was going to kiss her. When he said he wasn't going to touch her again after that, the electricity sparking through those same nerves froze. It was oddly painful, but if physical avoidance was what it would take to stay here, then she would accept his terms. "All right," she agreed quietly.

"Second," Nick continued, "I want you to be cautious with Jess and Amy. Don't try to be their mom. Don't spoil them. Don't get too close."

"That might be hard." She understood that he was trying to protect them, but how could she not care for those girls if she was living in the same house with them?

"I know," Nick said, his thumbs massaging her wrists where he held them against his chest. "Just tell me you'll try."

"All right. I'll try."

"Good. Finally, as a condition for this partnership, we need to agree that Jeff and I continue to run the ranch according to our own principles. Even if something like using growth hormones looks like it might increase profits, we won't do it. This is an organic operation."

She smiled. This was a condition she could agree to wholeheartedly. "I have no problem with that. We can write it into the partnership agreement."

"Good." Nick didn't smile. He stared at her mouth again. "I still think this is a foolish thing to do."

She paused a split second. "Kissing me?"

"Going into partnership. And, yeah, probably, kissing you, too."

"Then why do you want to do it? Kiss me, that is?"

"Why do you want me to?"

She didn't intend to answer that question.

He looked at her intently, and her breath caught as she waited for the promised kiss.

He lifted her arms, placing them around his neck. Then he slid his arms around her shoulders, pulling her close. He was so firm, so warm. He lowered his face, nuzzling his cheek along her jawline, and she breathed deeply at the gentle rasp of his beard. He remembered how sensitive she was along her jaw, and beneath her ears. His tongue snaked out, lapping at her earlobe, and a shudder ran down Dacy's neck and shoulders. Arching her head to give him better access, she buried her hands in the long hair curling over his collar, holding him to her. It had been so long since she'd felt this way, since she'd felt such sharp pleasure in a man's embrace.

Then he guided her head so that he could claim her lips. Resilient and soft upon hers, his mouth communicated a passion that his kiss last night had only hinted at. This time, his kiss was different. Tonight, his tongue searched her mouth, questing for a satisfaction of needs he didn't want to acknowledge. Dacy reveled in him, taking all he gave, and demanding her due in return. Their tongues twined, darted apart, found lips, teeth, and met again in absorbing play. All her fears and grief receded in that kiss. Her need was as strong as his, and together they held the shadows that dogged their daily lives at bay.

Dacy didn't know how long they stood in front of the counter, their lips together, their hearts open. Nick pulled away at last, and she became aware that his heart was hammering wildly under her palm.

"I heard footsteps on the porch. They're coming back in," he whispered, dropping his forehead to rest briefly against hers.

She couldn't speak.

He stepped back, untangling her arms from around him. A sad smile lit his smoky eyes. "Are you all right?"

She wasn't, but she nodded, anyway.

"Good." Nick dropped her hand, breaking physical contact. Both of them stared at the space where their hands had been joined. "If we both try, this won't be so hard."

Dacy didn't know if he was fooling himself, because he certainly wasn't fooling her. If he was serious about their keeping their hands off each other, it was going to be harder than she suspected either one of them was up to handling.

All things considered, she'd give Ground Rule Number One about a month.

Two weeks later, Dacy walked across the kitchen, her booted feet resounding on the new plywood that had been tacked over the floor joists. After the rotting linoleum had been removed and the joists strengthened, Harley had laid down the plywood so they could use the kitchen until it was time to rebuild it. Restoring an old house was a process, Dacy was learning—a long, messy, noisy, chaotic process. She loved every minute of it.

She had spent the morning going over the disorganized financial records Nick and Jeff had been able to cull from their bank and insurance agent. She had also made some phone calls, trying to reconstruct the Reynoldses' list of buyers and find out why so many of them had canceled their orders in the past six months.

What she'd learned was disquieting and she needed to talk to Nick. To do that, she would have to track him down. True to his word, he'd kept as far away from her as he could. He was never around, except at mealtimes. Then he avoided sitting next to her at the trestle table Edna had loaned them. A few times she had brushed his shoulder or hand while putting food on the table, or passing something, and he had cringed. That hurt—more than she would have thought—but she hadn't been willing to talk to him about it yet. Hurt feelings aside, she was learning Nick's routines and she usually had a good idea where to look for him now. At three-thirty on a Friday afternoon, he'd most likely be at the corral over at his place, watching Dani teach Jessica to barrel race.

Dacy glanced up at the sky as the sunlight dimmed unexpectedly. A bank of dark clouds was rising in the west, the first thunderstorm of the season. Remembering thunderstorms from many summers past, Dacy reached for her raincoat on her way out.

"Afternoon, Harley. Guys," she called, skirting the trampled grass and mud where the crew was mixing cement to patch the foundation. "It looks like we might get a storm."

"The wind'll carry that south of us," Harley predicted, squinting at the clouds. "We'll have to wait a while before we see a good thunderstorm."

"Since the roof isn't fixed yet, that's good news." She laughed. "I'll see you later."

Pulling out of the drive, Dacy looked around with satisfaction. They'd gotten a lot done in the past ten days. The house was full of workers tramping in and out, tracking in mud and grass as they hauled in electrical wires, pipes, a new bathtub, a new stove and now lumber and other building supplies. Though there would be changes later, the downstairs bathroom, the laundry hookup and the kitchen plumbing had been brought up to functional standards. Harley's crew had now begun work on reinforcing the foundation and the roof.

The upstairs bedrooms were uninhabitable, but the downstairs parlor and dining room were in reasonably good condition. Nick had put Jessica and Amy in the dining room with the new beds, dressers and desks the girls had picked out from one of Dacy's catalogs. He'd scowled at the furniture, which Dacy had paid for, but he'd smiled at his daughters as they argued over where everything should go.

Dacy had set the old parlor up as an office with new phone lines, a digital answering machine, a fax machine, a computer and printer and two big cherry file cabinets and a matching desk that she had delivered from Minneapolis. In one corner, she placed a sofa bed, and the office served as her bedroom, as well.

Nick slept on a cot in the family room. Through the wall, Dacy could hear him moving around late at night and early in the mornings. On several occasions, she'd resisted the impulse to go talk to him, to try to recover the sense of closeness she'd shared with him her first night here. Nick wouldn't have it, she knew. So far, he'd held rigorously to his ground rules. He hadn't come within three feet of her, and when she approached, he moved away.

His avoidance was beginning to irritate her. Those first two days she'd been here, when Nick thought she would be leaving, they had shared a companionship that had been deeply comforting. She thought it had comforted him, as well. They had slipped into that so easily. Now Nick was denying the natural affinity between them, and it frustrated Dacy. Instead of harmony, there was an undercurrent of tension between them.

The girls didn't appear to be affected by it, however. Caught up in the excitement of the renovations and all the recent changes, they had been even-tempered and generous about including Dacy in their lives. They had had a few minor spats, but Dacy had let Nick handle it, and neither of the girls stayed upset for long.

Overall, Nick was coping as well as could be expected with the changes. In other words, when they were in the same room, he was civil, if cool. He grouched about the chaos and the plaster dust in his clothes, and he muttered under his breath about conspicuous consumption when he found out about the extra phone lines and what overnight shipping charges cost. In spite of his testy moods, he sat down calmly with Dacy and Jeff to go over the finances. The whole time, he'd looked as if he had a mouthful of spoiled sauerkraut, but he'd helped draft the partnership agreement and he'd made himself available to help reconstruct the ranch's financial records. Always, Jeff or the girls were present. Daçy hadn't been alone with Nick since the night he'd accepted her partnership offer and kissed her.

Dacy was disappointed with his withdrawal, but she was so busy she didn't dwell on it. By the end of her second week in her grandparents' house and as a partner in the Reynolds Ranch operation, she had paid all the outstanding debts and loan payments on the ranch and sworn Marv Petersen, the local banker, to secrecy. While they couldn't keep her involvement a complete secret in such a small community, she didn't want Earl to know the extent of her financial commitment to the ranch.

In addition, she had also renewed the lapsed insurance policies, and set up a computer system to manage the ranch's business. She had cooked dozens of meals, some with onions or tomatoes or herbs—she hadn't dared put them all together yet—and there had been an occasional grumble, but no mutinies. She had driven Jessica and Amy to school on days Nick had to be out early. A good portion of her time had been spent discussing plans for the house with Harley and the subcontractors he'd hired.

Although there was so much to do, she found time to walk along Badger Creek every day. This time was precious to her. Driving west toward the Reynoldses' home place, she glanced at the line of cottonwoods, plums, chokecherries and spruce trees that marched along the creek bottom. She recognized the tree where a great horned owl often perched at sunset. While Dacy worked hard to reclaim the house and her heritage, the land and the animals, in age-old, simple ways, helped mend her spirit and ease her grief over Charlie's death. As crotchety as Nick was about her presence and their arrangement, she was grateful that he hadn't let his pride keep her from this place. The trilling calls of meadowlarks and the raucous crows soothed her in ways that the crowded Manhattan streets, with their blaring horns and hissing hydraulic brakes, could not have done.

Rolling the window down, Dacy let the cool air rush over her. It smelled damp and grassy. Somewhere to the west there must have been a thundershower from that storm cloud. Blowsy and dark, it drifted southward, as Harley had said it would. She watched it as she drove. Twice she spotted streaks of lightning, and once, a few fat drops of rain fell on the windshield, but that was all. Ten minutes later, as Dacy pulled into the yard at the Reynoldses' home place, the sun was peeping out from behind the passing storm again.

She drove past the bare foundation of the burned house and parked near the corral. Nick and Jeff were both leaning against the high fence, forearms braced on the top rail, Stetsons low on their brows. They were watching Dani teach Jessica how to train her horse. Looking around for Amy, Dacy saw her in the cab of Nick's pickup, reading.

Picking up her notebook, Dacy got out of the car and walked to the fence.

"Hi, guys." Deliberately, she wedged herself into the space between Nick and Jeff. She decided to push Nick a little, just to see how he'd react. Her arm brushed his midsection, and he rapidly moved away with a muttered greeting. Dacy hid a smile.

"Hi, Dacy. What's up?" Jeff asked, tipping his hat back on his head. He looked the quintessential cowboy.

She flipped open her notebook. "I was going over the records we got from your insurance agent. I have some questions."

Nick hooked a boot heel on the lowest rail and winked at Jeff. "I told you it'd be business," he said over her head.

Jeff laughed, and Dacy shot Nick a look of mock impatience. That was a mistake. Her gaze lingered over the dark hair curling over his collar, and the way the worn denim of his jacket stretched over his broad shoulders. Never mind what that same worn denim looked like stretched over his legs and rear end. By the time she looked back up at his face, Nick's eyebrows were raised in question.

"Maybe this isn't business, after all," he said so softly, Jeff couldn't possibly have heard him clearly. "Remember Rule Number One, Dacy." He shifted a little farther away from her.

She decided to ignore him. Riffling through the notebook, she found the page she wanted. "According to the records, you signed contracts for the delivery of organic beef to five different companies the year before last. Right now, it looks like your only client is a Des Moines restaurant company."

"That's right," Nick agreed, watching Jessica guide her horse through the course inside the corral.

"These companies canceled standing orders after more than a year of satisfactory deliveries," Dacy continued. "Do you know why?"

"No," Nick mused, "I never figured that out. We produce good beef. It's the best there is in the organic market. The Denver group said they found another supplier closer to their stores. Reduced shipping costs made them more competitive than we were. The California group started demanding California state organic certification, which I couldn't get here in South Dakota. The others had a range of reasons." Nick squinted at the sun. "None of them made much sense, except the Denver group."

"Do you have state organic certification?" Dacy tapped her pencil on the notebook rings.

"We don't have a state certification program for any organic produce or meat here," Jeff answered. "There aren't even guidelines. Nick got the regulations from the toughest states, and that's what we use."

Dacy lifted some pages from a pocket in her notebook. "What does the state department of agriculture's 'Board of Organic Certification for Grain, Produce and Livestock' do?"

Both men laughed. "There isn't any such thing," Nick told her.

"Are you sure?" She frowned at the letter in her hand.

"Dacy, I know the state department of agriculture backward and forward. I know who runs each program and how open he or she is to environmental ranching. Believe me, there's no 'Board of Organic Certification' for anything in this state."

She handed Nick two faxes. "Then where did these letters come from?"

Nick began to read the first. "This is a letter to Health Right, the distributor for the Minnesota stores we used to sell to, on Department of Agriculture letterhead, informing them that Reynolds Ranch beef has not passed state certification standards for organic livestock production. Damn. If they believed this, no wonder they canceled their orders."

Jeff swore fluently, then said, "I suppose the second letter is to one of the other suppliers."

"Yeah," Nick concurred, looking it over. "It's to the Seattle company." He raised a hand to run through his hair, then caught himself before he sent his hat flying. "Where did these come from? There's no such board in the state ag department."

"They look official," Dacy observed. "They're on state letterhead. They certainly convinced your clients."

"Where'd you get these?" Nick asked tightly.

"I called the companies to check why they'd canceled orders. When they told me about the letters, I asked them to fax me copies."

"Damn," Nick swore again, shaking his head.

"Why didn't anyone ask us about this?" Jeff asked.

Nick was silent for a moment. "They did," he finally said. "The woman at Health Right asked me for evidence of state certification and she got real cold when I laughed at her and told her this was South Dakota, not California. She made some crack about how lying to her wasn't going to get me anywhere. This is obviously why the California group wanted me to show paperwork, too."

"Why didn't you follow up on any of these canceled orders?" Dacy asked quietly, trying hard to keep any trace of judgment out of her voice.

"It was last November." Nick jiggled his foot on the fence rung. "We'd sold a bunch of calves for a good price, and things seemed to be going well. I thought we wouldn't have any trouble picking up new clients."

Dacy smiled faintly. "This is why you guys need me."

Jeff laughed and Nick scowled at the fence. "She's got us there, Nicky," Jeff said. "So what are we going to do about these letters? Isn't this libel or fraud or something? They can't be legal. Who signed them?"

"Someone named Marielle Orbach," Nick read.

"Never heard of her." Jeff's eyes tracked Dani in the corral as he spoke.

Dacy took the faxed letters back from Nick. "I'm going to make some phone calls to the state agriculture offices to see what I can find out. In the meantime, I think a few calls to your former clients explaining what happened might get some of those contracts back. The people at Health Right still haven't found another supplier whose beef their customers like as well as yours."

Nick met Dacy's gaze directly. "It would help us a lot to get those contracts back, but I want to know who sent those letters."

Dacy noticed that Nick's eyes were the same color as the steely underside of the storm cloud receding in the distance. Absorbed in the problem of the letters, he wasn't on guard, and he took a step closer to her. Instantly, her skin felt as though it had surged past her body, reaching to feel him across the gap between them. It surprised her how much she reacted to that small step. Pushing her reaction aside, she tried to focus on the letters. "I know a lot of your neighbors are upset about that *Newsday* article, but these were sent months ago, before that was in the works. Is there anyone you can think of who would benefit from you losing business? Someone who'd be bold enough to do something like this? Anyone besides . . ."

Jeff and Nick spoke in unison. "Earl."

Chapter Seven

Dacy remembered her conversation with Earl Tally in the parking lot at Char's two weeks ago. The hostility. The smug assurance that Nick and Jeff faced ruin.

"Him and his daddy have wanted our lease land ever since our daddy can remember," Jeff said, settling his hat low over his eyes again. "I wouldn't put it past that old bear. He's got a mean streak, and he doesn't think anyone sees it. He thinks he can do whatever he wants. I've suspected for a while that him and that rotten kid of his have been behind our bull calf losses."

"It makes sense," Nick agreed. "I've wondered, too, but I don't like to accuse my neighbors of criminal behavior without proof."

Jeff settled one booted foot heavily on the fence rail and watched Dani follow Jessica through the course, calling out instructions and encouragement. "He's got easy access to our pastures. He or Cliff could come out at night, feed the calves something to make them sick and we'd never notice."

"Earl Tally is not going to drive us off his ranch," Nick stated with conviction. "Dacy, if Earl is behind this, he'll try to cover his tracks. Do you think we can connect him to the letters?"

Dacy closed the notebook and held it against her chest, crossing her arms. "If he's at all careful, probably not. But we can try. My guess is that when he finds out you figured out what happened to your contracts, he'll try something else. If he really wants you ruined, he won't stop."

"Then we'll have to make sure he doesn't get the opportunity to hurt us again." Nick's eyes blazed with determination. "Now that we know for sure that someone's gunning for us, we can protect ourselves and the ranch." He paused. "If we work together. It will take all of us to stop Earl and keep the ranch going. Are we together on this?"

Jeff nodded.

"Dacy?" There was a trace of hesitation in his voice.

Dacy looked at him steadily. "I have as much to lose as you do." *Maybe more,* she thought, although Nick wouldn't think so. "I'm a partner. I'm with you."

"All right. Good." He glanced from Jessica riding in the corral to Amy reading in the pickup. "Good," he repeated.

"What do you think he'll try next?" Jeff asked.

"It could be more stock losses. They've been steady over the past year or so. Or he might try to disrupt the Bureau of Land Management and Congressman Green's visit in July."

"What's that?" Dacy asked, opening her notebook back up.

"There's a big environmental rally in the Black Hills over the Fourth of July. Several of the top officials in the BLM from Washington are going to be there, along with some other political honchos. They want to visit the ranch to see what we've done here, especially in the pastures on the leased land."

"What's at stake?" Dacy knew Washington politicos didn't just happen to drop by a ranch that was this isolated.

"Federal policy changes that will do a better job of protecting fragile lands. There's a bill in congress we'd like to see passed. It's a good bill, but there's a lot of opposition."

Jeff interrupted. "From what you read me and from the dates on those letters, it looks as though Earl's taken advantage of the times when we were both away from the ranch."

"When will you be gone next?" Dacy asked.

"There's a weekend conference in Brookings in a couple of weeks. The state university is there. It's a center for agricultural development," Nick explained.

"I remember," Dacy said, jotting notes. "My dad went to college there."

"I don't know—maybe we should cancel." Nick and Jeff exchanged a meaningful look.

"No," Dacy said, thinking rapidly. "I think you should go. It's a perfect opportunity to see if Earl tries anything. I'll be here, and I can keep tabs on him."

Both Nick and Jeff shook their heads. "You don't know what to look for, or where," Nick argued.

"Nick's right, Dacy. You don't know the ranch well enough. But I don't have to go to Brookings." Jeff tapped the heel of his boot against the fence. We can still make like we're both going away. Then maybe Earl will feel safe enough to make a move. I can camp out up on the butte and see what happens."

Dacy had a sneaking hunch where Jeff was heading. She made no effort to stop him.

"That might work," Nick agreed.

Jeff's mouth twitched, as if he were trying not to grin. "Great. Then you can take Dacy with you. She can take the girls shopping to get their new clothes."

Tension radiated full-blown from Nick like a mushroom cloud. "No," he said a little too quickly. "I don't think that's a good idea."

He was certainly consistent, Dacy thought.

"Sure it is," Jeff continued, not giving her a chance to respond. "You won't have time to take Jessica and Amy to the mall. You know they'll want to go. They need new stuff. With Dacy along, you won't have to disappoint them."

Dacy waited for Nick to say something. He took off his hat, raked his hair, then replaced his hat. He took a step back, then a step forward. He scowled at the corral, the butte and at Jeff. Finally, he looked at Dacy. His mouth moved, but he didn't say anything.

She looked into his dark gray eyes and understood. He liked her. He wanted her. He was terrified of her.

In that moment, Dacy also knew that he wasn't entirely choosing to push her away. It was a habit. This was Nick's rhythm. It wasn't just her, it was all women, or at least any woman who threatened him with the possibility of involvement. He was protecting his heart, and this was how he'd done it for years.

It was time to change—for both of them. Dacy wanted to tell him not to fear her. She wanted to tell him not to fear his own feelings. She wanted him to tell her the same thing, that it was okay to feel this need, this power, even when they were simply standing beside the corral, with people all around.

Instead, she waited.

Nick searched Dacy's eyes. Pale glass green, they were unreadable. She didn't say anything, waiting for him to decide. Jess and Amy would love to have her come to

Brookings with them, but he didn't want her. There would be long hours in the car, close enough to her to smell her perfume, or for her to steal casual, not quite accidental touches. He'd noticed when she'd done that in the past couple of weeks. No, he didn't want her to come.

Then again, part of him wanted her to come. The past couple of weeks had been an exercise in restraint for him, but didn't he look forward to the time he was with her? She was so strong. He admired that. She was beautiful. He craved that. She was vulnerable. That nearly undid him at times. Many an evening he'd watched her walk off toward the creek at sunset, and it had taken every bit of self-control he had not to follow her. He knew she cried then. He knew that she remembered Charlie and that she mourned. He wanted to comfort her.

Instead, he reminded himself what an interfering busybody she was. He told himself how pushy she was. He told himself that he resented the hell out of her buying things for the girls and flaunting her money, but he knew it wasn't because he begrudged her anything. It was purely a selfish reaction to recognizing the gulf between them. She was going to be bored once the house was finished and the ranch back on its feet. There was only so much even a creative soul could find to do in Antelope County. Sooner or later, she would leave.

He didn't want her to leave. Not again. Damn it all. He wanted...something he couldn't put into words. He didn't dare put words to what he thought he wanted with Dacy.

Jeff and Dacy were both looking at him, expecting him to say something. He opened his mouth, intending to explain why it was impossible for Dacy to come to Brookings with him.

"Well, maybe," he muttered, surprising himself as much as anyone. "We'll talk about it later."

Dacy blinked at him. "Okay" was all she got out before he interrupted her.

"I told Harley he could have that old cream separator in the barn. I'd better go get it." He turned on his heel and marched off.

Jeff's quiet laughter followed him all the way.

At dinner, Jeff told Jessica and Amy about the trip to Brookings and that he wasn't going as he had last spring. Dacy was going instead. Nick didn't contradict him so Dacy decided that meant she was going. She wasn't sure why, because it really wasn't a big deal, but she felt as though it were an important victory.

She thought the same thing when Nick stuck his head in her study door after making sure the girls were doing their homework.

"Hi," he said, pushing the door open wider.

She swiveled in her chair to look at him. He was nervous, tapping long fingers against the edge of the door.

"I noticed that you didn't get your walk in yet tonight." He braced one shoulder against the frame in a visible effort to relax.

She closed the file she had been studying. "No, I didn't. Dani called. We talked longer than I realized."

He was still for a long moment. "Want to go now?"

Dacy's stomach did a little flip-flop. "With you?" she asked cautiously.

He looked faintly alarmed, but he stood his ground. "Yeah. Come on. Get your jacket. Jeff will stay awhile longer with Jess and Amy."

Dacy rose and approached him. He didn't back away when she stopped right in front of him. "Why?"

His expression wavered, then settled into a half smile. Ah, she thought. He didn't know.

"Do you need a reason?"

Dacy decided she didn't just now. "No. Not tonight." It felt good to be sought out.

Walking side by side, they didn't touch, but they were close enough that Dacy had only to put out a hand and Nick would be right there. They didn't speak, either, as they walked over springy new grass into the shadowed cottonwoods in the creek bottom. The sun was already down, and the air was still and clear, all traces of the earlier storm clouds vanished.

About a mile west of the house, Nick led her up the creek bank and they climbed a low rise. It was nearly dark, with only a thin band of blue-green light still glowing along the horizon. The stars were bright when they looked away from the security light by the house.

"Can we put that light on a switch so we could turn it off to look at the stars?" Dacy broke the silence without intending to.

Nick took a long breath before he answered. "Sure. It costs more, but I guess that doesn't matter now."

She heard censure in his words. "Why does my money bother you? I worked for it. I didn't do anything illegal to get it."

"It's not the money, Dace. It's the difference it signifies between us. Money and access to the things it buys can change people's values. The simple things may not be enough anymore."

"You think money has changed me?"

He didn't answer immediately, and when he did, he sounded tired. "No. I guess not." It was too dark to see him clearly. She had only his voice, deep and resonant, to give her clues about what he was feeling. "I meant that the simple things are what I know. They're what Jess and Amy have grown up with. It's not the things or the money that bother me as much as the easy way you give it away. You make it seem as if money is the answer to everything."

"Money can make some things easier, sure," Dacy agreed. "But not the most important things. Money didn't give Charlie a long life. It didn't make me happy in Manhattan. If it makes life easier for you and the girls, isn't that what it should do?''

"I don't know," Nick said quietly. "I worry about it. My girls will probably have to work hard for a living someday, and I want them to do things they love, things they think are important. I don't want them to choose a career based on how much money they'll make. Not every job worth doing pays the kind of money that lets you call up Neiman-Marcus on Monday afternoon and have a house full of new furniture by Tuesday evening. I worry about them coming to expect that."

"Even with money, you can only do that if the store has what you want in stock." She teased him, but she did it gently.

"You know what I mean."

She sighed. She did know what he meant. "Most jobs worth doing don't pay as well as what I did in New York. Social and personal value and monetary reward don't always go together. I know that, Nick."

"I know you used to. Remember when you wanted to be a social worker?"

That made her smile. "I did, didn't I? I'd forgotten that. I was going to save runaway children and orphans. Then I discovered the excitement of high finance, and now I have my hands full trying to save myself."

"And my ranch," Nick added with a wry chuckle. "And two little girls who lost everything they owned in a fire."

"I think we may have discovered a pattern here." She laughed easily at herself. "What about you, Nick? Can I save you, too, while I'm at it?"

She sensed more than she saw his smile fade. "No, Dace. I don't need saving."

She wasn't so sure about that.

"I guess I was pretty idealistic when I was in high school," she said, switching to the safer topic. "Nick, have I changed a lot since I was seventeen?"

He thought for a moment, and she felt his scrutiny. "In some ways. You're more confident. You're sadder."

"Yes." That was true. "I feel more powerful, but less in control. Does that make sense?"

He chuckled, a warm, indulgent laugh that sent shivers into Dacy's belly. "Yeah, it makes sense. More powerful, but less in control. Do you want to be more in control?"

"Sometimes." With him, she did. She wanted him to be more open with her. She wanted him to let her rescue him. He wasn't cooperating.

"You know pretty well how to get what you want," Nick said softly. There was a slight edge to his comment.

"Up to a point, I did," Dacy admitted. "I'm past that point, Nick. I can't get what I want now without a lot of help."

"I thought you had what you wanted. The house. Your grandparents' ranch."

"The house is a big part of it. It's part of the connection I want, a tie to my family, to our past, to the land. But I want something else, too. I want to be connected *now.* In the present. The way you're connected to Jeff and to Jessica and Amy."

"You want a home. You want kids, a family. You want roots. You want challenges, too."

"Wow." She thought for a moment. "That sounds so old fashioned, doesn't it? Kids and a family."

"It's what you want." It was a statement, not a question. "Charlie's death made you realize it. How come you didn't marry him and have some kids?"

Dacy furrowed her brows. "I've been wondering about that lately. I don't know for sure. Our lives were so taken up with work. I think Charlie didn't want to get married. He didn't really want kids. We talked about marriage once or twice, but even when we talked about quitting our jobs and moving to the country, we didn't talk about kids."

"Maybe it was you who didn't want to get married."

"No." Her response came before she had time to think about it.

She heard the smile in Nick's reply. "Maybe you didn't want to marry Charlie, then."

Dacy turned away from him and lost herself in the black night.

"Dacy?" He moved closer to her.

"You're right. I didn't want to marry Charlie." A tear slipped down her cheek. "He was my friend, always. I loved him. But I didn't feel for him..." *What I used to feel for you,* she thought. *What I might feel for you again.* "... the kind of love I want to feel for a husband. Something was missing. Both of us knew it, but neither of us had what we really wanted so we made do."

She heard the rustle of his jacket close behind her. She thought he was going to touch her, maybe put his arm around her. He didn't.

"But you still want that kind of love. The connection. The family." He sighed. "And the challenges."

"Yes," she admitted. "That's what I want. Is that so much?" She sounded wistful to her own ears, belying that she thought it *was* too much to ask.

"No, it's not so much to want," he said softly, almost regretfully.

"You don't think I can get that here."

"I don't think you'll be satisfied with the kinds of connections you'd find here. Not for very long."

"Are you calling me a snob, Nick?"

"No. I'm being realistic."

"I was realistic with Charlie. It didn't get me what I wanted. Now I'm going to dream."

Nick moved away from her. "Don't dream about me."

His words hung in the air, adding to the chill she felt. "I can have connections without you, Nick. Who knows who I may fall in love with? It doesn't have to be you. I didn't come back here to pick up where we left off. I didn't know exactly what I came back here for, but you're right, I want a family. A husband, and children. Here. But it doesn't have to be you," she reiterated.

That got a reaction. He whipped around to face her, his features visible now in the light of the rising moon. "Then who? You're living with me and my kids, you're partners in my ranch. If it isn't me or Jeff, then I don't know who you'd have time for."

"I don't know. It doesn't matter. When the right guy comes along, I'll let you know." She paused dramatically. "Do you think Jeff would have me?"

Nick actually sputtered. Dacy laughed.

"Nah," he said, finally grinning at her through the darkness. "He's too hung up on your cousin."

"I wondered about that," Dacy mused. "He tracks her without really looking at her. That's usually a dead give-away. Doesn't Dani like him now?"

"I think she asked him to marry her and he said no."

That didn't surprise Dacy. Dani had had a crush on Jeff since she was a baby. "Why'd he turn her down?"

"Inferiority complex."

"That seems to be a problem with you Reynolds boys."

"I don't feel inferior."

"Oh, that's right. You're the scared one."

"No, I'm the realistic one."

"Jeff probably thinks he's being realistic, too. Love isn't always realistic, though." Dacy sighed. Then she threw caution to the winds. "What would you do if I asked you to marry me now? For love? Not that I'm asking. Just a 'what if...'"

He didn't even pause. "I'd say no."

"That was too quick an answer. Think a minute. What if I fell in love with you again, and you loved me back. Would you still say no?"

He thought a minute, and as he did, Dacy had that same sensation she'd had at the corral when it had felt as if she had expanded past her skin to feel him without a touch. She was sure he felt the same thing. Emotion sparkled between them, bittersweet and yearning. Tears welled so suddenly in her eyes that one spilled before she could wipe it surreptitiously away.

"This is a risky game, Dacy. It'll only hurt."

She was stubborn. "If there was love, would you marry me now? Yes or no?"

She waited, hoping as only a fool would hope, knowing what he would say, but craving the tiny window of possibility the waiting opened to her.

"No." His whisper closed the window.

They had been standing side by side. Now she faced him and moved close. She cupped his cheek in her hand and smiled sadly up at him. Rising on her tiptoes, she placed a warm, gentle kiss upon his lips. "I'm breaking Rule Number One. Good night, Nick," she breathed, against his mouth. "Thank you for the walk. Don't dream about me."

She left him standing on the rolling prairie, as high as the highest trees in the creek bottom below, with the moon rising behind him in the east. Of one thing she was certain. In love or not, be they richer or poorer, more frightened than courageous, she and Nick were connected *now*, not just in the past. Time alone would tell how strong those ties were.

Chapter Eight

Don't dream about me, she'd said.

Hah, Nick thought, turning into the drive one evening a few days after their walk. He dreamed about her every night. Worse, he dreamed about her every damned day, with his eyes wide open. The eyes-wide-open dreams at night were the worst, though. With only a wall between them, he could hear her unfolding the sofa bed, then climbing into it. In his mind, he saw her in her flannel nightgown. Who ever said flannel wasn't sexy? Dreaming about what she felt like under it, it was sexy as hell. He dreamed about her green eyes half-closed, making her look sleepy and desirable, masking the intensity of her own desires. Oh, how he dreamed.

Knowing that she probably wouldn't turn him away was a torment to Nick. It kept him thinking about her constantly. He imagined her sitting at her desk, staring intently at her computer, tapping her pencil and making faces at the numbers she was always running. He thought about her cooking dinner for him and his daughters in that disaster of a torn-up kitchen, cheerfully dodging workmen and debris.

Getting out of his pickup, he walked toward the house, thinking about what it would be like to love her again, heart and soul, the way he had when they were kids. He dreamed about making love to her in the bed of his pickup, parked in an out-of-the-way gully up on the butte, just like he had so long ago.

It was agony. He craved her, and when he told himself he should stay away from the house, find any excuse to be gone from her presence, he did just the opposite. Like now.

Nick stepped up onto the porch, looking through the glass in the door. Dacy stood in front of the counter, stirring something in a bowl while Jess poured liquid into it. No doubt it was another of Grandma Fallon's cake recipes. The work crews were getting spoiled.

He opened the door and stepped inside.

"Check your feet," Dacy commanded without turning around.

"Yes, ma'am." Nick was a hair too polite.

Both Dacy and Jess looked over their shoulders at him. Both of them grinned. So did he. This warm feeling of content was why he wasn't hauling his butt into town looking for that pump flange he needed for the southwest pasture.

He raised his boots up for them to see, and was rewarded with more smiles.

"You are an angel," Dacy declared.

"Yes, ma'am," he agreed.

Jess laughed. "No, he isn't. Not *my* dad."

"Hush, girl." Nick put the boots down and ambled over to the sink. "Never contradict anyone who wants to think well of me." He tickled her back and she squirmed away, leaving room for him to get closer to Dacy. He didn't even think about violating Ground Rule Number One until it was too late. He nudged Dacy's elbow and looked into the bowl.

"What's this?" Lightning fast, he stuck a finger into the batter and scooped it into his mouth.

"Don't!" Dacy batted at his hand with the spoon. She missed.

"Dad!"

Nick's mouth filled with a gritty mixture that tasted mostly like salt and alka seltzer.

Dacy and Jess laughed when he leaned over the sink and spit it out. He grabbed a glass and rinsed his mouth about six times while they kept laughing.

"That's what you get for being greedy," Dacy said piously.

"What is that stuff? Nothing I'm expected to eat, I hope." He coughed and made a face.

"It's salt dough. We're experimenting. We're going to make backgammon pieces and checkers out of it," Jess explained.

"Why?" Nick filled his glass again and drained it.

"We don't have any anymore," Jess said. "I wanted to play backgammon, and Dacy said we could draw a board on paper and make the pieces."

"Why didn't you just call up one of those catalog places and have them ship you a new backgammon set?" It seemed as though Dacy did that with everything else.

Jess was patient with him. "This is more fun. See, we can use food coloring for different colors, and a glaze to make them shiny."

Dacy grinned and shrugged. "Rule Number Two—no spoiling?"

Nick wiped his mouth with the back of his hand. He felt conspired against. They were trying to make him crazy. He loved it. "Didn't you make a cake today?" He sounded hopeful.

"No. We wanted ice cream instead." Jess was starting to sound bossy the way Dacy did.

"Nobody asked me," he complained.

Dacy looked him square in the eye. "Then I'm asking. What do you want, Nick?"

He froze. He wanted to run his hands up over her rear end and under her sweatshirt. He wanted to unhook her bra and feel her bare breasts fill his hands. He wanted...a lot of things.

"Anything sweet will do," he said softly.

"Anything?" Dacy arched her brows.

He licked his lips. It occurred to him that if he married her, they could flirt like this, and then at night, when the girls were tucked away in bed, they could do something to ease the sort of need he was feeling.

Until she left.

The thought sobered him.

"Ice cream is fine." He smiled reluctantly and ran his finger down her nose because he wanted to touch her and that seemed the safest way to do it. "Where's Amy?"

"Doing her homework." Dacy stuck the spoon back in the dough and sighed.

He moved away from her. He had reminded himself about the leaving in time. This time. More and more often now, he was forgetting about it. That was foolish.

Even so, Nick wasn't sure how long it would be before all the dreams and thoughts and moments prodded him into rash behavior. A man only had so much control, after all.

Don't dream about me, he'd told her.

Fat chance, Dacy thought. How was she supposed to control her dreams? How was she supposed to control her mind when her body loved thinking about Nick? Her stomach got all excited and her heart fluttered. He wasn't helping matters much, either. He flirted with her. He broke

Ground Rule Number One all the time now, even if he did it in sneaky little ways, like running his finger down her nose, the way he would to one of the girls. The rat. He was tormenting her. Her only consolation was that she knew he was tormenting himself, too.

It was Friday afternoon again. In a week, they would be driving to Brookings. Now she was perched on the corral fence, watching Dani and Jessica weave through the barrel course they had set up. Jeff stood idly down by the cattle chute, faithfully tracking Dani, who never so much as glanced his way. Dacy reminded herself to ask Dani why that was.

Nick and Amy walked over from the barn, Amy with a book under her arm. When they reached her, Nick lifted Amy up onto the fence beside Dacy before climbing up himself. Amy immediately flipped her book open.

"Did you know that the Sioux Indians lived here thousands of years ago?" Amy shared everything she learned. "My teacher said they came only two hundred years ago, but Jeff said they were here before, then they came back. I found this book in the library that says some of the rock paintings, like in Badger Gulch, are thousands of years old. Did the Sioux make them, Dad?"

"Maybe," Nick answered. "That's what Jeff thinks."

"How long has our family been here?"

"A little more than a hundred years. Your grandpa's grandpa came out to Dakota Territory when he was a little boy. His daddy ran a general store down in the Black Hills during the Gold Rush in the 1870s. He moved up here when he got married. It was lonely country back then."

Dacy looked out across the rolling prairie to the horizon. The road was hidden from view by a rise of land. In the distance, the dark shapes of cattle dotted a green hillside. There were no trees, no buildings. It was lonely country now.

"What about you, Dacy? When did your family come here?" Amy wanted to know.

As much as she tried not to, Dacy felt like a family then with the three of them perched together, Amy running them through familiar narratives of place and family, all of them watching Jessica and Dani. It was a good feeling, sinking deeply through her, down into the hard ground. It was a feeling she wanted to keep.

Shielding her eyes against the afternoon sun, Dacy recounted her family's history for Amy. "The Fallons came to Montana in the 1870s, when the army opened up traffic along the Yellowstone River and the big cattle drives were on. They had a ranch west of here about a hundred miles. When this land was offered to settlers in the 1890s, my great-grandparents moved here. They built the house we're living in now in 1895."

"That's an old house," Amy said solemnly.

"For this country, it is." Nick placed a hand on her back.

"On the east coast, there are a lot of houses that are much older," Dacy said.

"Two hundred years old?" Amy's eyes opened wider.

"Some of them even older," Dacy said, nodding. "Like Mount Vernon, George Washington's house, and Monticello, where Thomas Jefferson lived."

"A girl in my class went to Mount Vernon last summer with her family. Dad said maybe we could go sometime. Dacy, will you take me to see Mount Vernon when we go back east?" Excitement lit Amy's eyes.

Dacy caught Nick's warning look over Amy's head. The illusion that they were a family shattered. "Maybe your dad can take you, honey." She tucked an arm around Amy, to console herself more than Amy. As she did, she brushed Nick's hand where it lay on Amy's back. He started, but he didn't pull away.

Amy seemed content with the answer. "You can come, too," she stated.

Nick gazed at her steadily, his expression unreadable. Dacy held her breath and didn't answer.

Nick did. "We'll see, Tiger." He turned his head back to watch Jessica take the barrel course one more time.

For once, he hadn't said no outright. He was making it harder than ever not to dream about him.

As the days passed, Dacy found it more difficult to tell what Nick was thinking. He was around more, and he was more relaxed—sometimes. Other times, he was cool and withdrawn. A week had passed and, in the morning, they would be going to Brookings for the conference and shopping trip. Dacy had little idea what to expect from him.

Turning off her computer monitor, she stretched and rose. It was after ten o'clock and light still streamed across the hall from the dining room where Jessica and Amy should have been sleeping.

In the hall, she caught Nick shutting off the light and closing the pocket doors. He signaled for her to follow him into the kitchen.

He flipped on the burner under the kettle, which was still warm, and found the chamomile tea in the cupboard. Dropping a tea bag in each of two mugs, he handed Dacy one.

"I thought we should talk about the weekend." His voice was low. "I don't want people to get the wrong idea at the conference."

Dacy stiffened. "What idea would that be?"

"Don't get snippy, Dace." The kettle began to rumble. "We're business partners, not lovers. I just want to make that clear."

"I see." She tapped a finger against the mug. "So you're afraid if your friends realize that we live in the same house, if I take your daughters shopping while you work, if they see us acting as a *unit*—" she stressed that word hard "—they'll think we're lovers."

The kettle boiled. Nick switched off the heat and flipped up the spout. "Right. Hold out your mug."

She thrust her mug toward him impatiently and he filled it, then his own. The grassy tang of chamomile filled the air. It reminded her of her first night at the ranch, more than a month ago now. So much had changed, but not Nick's stubborn attitude about her.

"Why do you care what anyone thinks?" She brought her mug close and inhaled the fragrant steam. "Why don't you worry about what people around here think?"

"People around here know what's going on."

"Well, then I wish someone would tell me," Dacy grumbled too softly for him to hear. "Look, Nick, I don't want to sully your reputation. If it's easier, just tell everyone I'm your cousin or something."

Nick looked appalled. "That's a lie. Nobody would believe that."

"Then tell them the truth if they ask. If you can figure it out."

"What's that supposed to mean?"

Dacy really didn't want to talk about this anymore. "I don't know, Nick. This is a pointless conversation. I won't act like your girlfriend, all right? I get the message." She took a sip of tea. "Come outside a minute. I want to show you something."

Carrying her mug with her, Dacy went out the back door into the yard. "Follow me," she said quietly, threading her way between the piles of trash and lumber Harley's crews had left. When she stopped, Nick came up close behind her. "Watch." She pushed a switch and the light snapped off, leaving silent darkness in place of the buzz and glow of mercury vapor.

The night closed in around them, dark and clear, with stars as thick as hoar frost without the light to dim them. Nick moved even closer than the darkness, fitting Dacy's shoulders against his chest, and she leaned into him without protest. One of his arms curved around her waist and she tucked her head under his chin.

"You're a master of mixed messages, Nick. What are you doing?" Part of her wanted to move away. He might hold her now, but he would withdraw again.

"I don't know," he murmured. "Breaking Ground Rule Number One." His free arm snuggled up to her middle, but he didn't lift it to where it would touch her breasts.

"It's your rule. I guess you can break it if you want." She noticed that he was careful how he held her. "But why?"

He took a sip of tea over her shoulder before he answered. "I never said I didn't *want* to touch you. Sometimes it's too hard to fight the need to touch. To be touched. Can't I just hold you? Can that be all there is to it?"

"No." She placed her left arm over his, at her waist, her hand over his. "Not for us."

He didn't move. "Look." Using his mug, he pointed to the southern sky. "There's Scorpio."

She remembered him pointing out the scorpion many, many years ago. "The yellow star is Antares."

"You remember."

"I remember lots of things."

He breathed deeply, his chest lifting against her back. He was hard, warm and male. "Me, too," he whispered. "Tell me what else you remember."

Tonight Nick was playing the dangerous game, rousing the burn of long ago passions and dreams. "Why? So you can tantalize yourself and then push me away? So you can tell yourself how virtuous you're being by resisting me when I'll only hurt you in the end?" Her quiet laughter was tinged with bitterness. "No, Nick. Not tonight."

His sigh stirred the hair at her temple. "I don't want to hurt you, Dace. I'm sorry. I tried to explain before—"

She cut him off. "I know. I just didn't think it would be like this."

"How?"

"Close but not close. Here but not really part of things."

"It takes time to be part of things."

"I know. And I have to make my own life. I'll do that. I'm not sorry I'm here." She fell silent.

After a minute, Nick spoke. "Sometimes lately I don't feel like I have my own life anymore."

"Because of me?"

"Partly. It's more than that, though. It's Earl scheming against us, hurting the ranch, and I didn't even realize what was happening." He paused to sip his tea. "It's the time away speaking, the magazine articles, the time on the telephone instead of in the barn or out in the pastures." He took a deep breath and squeezed her. "And then this pushy redhead with too much money and brains lands on my doorstep and refuses to leave."

"Maybe it's not your life anymore." She pried his arm away from her and threaded her fingers through his.

"Whose is it, then?"

Turning, she faced him. His features were hard to see in the dark. Knowing hers were, as well, she smiled.

"Ours." She squeezed his hand and released it. "Good night, Nick." She practically ran back to the house then, not caring to get into a discussion of what she meant. *Let him stew about it,* she thought as the screen door whispered shut behind her.

* * *

That one word haunted him all the next day, during the long drive to Brookings. *Ours.* Maybe it wasn't his life anymore, maybe it was... ours. Whatever that meant.

He looked over at Dacy where she sat in the passenger seat of the Suburban. Her hair fell forward, shielding her face, as she bent over the map she studied intently. Picking up the sunlight, it glowed with coppery highlights.

Nick looked back at the road.

"Did you know that we've lost three hundred feet in elevation since we crossed the Missouri?" Dacy asked without looking up. "The road looks flat, but it isn't."

Amy immediately leaned forward over her shoulder. "Look. It goes back up again by the time we get to Brookings."

Listening to them discuss what kind of geological history had shaped the Missouri valley, Nick thought Dacy and Amy were a lot alike. They liked those pokey details, such as elevations, that women like Tammy ignored.

He glanced back over at her. In jeans, boots and a royal blue button-down shirt, Dacy looked like a rancher today.

Or a rancher's wife.

Ours, she'd said. Did she know what she was saying?

Unconsciously, Nick raked his hand through his hair. This was not a good line of thought, he told himself. Not good at all.

Jess leaned over the front seats. "Dacy, look." She pointed out the window toward a field. "There's a horse. Near the fence. See it?"

"I see it." Dacy said. "Can you tell what breed it is?"

"It's big," Amy commented.

"I think it's a Percheron. Did you see how long its tail was? Cool," Jess breathed. "Dad, how come we can't get a Percheron?"

"Tractors are cheaper to feed," he quipped.

"Horses are easier to fix," Dacy said, chuckling.

"Not always," Nick insisted.

"Horses have foals," Jess said. "That's what I want."

"She's got you there, Dad." Amy giggled. "Tractors don't have babies."

"Sure they do," Nick claimed. "Where do you think toy tractors come from?"

"F.A.O. Schwarz." Dacy put down the map and laughed.

In the rearview mirror, he saw Jess and Amy roll their eyes.

"You guys are sooo lame," Jess groaned.

"We're entitled to be lame. We're—" He broke off. He'd been about to say, "We're parents." "Old," he finished.

"Speak for yourself," Dacy said, lifting her chin in mock indignation.

He looked at her helplessly. It was a good thing the road was as straight as a ruler because he almost forgot it was there. *Ours,* she'd said. It wasn't his life anymore, it was...ours. His ranch, his kids. Her house, her car. His brother. Her cousin. Now the ranch was hers, too. Ours. The girls were building a relationship with her. Had he really almost said, "Because we're parents"? It was a slip, an honest mistake. It was like calling your grade-school teacher Mom. It happened. It didn't mean anything.

Ours.

Oh, God, he thought. He was going to fall in love with her again. It was probably already too late.

He looked back at the road.

"Nick?" Dacy's voice was cautious. "How fast are we going?"

He glanced at the speedometer and his foot came off the accelerator immediately.

He was doing eighty-five and he hadn't even noticed.

Chapter Nine

The auditorium was packed. More than five hundred people had shown up at eight o'clock on a Saturday morning to hear Nick give the keynote address for the conference. It wasn't at all what Dacy had expected. She had thought there would be a couple of dozen ranchers in jeans, boots and bolo ties, getting together for a casual schmooze. Despite the fact that she had spent the past month dealing with the Reynolds Ranch's business operations, it hadn't hit her until now that ranching was not only big business but big politics.

Name tags identified a number of elected officials from surrounding states, and representatives from several large corporations. There were executives from major environmental groups, as well, and Dacy thought she recognized a celebrity rancher or two. She was glad Jessica had insisted they get there early, and that the girls had told Dacy to bring something to wear besides jeans. Nick had simply told her to wear what she was comfortable in. How typically male, she thought.

Amy leaned over and spoke right in Dacy's ear. "See the blond guy in the green suit next to the lady with the diamond pin? That's Mitch Avery and Annamaria Mattei," she said, naming a powerful communications mogul and his Italian actress girlfriend. "Mitch has a place in Montana that he's going to make a buffalo commons. That's where the buffalo roam free. He was here last year, too. They took us out to dinner."

Annamaria happened to look over just then. She waved and smiled at the girls, who waved back.

"It seems as though you two are used to hobnobbing with the rich and famous," Dacy commented, remembering Nick's concerns over his daughters' reactions to wealth.

"Sometimes," Jessica said without much interest. "Dad knows lots of famous people. Look, there he is. Down in front of the stage. That guy he's talking to? He's a senator. He came to our place to look at the petroglyphs in Badger Gulch."

Dacy didn't know which man was the senator, and she didn't especially care once she caught a glimpse of Nick. It was the first time she had seen him wearing anything besides jeans. In a dark suit and silk tie he was...riveting.

"Wow." Dacy stared.

"Yep," Amy agreed. "He looks good, huh?"

It took a few seconds before Dacy noticed how closely the girls were watching her reaction. "He certainly does," she said, quickly looking away.

It was no use. After one sweep of the room, her eyes landed on Nick again.

Jessica squinted at him. "That's a new suit. Dad had it delivered to the hotel last night. All of his good clothes burned up. That's a new tie, too. He doesn't usually wear such bright ones." The tie was magenta and purple. "I like it."

"It's not Dad," Amy countered. "I liked the old green-and-blue striped one. Especially with the diamond tie tack."

Jessica continued to chatter about people's clothes while Amy scrutinized the crowd for gems. Seated on either side of Dacy, they talked across her. She watched Nick.

Gone was the disheveled rancher who clomped mud through the kitchen and complained about plaster dust on his Stetson. Gone was the bumbling businessman who lost contracts and let his insurance policies lapse.

In his place stood a leader. Shaking hands and trading quips with politicians and corporate magnates, he could have been the CEO of any of a hundred corporations she had worked with through the years. He exuded confidence, and his warm smile welcomed questions and comments from the milling crowd.

Dacy was fascinated. Why did Nick bother with ranching? Clearly, he was in his element here.

She watched him excuse himself and disappear. A few minutes later, the auditorium lights dimmed and the governor introduced Nick as one of the country's leading experts on new ranching. Beside her, Jessica and Amy beamed with pride. Dacy couldn't help feeling proud of him herself.

When he spoke, she heard his passion. She heard his intelligence, and his wit. He played the audience masterfully, drawing vivid pictures of the dying west, where ranchers struggled to make a living, their cattle and sheep tearing up the land, fouling streams and eroding topsoil. He painted contrasting images of the new west, the west of the future he envisioned, where people and animals worked together to make a living *and* protect fragile resources.

But as he spoke, an emotion stirred in her that had nothing to do with pride or affection. While the crowd hung on his every word, Dacy began to fidget. When he told about a ranching cooperative in Oregon that had successfully turned to new ranching to provide organic beef to a Japanese restaurant chain, she remembered him telling her that too wide a gulf separated them. How wide, she wondered? As wide as the Pacific Ocean that separated the Oregon ranchers and their Japanese executive clients?

When he talked about the way the buffalo had been saved from almost certain extinction, she remembered him telling her it wasn't realistic to think she would be happy living in Antelope County. A hundred years ago, who would have thought it would be realistic to talk about wild herds of free-roaming buffalo again? Yet Nick was talking about it. People like Mitch Avery were doing it.

Dacy grew angrier and angrier listening to Nick. He was a dreamer. He sounded like a damned prophet up there, talking about a utopian future where people fit more cooperatively into the west, but he couldn't envision happiness for himself. He would hold her at arm's length and morosely prattle on about how she would never be happy on the ranch for more than the time it took to renovate the house and put the ranch in sound financial shape. He would fuss about the distance between them, which she now recognized for the utter poppycock it was. All the while, each of them would be yearning to hold the other tight, to touch each other as they once had, with so much more than dreams. All this, Nick denied. He was a dreamer, but he failed to seek his own heart's dreams.

Dacy wanted him to find those dreams, the dreams they had had at seventeen. She couldn't have been more right when she'd told him he was scared. He was afraid of getting hurt, and it blinded him to some very real possibilities.

Applause erupted around them. Nick was finished. Automatically, Dacy rose with the crowd, clapping, watching him smile at the audience. Amy waved at him, and he waved back. His gaze lingered on the three of them, and his smile faded just a little. What was he thinking? Dacy wondered. That she was getting too close to the girls? Was he thinking about all the things that were wrong about her? Was he thinking that he would be a fool to see where their feelings for each other might take them? Probably, Dacy thought, and it just made her madder.

"That was great," Jessica said, interrupting Dacy's inner dialogue. "Let's go to the mall now. The stores will be open by the time we get there."

Both girls made a beeline for the exit.

Dacy tossed a malevolent smile in Nick's direction. She knew a surefire way to get his goat. Letting Jessica and Amy have free rein today would do the trick nicely.

Staring numbly at the heap of bags surrounding her feet, Dacy considered that she had underestimated her charges. It was just as well she'd decided this morning to let them do whatever they wanted to, because she seriously doubted she'd have been able to deter them had she cared to. She'd never have believed girls their age could be such determined shoppers. It was four o'clock and she was exhausted. Her feet hurt and she had a headache. Jessica and Amy, however, revived by a dose of junk food, were raring to continue.

Amy pulled out a list and a pen from her fanny pack, and Dacy had to smile. They were alike in many ways. Amy's mission today was to replace as many of their possessions as possible, and she attacked each task with vigor.

"Okay." Amy was all business, checking off one item after the other. "We've got new summer clothes and shoes. All the coats they have now are ugly, so we'll have to wait until back-to-school sales to get good ones. Jess got her stuffed animals and Barbies, and I got a new rock polisher and telescope. We replaced the CDs and got some new ones, and we got some new posters. We've still got to go to the bookstore, and then we're getting manicures and haircuts at the Herberger's salon."

"I think manicures are a bit much," Dacy said faintly.

"We always get manicures," Jessica explained patiently, not for the first time. "Our mom runs a string of nail shops. We like manicures, and we always have to do it ourselves at home. It's fun. Besides, we have plenty of time."

"I never heard of nine- and eleven-year-olds getting manicures." Dacy stirred her diet pop with the straw. "I've never seen kids who are as serious about shopping as you two."

"You haven't been around kids much," Jessica reminded her.

"And our mom trained us," Amy cut in. "She loves to shop. When we go to stay with her in Denver, we go to the mall every day."

"Why?" Dacy couldn't imagine doing this every day. It would be hell. She fished a couple of aspirins out of her purse.

"To look at what's new. To get ideas." Jessica slurped hard on her straw to get every drop of her milkshake.

"Catalogs are more efficient," Dacy insisted. Over the past ten years, she'd shopped infrequently, and then mostly in exclusive boutiques or from catalogs. She hadn't had time to take whole days to shop.

"But with catalogs, you can't try things on or see what they're really like," Amy said with irrefutable logic. "This way, you know exactly what you're getting."

Dacy smiled. "I'm beginning to understand why your dad worries about you two being corrupted by materialism."

"He's a worrywart." Amy dismissed her father's concern with a wave of her hand.

"He thinks we're going to be like Tammy," Jessica added, rolling her eyes.

"Tammy? Your mother?" Dacy was startled that Jessica used her mother's first name.

"Yeah, she likes us to call her Tammy. It makes her feel old to be called Mom," Jessica explained.

Dacy decided to risk the question. "Is it bad to be like... Tammy?"

"No, but it scares Dad," Amy said. "I mean, she left us, you know?"

"I love my mother," Jessica said in a very adult tone, "but she doesn't have much time for us. Her business takes a lot of time, and then she's got to shop, and she goes to lots of parties. She likes to travel, too. She likes to see new places all the time. She went to Brazil in February."

"To Rio for Carnival," Amy added. "She brought us back masks. They burned."

"Yeah," Jessica continued. "Mom loves us, but she doesn't like being a mom. I mean, she likes that she's our mom, but she doesn't like the boring parts, like making dinner every night, and driving us to school things, and getting up early every morning. She told us so. She says it's boring, and she thinks Dad is boring. She said he's nice, and he's a good dad, but he's not really exciting, like a good boyfriend should be. Mom hates the ranch, though. That's mostly why she left us. She said the plains drove her batty. Always the same, always dull, always the same people, same hills, same everything. She's happier in Denver."

Dacy didn't know what to say.

"I like it on the ranch," Amy said quietly. "I like the same people and the same place."

"Me, too," Jessica concurred. "But Dad's afraid we're going to hate it like Tammy did. That's why he doesn't like it when we go bananas at the mall. He thinks it means we're like Tammy, and he wants us to stay with him and love the ranch the way he does."

Dacy listened carefully as the girls talked about their mother and Nick. Saying anything seemed like stepping into a mine field.

Amy interrupted her thoughts. "Dad's afraid you'll get bored and leave." There was a subtle challenge in the statement.

Dacy took a sip of pop. "Yeah. I know."

Both girls gazed at her steadily, their eyes gray and solemn, much like their father's.

"Will you?" Jessica prodded.

"I can't say for certain." Dacy set her drink back on the table. "I don't get bored easily, though. I know that."

"How come you went away, when you were in high school and you and Dad were going to get married?" Amy didn't pull any punches.

Dacy's eyes widened. "How do you know about that?"

"Uncle Jeff told us," Jessica supplied. "Why didn't you marry my dad then?"

Dacy answered candidly. "My father made me leave. He found out your dad and I were planning to run away together, so he packed up all my things, forced me to get in the car and he drove me away in the middle of the night. He wanted me to go to college."

"Wow. Just like in the movies. Did you and Dad love each other a lot?" Jessica leaned forward on the table, her face intent.

Dacy nodded and she smiled, surprised to feel tears threatening. "Yes. We did. Even though we were so young, I think we cared deeply for each other. But my father did what he thought was right when he took me away."

"Couldn't you have come back?" Amy wanted to know.

Lately Dacy wondered what her life would have been like if she had. "My father made me agree to wait until after my first year of college was over. By then, I thought he had been right. I loved the university, and I wanted to stay there. I thought your dad would still be around when I was finished. My mother said that if what we felt was strong enough, it would still be there when I graduated." She felt as though she were answering an inquisition.

"Did you ever come back?" Jessica pressed.

In her mind, Dacy said, *Yes. I came back. I'm here now.* But that wasn't what Jessica meant. "No. I heard your dad got married."

"Did you still love him?" Amy looked at her with wide, gray eyes.

Dacy smiled again and nodded slightly. "Maybe I did, but I didn't think about it very much."

"Then you fell in love with Charlie," Jessica said. "How come you didn't marry him?"

The tough questions just kept coming. "Well, I think because, at first, I loved Charlie more like a brother than a husband. He was my best friend for years, and then one day, he told me he loved me." Dacy didn't know how to explain to the girls why she hadn't married Charlie.

Jessica put into words the thoughts that Dacy wouldn't admit. "Maybe it was because you still loved Dad. Maybe he's your one true love."

Dacy cringed inwardly. Her cheeks grew hot, and she didn't know what to say. She couldn't say, *Hah, that's preadolescent romantic delusion.* She couldn't dismiss either Jessica or her question, but she wanted to.

Amy didn't make it any easier. "Do you love him now?"

Dacy couldn't answer. A warm swell of feeling flooded her chest, and she thought she might cry, after all. Her body said maybe. Her head said no. Her heart wasn't sure. How did you answer a question like that, coming from a man's nine-year-old daughter? With as much truth as she could, Dacy decided.

"I don't know if I love him," Dacy told the girls. "I like him. I respect him. Your father's a good man. But I don't know if I love him now."

Amy sighed. "It would be easier if you did."

"What would be easier?"

"Everything."

Even though she'd had the same thought herself, right now Dacy wasn't at all sure about that.

"No, Amy, Dad needs to love her, too. *Then* everything would be easier," Jessica said with all the wisdom of an eleven-year-old sage.

Amy folded up her list and tucked it back into her fanny pack. "Well, I think he does. I think he's just being a worrywart. Anyway, I love you, Dacy. Even if you don't like shopping very much." She jumped up and gave Dacy a quick hug.

"Me, too." Jessica leaned over and put her arm around Dacy's shoulder and planted a big kiss on her cheek. "We're glad you came back to South Dakota. We're glad you're here, and we're glad you're part of our family now."

A tear did leak out the corner of Dacy's eye then. "Thanks, guys. I love you, too," she whispered, one arm hugging each girl.

Things got out of hand at the beauty salon. Two of the operators had cancellations and were bored. Jessica and Amy were old hands at the beauty game. In a matter of minutes, they had directed the unoccupied operators to give them pedicures while they had their manicures done.

"Wait a minute." Dacy tried to interrupt the proceedings. A blond teenager with very big hair took her arm and steered her toward the shampoo sinks.

"Oh, come on, don't be a spoilsport," she cajoled, snapping her chewing gum. "They're having fun." Miss Big Hair firmly guided Dacy into the chair, wrapped her head in a towel and flipped a cape around her shoulders. "Hi, Sharon!" she squealed when another teenager in a white lab coat walked in.

"My five o'clock makeover didn't show and the store's dead." Sharon perched on a swivel chair by the pedicurists. "Do you guys care if I hang out in here?"

Jessica pounced right as Miss Big Hair dunked Dacy's head under the nozzle. "Why don't you bring your stuff in here and do makeovers on us?"

"Sounds cool," Sharon said, hopping up.

"I don't think you should do that," Dacy said, her voice all but lost in Miss Big Hair's armpits. "Your dad won't like it."

"We do it all the time with Tammy," Amy called back.

That didn't mean Nick would approve. In fact, Dacy didn't think *she* approved. She was going to say so, but Miss Big Hair asked Amy who Tammy was, and Dacy couldn't get a word in edgewise. Between the five operators, Jessica and Amy, and Sharon the makeup expert, the chatter was more than Dacy could follow. She gave up and decided to enjoy the shampoo.

It felt good. She was practically prone, with warm water and soothing hands stroking through her hair. By the time Miss Big Hair, whose real name Dacy learned was Pam, had rinsed the conditioner out of her hair, Dacy was practically asleep.

She woke up when she saw Jessica and Amy. Laying back in reclining swivel chairs, each girl sat with her hands held carefully so the fingers wouldn't touch. Each one had cotton balls between her toes, and green gook all over her face.

"Facials?" Dacy asked tartly.

Sharon beamed at her, undeterred. "Why not? I'll do you too. Sit down."

Miss Big Hair pushed her into a seat. "I'll dry your hair when Sharon's done. Tina will give you a manicure, too."

Dacy gave up. Amy opened one eye and peered at her.

"You look like my dad did when he decided to let you stay at the ranch," she said with a giggle.

Dacy laughed in response. "I'm beginning to understand why your father gets frustrated with determined women." She turned her face toward Sharon and offered her hands to the manicurist. "Okay, ladies. Do your worst. We will simply have to bear the consequences."

There was no doubt in Dacy's mind that there would be consequences.

Chapter Ten

All that beautification took time. As a result, Dacy and the girls left Sioux Falls later than planned, and they had to rush to get ready for dinner when they got back to the hotel. Dacy escorted Jessica and Amy and a good number of their purchases to the suite they were sharing with Nick. She left them to dress while she went to her own room to change. They were all supposed to accompany Nick and some of his friends to a steak house. Dacy realized that some of those friends would be politicians and people like Mitch Avery, so she'd picked up a simple, black silk knit cocktail dress and a pair of pearl drop earrings that she thought would do nicely.

Dacy hurried. She wanted to get back to Nick's suite to make sure the girls were dressed appropriately before he got there. She'd insisted that Sharon use only the barest minimum of makeup for them—a little lip gloss, a tiny smudge of beige eye shadow and a whisper of mascara had seemed safe.

As soon as Dacy opened the door into the sitting area of the suite, however, she knew it wasn't. Both girls were sitting sulkily on the sofa. Nick sat on the coffee table in front of them, his back to her. The atmosphere vibrated with tension.

"Go wash your faces," he ordered.

"No." Jessica was equally determined.

Unwilling to walk into the confrontation, Dacy closed the door behind her and leaned against it.

Amy got up and went into the bedroom. She had on a red knit T-shirt dress, black tights and new red high tops. Her dark hair was pulled back into a short ponytail, held with a red bow. Her fingernails matched her dress, but otherwise, she looked like a nine-year-old. The makeup was hardly noticeable.

She looked at Dacy, shrugging elaborately. "All right. I'll wash my face. It's no big deal. Geez!"

Jessica, on the other hand, presented quite a sight. She had supplemented Sharon's efforts with eyeliner, a darker shadow and brighter lipstick. She had changed into a short royal stewart tartan skirt, a white blouse with lace ruffles down the front and at the cuffs and a snazzy little black suede jacket. She was also wearing thigh-high stockings that stopped an inch or two short of her skirt, and low-heeled granny boots. Her sandy hair was wound up in a French twist with long tendrils hanging in front of each ear. The overall effect made her look much older than eleven. Dacy understood why Nick was upset.

"Jessica, you are not leaving this room dressed that way," Nick insisted.

"There's nothing wrong with how I'm dressed."

"It's not appropriate for your age."

"You just don't want me to grow up. The girls at the store liked this outfit. They said it makes me look sexy."

"That's exactly what's wrong with it. Eleven is too young for sexy. Change the stockings. Wash your face. Take your hair down. Now. We're late."

Jessica glowered at him, folding her arms across her chest. "No."

Nick tossed a frustrated glance over his shoulder toward Dacy. "Is this your idea of appropriate attire for eleven-year-olds?" His tone was scathing.

"No, it isn't." She tried to keep her voice calm.

"You bought the clothes. As I understand it, you allowed the makeup person to do this."

Dacy walked into the room, dropping her purse and keys onto an end table. "Not exactly."

"Don't blame Dacy. She didn't do anything wrong. I put more makeup on here," Jessica admitted.

"Where'd you get it?" Nick demanded. He glared at Dacy again. "Did you buy makeup for her?"

"No!" Jessica exclaimed. "Sharon gave me some samples."

"Who's Sharon?"

"The girl who does makeovers at the store."

"Well, you're not wearing makeup out of this room." He turned back to Dacy. "How could you let this happen?"

She closed her eyes and took a deep breath, choosing not to answer him. "Jessica, you have too much lipstick and eyeliner on. It doesn't look natural or pretty. Your father's right. And the skirt would look better with regular tights under it."

Jessica relented somewhat. "I'm not taking my hair down, though."

Dacy looked at Nick.

"Fine," he agreed. "Go. Clean up. Be ready in five minutes. And shut the door behind you."

Dacy steeled herself for the onslaught that remark promised.

Nick didn't disappoint her. One hand raked hard through his hair, and he began to pace. "This is exactly the kind of thing I try all year to counter, and now here you are, dolling Jess and Amy up like a couple of lap dogs. This is just what Tammy does. You were supposed to replace some of the things they lost in the fire, not go on a makeup and manicure frenzy! I could have sent them to their mother in Denver if I wanted them to do that."

Dacy was every bit as angry as Nick, and too tired to control her responses. She snapped back at him. "We did replace the things on your list. The car is full of clothes, toys, CDs, posters and enough books to stock a children's store. Have you ever taken your daughters shopping?"

"Of course I have!"

"Then you ought to know that they have minds of their own. I tried to curb this so-called frenzy. I don't have a lot of experience with children. What was I supposed to do? Put them on a leash?"

"You could try saying no."

"No doesn't always work."

His expression grew sharp at that. "You're telling me. You should have tried harder."

Dacy's feet still hurt, and now her head was starting to pound. She dropped onto the sofa and looked reproachfully at Nick. "You have determined daughters and I didn't want to alienate them."

Nick's laugh was not a nice one. "Now you know how it feels. What's it like to be on the receiving end of the steamroller for a change?"

She knew exactly what he meant. "I did not steamroll you."

"Yes, you did. You came in and flattened me. I never stood a chance."

"If you hadn't been so vulnerable financially, I wouldn't have gotten anywhere." It was a cheap shot, and she knew it.

He threw both hands in the air, and made an inarticulate sound. "That's beside the point now. Dacy, with kids you can't always be their buddy. You have to set limits. You didn't do that today."

That was true. "Maybe I didn't want to."

His stopped pacing and stared at her. "What's that supposed to mean?"

"Maybe I wanted to make you mad."

"Why in hell would you want to do that?"

"Because you made me mad. You make me mad a lot lately."

"What are you talking about?"

Nervous energy made it impossible to sit. Now Nick was still, and she rose, stepping closer to him. "I'm talking about this morning. You stood on that stage, in the midst of politicians and all sorts of high-powered types, completely at ease. Jessica and Amy told me about having dinner with Mitch Avery and Annamaria Mattei as casually as they would talk about a family picnic. Then I thought about all the times you've fed me this baloney about how we come from different worlds now, about how you're determined to ignore the way we feel about each other because we're too different.

"And you know what? I saw what a lie that is. I'm mad, Nick, because you keep trying to shut me out. Because you don't want me in your life. Because you don't want me to build a life for myself in Antelope County, with *or* without you. Instead of being honest with me, you look at me with hot eyes, then shake your head sadly and tell me we're too different. That's a lie, and that's what I'm mad at you about! So maybe I didn't try as hard as I could have to stop the makeover girl. Too bad. Live with it."

Nick's mouth looked as tight as a newly strung clothesline. She turned away from him, suddenly not wanting this fight, not wanting the raw, exposed feelings, or the hurts, but it was too far gone to stop it now.

"I did not lie to you." Each of Nick's words was carefully enunciated. "I've been as honest as I could be from the beginning. You've forced your way into my life, you've demanded a partnership I didn't want and you've used my family to manipulate me into accepting you. Now you're encouraging my daughters in behavior I disapprove of. You're doing just what their mother does. She buys them ridiculous clothes, and lets them play with makeup. Then everyone acts like I'm an ogre for trying to stop it."

She whipped back around to face him. "I am not Tammy!"

"It doesn't matter, Dacy." He spread his open hands in front of him, in an impatient gesture. "You aren't the kind of woman I want to spend the rest of my life with. Even if we still want each other in bed, I don't want to deal with these kinds of conflicts any more than I already have to."

Dacy stepped close to him, crowding him so that she could feel the heat of his body. She knew he could feel her, as well. "You haven't bothered to really look at what kind of woman I am. You only see me through the screen of your fears."

His eyes dilated, and when she moved away, he drew her back, his hand on her arm. She didn't think he realized what he was doing. "Wise men pay attention to their fears, Dacy."

"Foolish men are limited by them."

He succumbed to her taunt, pulling her closer until they were pressed up against each other, breast to breast, belly to belly, thigh to thigh. His gaze fixed upon her mouth. She looked from his mouth, so inviting, so firm, to his cloudy, half-veiled eyes. Their breathing came short and fast, quickened now by desire more than anger. The change happened so fast, Dacy felt a little stunned. Nick swore under his breath. Then he kissed her.

His mouth was gentler than she expected. He licked her lips first, stroking insistently, lapping seductively, until she opened to him. He invaded her then, pressing, but not too far, demanding, but not taking anything that wasn't offered. She wanted his kisses. She kissed him back, chasing his tongue when he retreated, nibbling at his lips, opening for him when he advanced. Against her belly, he grew rigid, and she rubbed against him, arching her back, instinctively moving to enhance their desires. When his hand closed over her breast, she groaned aloud and pushed more fully into him.

The bedroom door swung open.

She jerked away from Nick. He didn't let go.

"Hey! What are you doing? We're late!" Amy sounded annoyed.

Jessica giggled. "Geez, you tell me my clothes are too sexy and look at you! Yuck. I may be too young to be sexy, but you're too old. Knock it off!"

Vaguely, Dacy noticed that Jessica was laughing at them. Neither she nor Nick were laughing. His eyes were dilated, making them look darker and more dangerous than usual, and his chest rose and fell rapidly. She knew her breathing matched his, breath for panting breath, and her lips felt swollen and sensitive. All of her felt ready for more of Nick, more kisses, more touches, more feelings, until there was nothing left between them but sensation and emotion.

Coming on the heels of their harsh words, it was too much. Confusion overcame her with the force of a summer thunderstorm. She'd thought she was in control of her feelings for Nick, that there was a strong rational side to how she felt about him. She was recovering from losing Charlie. Given their history, it was only natural that she would be attracted to Nick now. Combined with a chemistry that she couldn't deny, it all added up to an understandable attraction. At least, she thought she'd understood it.

There was no understanding this, though. One minute they had been arguing. She had been angry and hurt, and then they had gotten closer. That was all it had taken. He had touched her and her anger was lost in a tempest of powerful desire. Never in her life, not even when she'd made love with Nick when they were teenagers, had she felt anything like this. For a few minutes, there had been no rational control.

When she pulled away from Nick this time, he let her go, even though his gaze trailed her like a mountain lion stalking prey.

Edging away, Dacy found her purse and her keys and picked them up off the end table. "I don't think I feel up to going to dinner," she said slowly. "I'm more tired than I realized."

Nick cleared his throat. "All right."

He sounded relieved, she thought. He didn't want her along. Great. Digging deep, she found a smile for Jessica and Amy. "You girls take notes for me. I'll see you in the morning."

Slipping out the door, Dacy all but ran down the corridor to her room. As retreats went, it wasn't graceful, but it got her away from Nick, and right now, that was imperative.

They were going to have to talk about what had happened sometime, but Dacy didn't want to face him again tonight. Once in her room, she hurriedly changed into leggings and a sweatshirt. So much for the new dress and pearl earrings, she thought, putting the dress back on its hanger. On her way out, she scrawled a brief note to Nick, saying she'd see him tomorrow after the last session of the conference when it was time to go home.

Home. The thought was comforting. The old ranch *was* her home now, she reminded herself. It was also Nick and the girls' home. She and Nick needed to straighten some things out, yes, and they would. Tonight, though, she wasn't going to think about him anymore. Leaving the note at the front desk, Dacy flipped open a local newspaper she found in the lobby and scanned the movie listings. If she took a walk, picked up some dinner and went to a movie, she could be gone all evening. Tomorrow would be soon enough to deal with Nick. It would be soon enough to deal with feelings that went far deeper than she had suspected.

The conference was over at noon, and after a stop for pizza, Dacy, Nick and the girls were on the road west by one o'clock. Nick drove. Dacy tried to sit in the back, but neither of the girls wanted the front seat.

"We didn't get home until after midnight last night. If I want to sleep, there's more room back here." Jessica yawned to underscore her point.

Dacy felt a little stab of guilt. If she'd gone to dinner, she could have brought the girls home earlier and let Nick stay out as late as he wanted. Instead she'd watched a silly comedy and a big-budget action adventure movie that the critics had panned. Perversely, she'd liked it a lot, if only because the hero had long blond hair and pretty boy looks that were nothing whatever like Nick's.

Climbing into the front seat, Dacy fastened her seat belt and avoided looking at Nick. Every now and then, she felt his eyes on her. She asked the girls what Annamaria and Mitch had worn last night.

By the time they reached De Smet, the girls had finished telling Dacy about last night's dinner with Mitch and Annamaria and the congressman. Conversation lagged. Nick hadn't addressed a single comment to her, nor she to him. As the girls were lulled into a doze by the motion of the car, silence descended.

Before they'd reached Huron, both girls were slumped in the corners of the big back seat, pillows propped against the windows, sound asleep. At Redfield, Dacy would have liked to have stopped for a stretch, but she was reluctant to break the silence between her and Nick. It loomed as wide and flat as the prairie they were crossing. Taking a sip of water, she said nothing.

They reached Gettysburg a little after four. Amy woke up and asked for some water. Dacy passed a bottle back and looked over at Nick. His eyes stayed straight ahead, fixed on the highway.

"I'll drive anytime you want a break," she offered.

"I'm fine." He didn't look at her.

Amy handed the bottle back. "Are we at the river yet?"

"Almost," Nick answered. "Fifteen miles."

Amy went back to sleep before they crossed the Missouri River. The tense silence was driving Dacy nuts. Focusing on the landscape outside the window, she tried not to feel the knot in her stomach.

The land was dry west of the river. It was late May, and in a good year the grass would have been thick and green already. Only in the creases between the hills, where the water ran in gullies and draws, was it green. The tops of the hills still showed the dull brown of winter.

Thinking that she felt rather like the hills looked, a bit too dry, but coming back to life, waiting for the rains to come, Dacy risked a glance at Nick.

He was watching her.

In his eyes, she saw both fear and desire. Conflicting emotions lanced through her in the seconds that their eyes met before both of them looked back at the highway.

His fear made her impatient, angry, yet it also made her want to reassure him. Why was he so convinced she would hurt him? Why couldn't she have a simple, clear-cut response to his obvious fear?

Probably because the desire she saw in him made her ache. She thought of last night's kiss, of how volatile it had been. It had been like the west wind, powerful and full of promise, tempting them both past any semblance of control. Even as the west wind could become a dangerous hailstorm or tornado, passion could blow stronger than she had bargained for. Dacy had an inkling now that kisses like that might destroy people. Maybe Nick had good reason to be afraid.

She wasn't going to be afraid, though. Instead, she wanted the power of the desire she and Nick felt to excite her the way thunderstorms had excited her when she was a girl. Why be afraid, when she could let these feelings alert her to the possibilities of life?

Glancing back at Nick, Dacy's heart sped up a little. She watched him, thinking of all the good things she liked about him, and feeling the joy of that along with the pain of his resistance to her. He let her look, keeping his eyes on the road, but she knew by the way he shifted his shoulders that he was aware of her gaze.

She loved looking at him, she realized, and it wasn't just because she liked the dark hair curling over his collar, or the arch of his brow in profile. She liked looking at him because she liked him. She liked Nick as much as she'd ever liked anyone, despite his fears, his temper, and his insistence on pushing her away. She liked his honesty, his intelligence and his teasing sense of humor. She respected his commitment to ranching in a responsible fashion, and she admired his ability to share the vision he had for the new west. Nick had courage and compassion both, and Dacy thought that was wonderful.

She loved the way he interacted with his daughters. He was firm, yet generous, always willing to listen to them, always ready to talk, liberal with his hugs and kisses. She also loved the way he talked about the land, the way he knew the name of every plant, every bird and every creature that shared the ranch with them.

With a jolt, Dacy noticed how her thoughts had shifted from "like" to "love."

Did she love him?

Jessica and Amy had asked her yesterday and she hadn't known. She still didn't want to answer that question, but she knew what it was. With Nick, she felt things like with no one else. Some of those things hurt, yes, and even the hurts were more vivid, more intense, than anything she'd ever felt with Charlie. Then there were the good things she felt for Nick, the respect, admiration and affection. Those things warmed her in every cell of her being. Those feelings were like the west wind rising before the storm, enlivening awareness and awakening expectations.

Then there was the storm itself, the hot and liquid excitement that flowed like a growing, moving force within her. Nick fired her with a desire she had never experienced. With regret, she wished she had felt a fraction of that passion for Charlie.

As much as she missed Charlie, Dacy was glad to be where she was now. She was glad Nick was here, in spite of all their conflicts. Even now, with the tension between them, there was also a strong current of attraction. They shared a sexual passion that wasn't going to let them rest easy until they came to terms with it. This passion, layered in her heart with the affection, respect and frustration she also felt added up to an inescapable conclusion.

She had fallen in love with Nick all over again.

Chapter Eleven

In that moment of realization, Dacy was completely clear about what she wanted. As Nick had suggested that night on the prairie, she wanted a husband and kids. Specifically, she wanted *him,* and she wanted Jessica and Amy. She'd also like to have a baby with Nick. The thought of carrying a child within her body, a child they created together, out of love, made her eyes prickle with unshed tears.

Dacy wanted a life that she and Nick would make together, and she wanted all of them to live as a family in Antelope County, working the ranches that her's and Nick's great-grandparents had homesteaded. She wanted to combine their talents and resources and make something new, something they could share, and that would last. The house was only a first step. Now she knew what she wanted to follow it.

Last night, though, Nick had said again in no uncertain terms that she wasn't what he wanted.

Dacy didn't want to believe him. He wanted her. She could feel it in her very bones. She was fairly certain that he wanted the same thing that she wanted, but he didn't trust her. It galled her that he couldn't see her capacity to commit herself not only to the ranch, but to him and Jessica and Amy.

While she watched him, Nick's eyes remained on the highway as it dipped and curved through the rolling prairie, broken now by steep-sided gullies and an occasional cottonwood tree. *Look at me,* Dacy willed. *See my love for you and for this empty, open country of grass and sky. Feel my commitment with your heart. Know that I won't leave you... if you'll let me in.*

Nick was stubborn. He stared straight ahead into the lowering sun.

Well, Dacy thought, she had convinced him to sell her her grandparents' house. In his words, she'd steamrolled him. Now she was going to have to find out if he loved her, and if, as she hoped, he did, she would just have to convince him that she was a safe bet to stick around. If he wanted to call her determination "steamrolling," he certainly could, but it wasn't going to stop her. He would have to convince her in her heart that he didn't care for her before she would give up on him.

Twitching his shoulders, Nick wished Dacy would stop staring at him. It made him uncomfortable. Her gaze felt like a demand for resolution, but there wasn't anything he wanted to say to her in front of Jess and Amy. Truth be told, he wasn't sure he wanted to talk about what had happened last night at all. Seeing Jess dressed up like a teenager, wearing makeup that made her look years older, had shaken him for a couple of reasons. One was the realization that Jess and Amy weren't going to be little girls forever. That, he could cope with, he supposed. Every parent had to.

Much harder to deal with was the disappointment he had felt with Dacy. He'd experienced the same frustration he felt with Tammy, every time his ex-wife placed too much attention on clothes and cosmetics. Appearances and having fun had always been all that really mattered to Tammy. In his mind, it was all of a piece with being bored with life on the ranch, and with him, a rancher.

Even though he thought it was futile, he'd been nursing the hope that Dacy was different, that, despite her background, she might be able to be happy living in Antelope County—living with him. She was right, she wasn't Tammy. Even through his fears of repeating the past, he could see that. He could also see that the same potential existed for Dacy to grow bored with the ranch. The clothes and the makeup were only a small symptom of a potentially much bigger problem. As much as Dacy denied that that problem existed, Nick thought differently.

He wasn't completely sorry for the way he'd blown up at her. If she'd just listen to him once instead of assuming she knew what was best for everyone, it would make life a lot easier for all of them. Why wouldn't she accept that they weren't necessarily right for each other? It was as clear to him as a midsummer's day was long.

Or was it?

Nick didn't want to think she had a point that being a rancher didn't necessarily mean he was a backwater rube incapable of meeting a woman like Dacy on fair and equal ground. Yes, he had friends and colleagues who were powerful, influential people, but he wasn't living with any of them. He didn't depend on them for the kind of mutual trust and support he wanted with a wife.

Shifting his hands on the steering wheel, Nick could hear Dacy's breath hitch a little. For God's sake, if she was going to cry, he was going to get out and walk the rest of the way home. What the hell was she thinking about?

He didn't dare look at her. She made him mad, and she was impossible to deal with, but she was so pretty. She was so strong, so smart and so generous. He thought about kissing her last night, and his insides went all loose for a second and then as tight and hard as the packed earth in the corral. His jeans began to constrict. Damn her green eyes and I-told-you-so smile, Nick thought.

Impatiently, he punched on the radio and hit the search button. Within seconds, the car filled with a small-town deejay's voice.

"Ooookay, folks, that was Lynyrd Skynyrd singing "Sweet Home Alabama" for Roy and Tanya Flynn out at Faith. Happy anniversary, you guys, from your kids, Tommy, Christie and Julie. This is Wayne Cox and it's time for oldies. Call in your requests, folks. In the meantime, here's another one from the seventies."

The dark rhythms of a familiar song rolled from the car speakers. A woman's low, sultry voice almost chanted words that had played from the radio of a beat-up '65 Ford pickup while a pair of young lovers had learned the joys and pleasures of each other's bodies for the first time.

Nick stared at the radio blankly. He didn't see it, the highway or the new Suburban for a few seconds. He saw green eyes shadowed in the moonlight and heat lightning flashing in the distance. He felt young and strong and whole....

The entire summer had built to that one July night. Dacy had come to stay with her grandparents at their place a few miles up the valley. While he'd known her for years, that summer, there had been something different about her, something alluring that he hadn't been able to resist. He'd spent every moment he could spare and some he couldn't with her for two solid months. When they were apart, she was all he thought about.

Falling in love with Dacy Fallon had turned his summer to magic, and one night had been the most magical of them all.

That night he had planned to ask Dacy to marry him.

Until he died, Nick thought he would remember every detail of that evening. Late in July, the day had been hot and dry, but early evening thunderstorms threatened, flashing white lightning in towering blue-gray clouds. The sunlight fell in patches between the clouds, lighting the Fallon place in a pool of moving light as he drove in. He could smell the dust the pickup kicked up, the faint tang of the pines up on the buttes, and the sweet scents of cut clover and alfalfa in the fields.

More than anything else, he remembered how Dacy had looked, standing on her grandparents' porch. She'd had on a gauzy, pale green dress with a tie that ran under her breasts to make a bow in the back. It was sleeveless, and her hair had brushed her bare arms as she'd moved, making him ache to touch her. Her hair had been pulled back from her face in two tiny braids, held with narrow green ribbons at the back of her head.

To his young eyes, she'd been a vision, a beautiful princess, and she loved him. She'd told him so as they'd listened to the radio and watched the distant lightning flickering in the sky from a perch on Badger Butte. Her shy declaration had shattered him with joy. Then he'd asked her the question he knew he was too young to ask, yet too much in love not to.

Her answer rocked him.

"Yes, Nick," she'd said. "I'll marry you."

After that no more words had been necessary. Kisses communicated joy and the wonder of their love. By increments, as passion took them over, their touches had grown more heated. Everywhere he'd touched her, Nick's hands had burned, and he had been greedy. He'd wanted to touch her everywhere. Dacy was going to be his wife. He had wanted to know every precious inch of her.

And she had wanted him every bit as much.

"Sure?" he'd asked.

"Yes," she'd whispered. "Take me now."

On that distant summer night, as the song he heard now played on his old truck's radio, he had.

Nick tried not to look at Dacy, but his will seemed suddenly of no consequence in the face of the music's spell. He sought Dacy's gaze, wishing he didn't have to.

Dear God, she remembered. Knowing lit her cat's eyes. Worse, though, much, much worse, she was singing along. Her eyes bored into his with the same mixture of love and desire that he'd seen that long-ago summer night.

With his heart pounding, his insides spinning and his jeans getting tighter, Nick understood that whatever he might tell himself in his more rational moments, it was only a matter of time before they would once again take each other into a night made only for lovers.

Dacy didn't get a chance to talk to Nick about what had happened between them that evening. The charged moments during which she had sung to him had passed when Jessica awakened, wanting to find a radio station she could sing along with. Later, when they pulled into the drive at dusk, Jeff was there to meet them. He was obviously anxious to talk to them alone. Conversations of a private nature would have to wait.

In between carting armloads of new purchases into the house, Jeff caught Dacy and Nick together for a moment while the girls were in the house.

"Here," Jeff said, intercepting a couple of heavy bags of books as Nick was handing them to Dacy. "I'll take those."

Nick climbed out of the car. "Did Earl bite while we were gone?"

Jeff's nod was grim. "He sure did."

"What happened?" Dacy set the bag of stuffed animals she was holding on the ground.

"Earl and Cliff came out for a ride to their southwest pasture," Jeff began.

"Which borders our northeast pasture and the lease land where our breeder bulls are right now," Nick finished for him.

"Yeah." Jeff nodded. "If I hadn't been out there last night, we'd be short another bull calf or two today. After Cobie put the hay out for the bulls Friday evening, Earl rode in just about dark, hopped through the fence and added a few handfuls of his own." He pulled a handful of grassy stuff out of his pocket and handed it to Nick.

Nick swore.

"What is it?" It looked like any hay Dacy had ever seen.

"Loco weed and death camas. Any calf that eats this will get diarrhea and start upchucking until he's so dehydrated and confused he can't move. Damn! This is what's been bothering our calves, not scours. Earl's been poisoning our cattle for a year and a half!"

Jeff nodded in terse agreement. "It looks that way. If he tossed in a few handfuls at a time like this, only one or two animals would get sick."

"That's what's been happening." Nick took off his Stetson and raked his hand through his hair.

"Did you go to the sheriff yet?" Dacy asked.

"No. This isn't all." Jeff looked from her to Nick. "Earl and Cliff rode out to the meadow at the foot of the butte yesterday. I couldn't get close enough to hear them, but I didn't like the feel of it. They pulled up a few of the native grasses we've introduced, and paced off the meadow."

"Which meadow is that?" Dacy asked.

Nick answered. "If you follow the creek through Badger Gulch, it flows through an open meadow after a steep run down the butte. It borders the forest service land we lease, and for the past ten years, we've been restoring native plants to the area. We ripped out the junipers that had grown up along the stream after cattle destroyed all the natural cover. It's a showcase example of successful, ecologically sound range amd streamside management. It's part of what those folks from Washington are coming out here to see in July."

Dacy tapped her fingers on the head of a stuffed giraffe that protruded from the bag at her feet. "Does Earl know that?"

"It's no secret. Any BLM office around here could find out, and Earl's in tight with some of those guys in the regional office," Nick said.

"What do you think he was doing out there, then?"

Nick and Jeff exchanged a speculative glance. "If I had to guess," Nick mused, "I'd say he's got something up his sleeve to destroy that field. Was he spreading cheat grass seed around or something?"

"Nope." Jeff shook his head. "He was just looking. For now. I got a bad feeling about it, though."

"Me, too." Nick climbed out of the car. "How can we figure out what that old coot is up to?"

"Does he use cordless phones?" Dacy asked.

"Probably. Everybody else around here does," Nick told her. "So?"

"So listen in. It's easy, and it's legal."

Nick looked at her as though she was nuts. "Do you know how to do that? I don't." He planted his fists on his hips and looked at Jeff. "Jeff, do you know how to do that?"

"Nope."

"I didn't think so. Dacy?" He sounded impatient and angry.

"There's no need to get all bent out of shape. Dani has an old boyfriend in New York who's a private investigator. Why don't we call him and see what he says?"

While Nick appeared to consider this, Jeff instantly bristled. His eyes grew flinty. "That's a bad idea. We don't need help from some New York detective."

"I think we do," Dacy insisted. "Rafe's a great guy, too. If he's free, I'll bet he'd be glad to help us." She didn't say it, but she thought a little competition wouldn't hurt Jeff any. "Besides, Dani's been a little down lately. Maybe Rafe could cheer her up."

Jeff almost growled, but he turned the inarticulate sound in his throat into a grumble. "It isn't necessary. We can handle this."

"Call Dani and see what she thinks," Nick said, overruling his brother's objection. Dacy thought he looked suspicious as though he was hiding a smile. "If you don't mind paying for it, we can use all the help we can get. It's taken years to restore that meadow, and if it can help convince a few lawmakers and bureaucrats to cut loose some money for programs that encourage other ranchers to do the same thing, it's worth the price."

"As long as I'm paying," Dacy noted dryly.

Nick grinned at her. "As long as the lady is paying."

She gave him a long look before she picked up the bag of toy animals and flashed him a syrupy smile around the giraffe's head. Reaching over, she patted Nick on the cheek. "Your turn will come, sweetheart. Eventually, everyone pays the piper." She waltzed into the house, loudly humming their song.

Dacy awoke with a start. Something was amiss. Listening, she rolled to a sitting position and picked up her travel alarm. Three o'clock. It was silent. Ghostly light from the security lamp outside made shadows through the grape leaves that had overgrown the south window.

Then the faint sound of ice tinkling in a glass reached her ears. One quick glance revealed the source of her disturbance. Lounging against the frame of her opened door, Nick swirled the liquid in a glass, then took a sip. He wore jeans that weren't buttoned at the top and a gray sweatshirt, and no shoes over his woolen socks. As he lowered his glass, Dacy noticed that his hair was mussed. She watched him. His eyes never left her.

"Are you drunk?" Dacy was blunt, her voice scratchy with sleep.

"No. Just this one." He raised his glass toward her. "I couldn't sleep." He stayed where he was.

Dacy stifled a yawn and tucked her feet under her, inside the hem of her flannel nightgown, sitting back so she could lean against the back of the sofabed. "I suppose I've driven you to drink."

"Yeah, it's all your fault." He smiled over the rim of the glass.

He was in an odd mood. Dacy hadn't seen him like this before. "Do you want to talk?"

"About?" Sipping his drink seemed to occupy all his attention.

He was being dense. He was baiting her. "You know."

The mysterious smile reappeared. "Do I?"

"Nick. Either stop playing with me or go to bed."

"I thought you might want me to play with you in bed."

She blinked. "Is that why you're here?"

He glanced at the ice cubes on his glass, then back at her. "Only in my weaker moments."

Dacy pulled a pillow under her head and leaned her cheek against it. "I'm tired, Nick. I don't want to spar with you. If you want to talk about what happened when you kissed me, I will. But I'm too sleepy to trade quips." Her eyes drifted closed. A moment later, the mattress sank under Nick's weight. Opening her eyes, she found him sitting beside her. Heat radiated from him, and she fought the urge to snuggle her feet under his thigh.

"What were you doing in the car when you sang that song to me?" Anguish colored his tone. "Why did you do that?"

He wasn't quite touching her. Moving her knee slowly, she brought it up against his hip. Warmth spread out from him, making her want to curl up in his arms. Instead, she touched one finger to the back of the hand that held his glass. It was warm, too.

"Why, Dacy?"

She studied his hand. "Because I want you. Because I care. Because I'm not seventeen anymore and I want you to know me as a woman, not a girl."

His free hand raked his hair, and he leaned his head back, eyes closed, mouth drawn taut. "Did you hear anything I said to you the other night?"

"Yes." She traced the outline of his thumb, feeling the roughened skin, the smooth nail. A bead of moisture from the glass caught on her finger, and she rubbed it back over the tip of his thumb. "You said you don't want me." Her finger slid over the base of his thumb, tickling the inside of his wrist. "Tell me you don't want me now."

Dropping his head, he stared at her finger. "I don't want you, Dacy."

Pressing gently, she found his pulse point. "Then why is your heart racing?"

He turned to look at her.

"Why are you here, sitting on my bed in the middle of the night?"

Bending, he set his whiskey on the floor. When he looked back at her, a fire from within lit his eyes. Dacy's breath caught in her throat, and she was suddenly completely awake, completely alive. When Nick's strong fingers, cooler than his palm from the glass, closed over her hand, she laced her fingers with his and matched his fierce grip.

"Because the middle of the night belongs to lovers," he whispered, lowering his head, eyes fixed on her mouth.

"Do you want to be lovers?"

He made an inarticulate sound.

"Do you love me, Nick?"

He paused, raising his eyes in a questioning glance that shot straight to her heart. "I don't want to." He touched his nose to hers. "But I want you."

"Then take me now," she whispered.

"Take me, now," he repeated as their lips met.

His kiss was not gentle. Their hunger was impatient, needy, driven to press, to take, to demand the most that each had to offer, and then more. Nick's mouth, firm and resilient, held the tang of Irish whiskey and the sweet muskiness that was his own taste. Delving deep into his mouth, Dacy twined her free arm around his neck, urging him closer. He came easily, and when his weight pushed her back into the pillows, she reveled in his strength and size. Their kisses melded surrender and conquest into a fever of excitement.

She wanted more. More skin, more of him to touch. She wanted to kiss him everywhere, and she wanted his mouth to touch every curve, every hollow of her body. They would devour each other with hot, starving kisses fueled by Nick's resistance and her own need.

He nipped her lip and she cried out, tossing her head back, giving him access to her neck. Shivers rippled through her as he licked and nipped at the sensitive skin under her ear. His kisses were wild, almost past the limits of control, but she wanted him this way. Matching his intensity, she dug her fingers into his hair, pulling his mouth back to hers, making him hold still while she kissed his jaw and his earlobe as he had hers. She had no conscious thought, just impetus to act, to touch, to kiss, to hold, and to receive Nick's touches, his kisses, his weight upon her.

Rearing back a little, Nick focused his gaze on the row of tiny buttons that ran down the front of her white flannel gown. Disentangling his hand from Dacy's, he ran the backs of his knuckles down the line of buttons. Then one by one, he flicked them open. Slowly, he spread back each half of the gown to reveal her breasts. Already tightened by the desire ignited by Nick's kisses, her nipples hardened more as the cool air washed over her chest.

"You're even more beautiful than you were at seventeen," he whispered, cupping her left breast and raising it up to meet his tongue.

Both of them groaned aloud when he took her nipple into his mouth.

Images flashed through Dacy's mind of that summer night, so long ago, when Nick had first caressed her breasts and told her she was beautiful as he made love to her. This was a very different night. They weren't kids. There had been a sweetness that night, an innocence that was gone now. In its place was a raw and powerful yearning, made more poignant by the intervening years that had brought each of them disappointments, sharpening their need for the very innocence they lacked.

A deep shudder wracked Dacy, and a wave of grief overcame her. Nick kissed her bare breasts, and she knew how vulnerable they both were. She understood his resistance. She also knew he would withdraw from her again, no matter where this night took them.

"Nick, stop."

He lifted his head. One look at her face, and he drew back, releasing her breast.

"What happens afterward if we make love now?"

Taking a deep breath, he looked away from her.

"Are you ready to face what we feel for each other?"

Deliberately, he pulled the edges of her nightgown together and buttoned each small button. Then he hoisted himself up so that he was sitting beside her, one arm on either side of her. "You know I'm not, Dacy."

She reached up to touch his cheek, and tried for a smile. It didn't hold. Neither did the tears she was trying not to let spill. "Do you remember that first night I came back? I asked if you'd have had things be any different in the past. You said, some things, and I thought you were wrong to say that. But right now, I wish I could go back. I wish I had fought my dad and stayed here with you. I wish things had been different. But we can't go back there, Nick."

Gathering her into his arms, he held her close. "Shhh, honey. It's okay." He rocked her lightly.

Through her tears, Dacy clung to him. "You'd just push me away again, Nick. But you wouldn't have then."

"Dacy, that time is gone. We've changed."

"We still care about each other." She couldn't quite say, *we still love each other,* but that was what she meant. They both knew it. "Why do you have to be so damn stubborn?"

"I must have learned it from those danged bulls we raise," he said, smiling into her hair.

She sat back and held him at arm's length. "Are you ever going to get over it?"

Sobering, he met her gaze. "I don't know."

Dacy sighed. "That's what I was afraid of."

He stood. "I won't do this to you again. It was wrong of me. It's just that..." One hand raked into his hair. "Oh, hell, never mind." He walked out without another word.

Dacy picked up his whiskey and soda and drained it before crying herself to sleep.

Chapter Twelve

To Dacy's way of thinking, she and Nick had resolved little, but he acted as if there was nothing more to talk about the next morning. They each went about their business, and Nick was maddeningly cheerful. He and Jeff were getting ready to bring all the new calves in for branding. Their excitement put her in a bad mood, so she called Dani to get Rafe's number. She might as well put her irritation to use thwarting Earl Tally.

A round of phone tag finally ended around noon when she located Rafe in Denver, of all places. He agreed to drive up at the end of the week when he was finished testifying in a court case, but only after he had received Dacy's assurance that Dani hadn't married that cowboy she was so hung up on. Taking perverse pleasure in the prospect of irritating one of the reluctant Reynolds brothers, Dacy was looking forward to Rafe's visit.

The workmen were framing the new walls for the second-floor bedrooms and the house was filled with the sounds of hammers and nail guns pounding, radios blaring and workmen and women hollering back and forth. Dacy decided it would be a good day to visit the Gas'n'Gitit to catch up on local gossip. Calling Dani again, she arranged to meet her for coffee. Maybe she needed to talk to another woman about what was happening with Nick.

An hour later, Dacy and Dani were huddled in a corner booth at Char's, sipping weak coffee and picking at a bear claw between them.

"Ugh." Dani grimaced after a swallow of coffee. "Maybe we should chip in to get Char a cappuccino machine."

Dacy laughed. "No one would drink it but us. You can't drink two gallons of good coffee a day without going through the ceiling from the caffeine. You know how everyone here always has a big thermal coffee mug in hand."

"Yeah, I know. There aren't too many things I miss from New York, but good coffee is one of them." She dumped a packet of sugar into her cup, then a generous dollop of real cream. She grinned. "Camouflage."

Dacy sipped her coffee black like a stoic. "How do you feel about Rafe coming?"

"Fine. It'll be nice to see him. I like Rafe. What did he say when you talked to him?"

"He wants to see you. He wanted to know if you'd married that cowboy. I assume he meant Jeff."

"Hmmm." Dani stirred her coffee. "I expect you told him I hadn't."

"Did you want to marry Jeff?"

Dani nodded slowly.

Dacy broke off a piece of pastry. "What happened? He watches you like a hawk when you're around."

Shaking her head, Dani fixed her gaze on the tabletop. "A year ago, I came back here because Rafe wanted to get married. He made me think about what I wanted out of my life—career, relationships, everything. He said he didn't want me unless I was sure I wanted him. So I thought. I'd done most of what I wanted to in my career. I could go further, but I'm not that ambitious. I was tired of New York and Milan and Paris. I wanted to ride horses and talk to my mom and chase after cattle for a while.

Dacy smiled. "That sounds familiar."

"Yeah. We're predictable, aren't we?" Dani caught her eye and laughed. "Unfortunately, I also had to face the fact that much as I liked Rafe, I was still hung up on Jeff. I don't know what it is about that man, Dace, but he just makes me hum. It's like there's a switch in me that only he knows about and when he hits it, I feel more alive, stronger, more powerful, and, at the same time, just so vulnerable."

"I know what you mean," Dacy agreed softly.

Dani tossed her braid back over her shoulder. "So I set about trying to seduce Jeff."

Dacy licked a crumb from her finger. "Did you?"

"Oh, yeah." Dani sat back and looked out the window as a semi roared by on the highway. Her voice dropped. "Afterward, I told him how I felt about him and that I wanted to get married. To him."

Dacy waited.

"He didn't want me." She shook her head as if she was still baffled by his reaction. "He said he loved me, but that it wouldn't be fair for me to be tied to him. He's got some stupid idea that he's not good enough for me somehow." Dani put her chin in her hand. "Damn fool man. I couldn't change his mind."

"But what about you? What's been going on? Have you jumped Nick's bones yet?"

Dacy rolled her eyes. "I don't know what I'd call it. I want to. A few times we've gotten real close. Then Nick pulls away and insists I'll eventually hate the ranch and want to leave, and so he can't get involved because he doesn't want anyone to get hurt. Last night he came to my room in the middle of the night and we almost..." Dacy discovered that the trucks passing on the highway were infinitely more interesting when the words came hard. "I was the one who stopped it."

"Why?" Now Dani's voice was quiet.

"Because he wasn't ready and I didn't want him to push me away when the passion cooled." She looked back at Dani. The empathy in her cousin's face brought the tears back.

Dani fished through her purse, then passed Dacy a tissue. "I don't know what's wrong with those two. You'd think they'd been abandoned as children or something horrible, as shy of relationships as they are. But we know their parents. They didn't get warped at home."

"That's right, they didn't," Char said, looming suddenly with the coffeepot in hand.

"How long have you been there?" Dacy asked, discreetly trying to dab away her tears.

"Long enough," Char said tartly as she refilled their cups. "As good as their upbringing was, both those Reynolds boys have been abandoned by women. Nick's wife took off on him. In fact, each of you abandoned them."

"No, we didn't," Dani denied.

Dacy's heart sank. "I did. I didn't mean to, but I did."

"You were only seventeen. Your dad made you leave," Dani insisted. "That's not abandonment."

"I never came back. I was having fun at college. It might have felt like abandonment to Nick."

Char pulled over a counter stool and perched at the end of their table. "That's right. You probably don't know this, but Nick had a few wild years after you left. He knew you didn't leave because you wanted to, but it still tore him up. He took to the rodeo circuit for a couple years, riding bulls, and he ran around with a rough crowd. Lots of wild girls, too. That's where he met Tammy. He finally settled down and went to college back east, but in the summers, he still rode bulls. Tammy got herself pregnant before his junior year so he'd have to marry her. She wanted to move to New York with him. I bet you didn't know all that."

Dacy hadn't known. "No, I didn't." She did some quick figuring in her head. "Jessica isn't old enough to have been that baby, is she?"

Char's gray curls bobbed when she shook her head. "Tammy miscarried. Or so she claimed. I'm not sure myself she was really pregnant. Jess came along later." Char turned her eye on Dani. "And you, Miss Model, you left Jeff, whether you want to admit it or not. Once you won that contest and took off for Miami, we didn't hardly hear from you for five years."

Dani bristled. "I was pursuing my career! What's wrong with that? Women don't sit around waiting to get married anymore, Char, and I couldn't very well be a model in Antelope County. And then when I was traveling constantly, I always wrote Jeff. I called him more often than anyone except my parents. Just because he didn't want to leave Antelope County, that didn't mean I had to stay here forever."

Char laughed. "Don't get all worked up into a dither, girl. I know that and you know that. That boy doesn't know it, though. He wanted to be the center of your world, and he didn't think about how silly that is. That's how some men are. They want to please you so bad, they want to give you the moon. You have to show them you're happy with being held and loved and listened to."

"How do we do that?" Dacy leaned forward. "They're both so stubborn."

"You hold 'em and love 'em and listen to them," Char said as if it was the most obvious thing on earth. "For a pair of smart women, you two have about as much man sense as a pair of panty hose." Char hoisted herself off the stool and picked up the coffeepot. "Those boys are starved for loving, girls, and I don't mean just sex. But I'd start with sex. They are men, after all." Char waltzed back toward the register at the front of the store. "And, Dacy? It wouldn't hurt you to get involved in the community more. If Nick's worried you'll leave, put down roots."

Both Dacy and Dani watched her retreat, then shared a speculative glance.

Dacy furrowed her brow. "I think I'm going to take Char's advice. On both counts. I love him, Dani. Maybe making love can get us past some of his resistance, and if he sees that I mean to stay here, with or without him, maybe he'll see reason."

Dani raised her coffee cup and touched it to the rim of Dacy's in a toast. "Here's to better luck than I had."

"Thanks. I'm going to need it if I'm going to find a time and a place for a seduction in the midst of the renovations, Jessica and Amy, Jeff and all the work we have to do."

"You'll know when the right time comes," Dani predicted. "What kind of community involvement did you have in mind?"

"Country Culture Club?" she ventured, naming a ladies' group that their grandmother had helped found in the 1920s. Each month they got together to share desserts, conversation and some tidbit of cultural enrichment. The youngest member was at least seventy-five years old.

"It's a start," Dani said, chuckling.

"Church?" Dacy suggested.

"Good choice," Dani concurred. "And the girls' athletic league needs a coordinator."

Dacy rose, gathering up her cup and napkins. "Lead the way, cousin. A civic-minded citizen has been born."

* * *

Late Thursday afternoon, Dacy was sitting in a lawn chair at a table made out of two sawhorses and a sheet of plywood, thumbing through the songbook used by the Country Culture Club. Lazy cloud shadows drifted across the sun, skimming along in a breeze that didn't reach the surface. Still and warm, it was a perfect summer afternoon, punctuated by the sounds of workers in the house and meadowlarks in the fields.

A plume of dust rising from behind a hill on the road heralded a visitor. Dacy looked up to watch, smiling when she recognized Dani's 4-Runner. In a minute, Dani strode across the lawn to greet her.

"Hi, cousin."

"Boy, am I glad to see you," Dacy said, shielding her eyes against the sun. "Which do you like better—Columbia, the Gem of the Ocean,' or 'America the Beautiful'?"

"What?" Dani gaped at her.

"I have to pick the song for the Country Culture Club meeting tomorrow afternoon. Since Flag Day is in June, they picked a patriotic theme. What do you think?"

"I've never heard of 'Columbia, the Gem of the Ocean.' Is it a ship?"

"I have no idea. 'America the Beautiful,' then." Dacy wrote it down on her program list.

"You certainly act fast when you set your mind to something," Dani noted. "Have you . . . ?"

"No, I haven't. No chance. If the girls aren't right here, Jeff is, or Nick isn't. He's inside now, making calls to new clients, but so is Jeff and Harley's crew. I may have to wait a couple weeks until the girls go to Denver to visit their mother," Dacy confided. "Maybe we'll get some time alone then."

"I'll bet Nick's thrilled about the girls going to see Tammy," Dani said.

"I think he's okay with it. They go every summer, and she is their mother. Look—" Dacy pointed toward the road "—someone else is coming. Do you recognize that van?"

Dani squinted at the older, dark blue van turning into the drive. Then she gave a squeal and began waving both arms. "It's Rafe! Come on, Dace, come meet him!" Dani trotted back to where the cars were parked.

Dacy rose in time to hear the screened porch door snick shut. Both Nick and Jeff stood on the porch, Nick looking uncharacteristically chipper, while Jeff looked about ready to put his fist through the screen.

Clapping Jeff on the shoulder, Nick grinned at Dacy. "Come on, people. Let's meet our private eye." He almost skipped down the steps to Dacy's side, where he took her arm and steered her toward the van.

"This'll be a nice change of pace," he whispered in her ear. His breath was warm and it tickled. A shiver ran down her neck. "My brother has been enjoying watching us figure out what to do with each other. Now we get to watch him squirm." He chuckled.

"What *are* we going to do with each other?" Dacy asked, all innocence.

"Meet the private eye." Nick's lips tickled her ear again.

Hunching her shoulders in defense, but not moving even an inch away from him, Dacy wished he was always like this.

Rafael Saavedra had to be the second sexiest man Dacy had ever seen, excepting only the man at her side. More than six feet tall, Rafe was built like a model himself with a rock-solid chest and thighs like strong young oak trees, with both shown to advantage by his army green tanktop and khaki shorts. He wasn't a classically handsome man. His eyebrows were a little heavy, and if he ever gained weight, he might become jowly; nonetheless, he seethed sensuality. With his long, dark brown hair tied up in a ponytail and soulful brown eyes, he looked like a weary warrior of old. When he smiled, his eyes twinkled, but there was just a hint of sadness that didn't disappear. Dacy didn't know how Dani had resisted this man.

"Ah, this must be the beautiful Dacy Fallon." Rafe stepped forward and took her hand gently. His deep voice held the slightest trace of an accent.

Nick stepped closer to Dacy and put his arm around her shoulders.

"It's nice to meet you finally, Rafe." Dacy snuggled herself into Nick's side, making it clear where she wanted to be. Rafe's eyes lit with tacit understanding. "Welcome to the Fallon-Reynolds Ranch."

"This must be the Reynolds half of the operation, then." Rafe held out a hand to Nick.

Nick accepted it. "Half of the Reynolds partners. Nick Reynolds. My brother Jeff's on his way over. We're real pleased you could help us out on such short notice."

Rafe raked Dani with an appreciative glance. "It's worth it for the chance to see Dani again." He ruffled her hair with one big hand. "I feared I drove her from the city last year."

Dani looked at him with affection. "No, you just gave me the excuse I'd been looking for."

Jeff joined the group then. He looked as if every hair on his body was standing straight up, and when Rafe held out a hand, he made an inarticulate sound that might have been a snarl.

Nick pushed him gently and Jeff grudgingly accepted Rafe's handshake. "Jeff Reynolds." His voice was low, only barely polite.

"Rafe Saavedra." He rolled the *r* in his last name. "You must be the cowboy."

"We're all cowboys out here." Jeff widened his stance and perched one fist on his hip.

Dani looked flushed. "Well, now that you've met everyone, Rafe, I'll bet you'd like something cold to drink."

The smile Rafe gave Dani could have powered the state of South Dakota for ten years. He slung an arm around her waist and kissed her forehead. "You haven't lost your ability to read my mind. Show me the way, woman."

Dani led him toward the house while Jeff seemed to be choking on something.

Nick hit him on the back a little harder than was necessary. "This is your own fault."

"Shut up," Jeff growled. "Just shut the hell up."

"Come on, Dace, let's go fill Rafe in on the details and find out what he's got up his sleeve." Nick's arm slid down her arm and he took her hand, tugging a little.

Dacy went, thinking there might be more advantages to having Rafe around than she had imagined.

Over cold drinks and chips eaten at the makeshift picnic table, Rafe explained that he had borrowed the van and some surveillance equipment from a fellow detective in Denver. After listening to Nick and Dacy recount what they knew about Earl's attempts to undermine the Reynolds Ranch, he also took the faxes Dacy had from Nick's former clients.

"I can find out where these came from, if you want," he offered. "If the most substantial charges you have against Tally are trespassing and vandalism, you won't be able to get him off your back. Forging state documents could put him away for a while."

Nick took a healthy swallow of beer. "What if the land he was trespassing on was federal property instead of private land? Would that make any difference in the severity of the penalties?"

"I can find out," Rafe said. "Why do you ask?"

"Half of that meadow we're worried about is part of our forest service lease. It's federal land. We took out the fencing when we reorganized our grazing program a few years ago," Nick explained.

"I'll look into that, too. In the meantime, I'll set up the van near Earl's home. Can any of you take shifts listening?" Rafe looked at Dani.

"Sure," she said.

"I can help, too," Dacy added.

"I don't think Jeff or I can get away. We're about ready to start branding, and then we've got to start moving the cattle through the pastures," Nick told him.

"That's okay. I think the three of us can cover it. In fact—" Rafe grinned "—I may ask one of these women to take over one day so I can play cowboy with you."

Dani plucked Nick's hat off his head and dropped it on Rafe's. "What do you say? Does he look the part?"

Nick and Dacy laughed. "He sure does. I'd better watch it or he'll have my job."

Rafe tipped back the Stetson and snatched up a blade of grass, which he stuck between his teeth. "Don't worry, pardner. The lovely Danielle can keep me happy here for a week or two, but then I'll be glad to get back to New York."

"I know somebody who'll be glad to hear that." Dacy reached past Nick to dip a chip in the bowl of salsa. Her arm brushed his. He didn't move away.

Dacy liked Rafe's being there. She really did.

Chapter Thirteen

Sunday afternoon, Dacy found herself sitting in Rafe's van, parked in an out-of-the-way gully near the top of the butte, with headphones on, listening to Earl Tally tear his broker away from a golf game to take some abuse over stock market vagaries. Musing over how much damage she could do to Earl with the information she was hearing, Dacy regretted that she was such an honest soul. If she weren't, she could fix Earl's wagon but good with a little hacking and what she knew about the markets. She wouldn't do that, though. They would get him fair and square, with Rafe's help.

Being cooped up in a parked van wasn't the ideal way to spend a Sunday afternoon in June, but it had been Dacy's choice. After attending church that morning with Jessica and Amy, she had wanted some time alone to think. More than one parishioner had made an acerbic comment about Nick and Jeff and their ideas about new ranching. It seemed that Earl Tally wasn't the only one of their neighbors who wasn't enthralled with protecting grazing land, or with forgoing growth hormones and antibiotics.

Dacy got the distinct impression, however, that some of the people she talked to were more bothered by Nick and Jeff's limited involvement in the community than they were genuinely annoyed by their politics. Ermaline and Ross Kincaid, parents of one of Amy's friends from school, had asked Dacy if she might be able to get Nick to come out to their roping club to do a demonstration for the younger boys. When Dacy was reluctant to answer for him, the Kincaids assumed it was because Nick thought he was too good to help out his neighbors now that he was hobnobbing with senators and millionaires, and they said as much. Dacy had had to let it go since she didn't want to try explaining her and Nick's relationship.

That was another sore point. Carol Jean Willey, who had gone to high school with Nick, had asked her point-blank whether she and Nick were sharing sleeping quarters. Luckily, Jessica and Amy hadn't been at her side to hear that, but later, in the car on the way home, Jessica reported that there was widespread speculation about the state of Nick and Dacy's relationship.

"I just shrugged my shoulders and told them I had no idea," Jessica said with infinite patience over the foibles of adults. "But I did tell them you didn't sleep together, and as far as I know, you haven't had sex."

Dacy's face had flushed hot at that. She'd managed a strangled and sarcastic, "Thank you."

Amy wasn't to be left out of the conversation. "Have you?" she asked, all innocence. "Had sex with my dad?"

Dacy made an exasperated sound and refused to look at her.

"You aren't supposed to ask straight out like that, Amy," Jessica explained from the wise vantage point of an eleven-year-old. "It's personal."

"Oh. Sorry, Dacy. I mean, it is our dad, so I figured we should know."

"We do know," Jessica countered. "I heard Rafe tell Dani that they'd be able to tell in a second when Dad and Dacy finally did it because Dad might actually sit down in the house for more than a minute at a time."

"All right," Dacy interrupted. "That's enough. I'm so embarrassed I'm going to melt right here and you two are going to have to walk the rest of the way home."

The girls had laughed, and mercifully, they'd stopped.

The upshot was that Dacy had a lot to think about. She was concerned about the lack of support for Nick and Jeff in the community at large, and she didn't like being the subject of gossip. The latter was probably inevitable, she decided, and impossible to quell. She and Nick would either work things out or they wouldn't, and in a community the size of Antelope County, everyone who cared would know about it.

The former, however, Dacy thought she might be able to do something about. Nick needed greater community support. Although he hadn't said so directly, she knew from handling some of the correspondence that the delegation from Washington was expecting a show of local support. Without other ranchers willing to make changes, there would be no point to the legislation supporting new ranching.

Tapping her fingers on her leg, Dacy began a mental inventory of who she should talk to first. The ladies in the Country Culture Club would make a good start. She thought she could take them into her confidence and get their ideas, as well. They knew everyone in the community and all the intricacies of past feuds and alliances. They could guide her.

Marshaling support for the delegation visit would help build the community ties Char had told her to pursue, as well. Dacy hoped the older woman had been right, and that if Nick saw her working to build relationships in the community and getting to know people, maybe he would come to see that she didn't intend to bolt as soon as the house was completed. Crossing her fingers in a girlish gesture, she prayed that he would be able to trust her commitment to staying in Antelope County and, eventually, to trust her love for him, for his daughters and for the land they lived in.

Most of the afternoon passed in a blur of Tally household phone calls, all duly recorded, most of them short, boring rambles about the weather and cattle futures and an upcoming stockmen's dinner. At six o'clock, Rafe appeared to take the next shift.

"Hello, beautiful Dacy," he greeted her, climbing into the back of the van.

"Hello, beautiful Rafael," she teased.

"You don't take me seriously, I see." He lifted the headphones from her head. "But you like it when I flirt with you in front of Nick."

Dacy chuckled. "You noticed that, did you?"

"I'm not a private detective for nothing, sweetheart." He put a Humphrey Bogart twist on the endearment. "Did you hear anything useful?"

"No, but I heard enough that if I didn't already think Earl was a complete skunk I'd be convinced now," Dacy said, handing him the notes she'd taken. "Earl's cantankerous, but careful. Cliff should be back tonight, though, and he's more likely to shoot off his mouth. Maybe you'll have better luck."

"Let's hope so, but experience tells me we may have to wait quite a while." Rafe glanced over her notes. "Your boyfriend got back just before I left. You should hurry home if you want to catch him."

Dacy felt her cheeks heat up. "Nick's not my boyfriend."

He laughed. "All right, your lover. Whatever you want to call it." He took one of her arms and guided her out of the seat.

"No, you don't understand," Dacy protested.

Rafe smiled his slightly sad, infinitely amused smile as he sat down. "Yes, I do understand. For reasons that I cannot fathom, Nick and Jeff Reynolds love and are loved by two of the most intelligent, most attractive women I know, one of whom I would cast aside my freedom for in a second if she would have me. Fools that they are, these cowboys are compelled to drive these women away." He raised a speculative eyebrow. "It might be a good strategy, though. With women like you and Dani, playing hard to get may be the only way to hold you."

Dacy stared at him. "What?"

"You get things easily. They know that. Maybe they don't want to be taken for granted." He adjusted the headphones and a couple of knobs on the tape recorder.

"So you think Nick is being stubborn on purpose, just so he can be sure I really want him?"

"Not on purpose. Neither of those cowboys is that calculating. It's subconscious instinct." Rafe looked up at her. "Of course, Nick could just be incredibly stupid. I know his brother is." He shook his head, lost in thought for a moment. Then he smiled at Dacy. "You better scoot on out of here. If you give him too long, that cowboy of yours is going to elude you again."

Dacy patted him on the arm and went. Maybe tonight, she thought. Maybe tonight she would find Nick alone and then . . . Butterflies erupted in her stomach as she imagined what she wanted to do. *Dear God, please let this work,* she prayed. *Let Nick love me. Let him trust me enough.*

* * *

Luck wasn't on Dacy's side that night. Nick was on his way out when she arrived at the house, and Jeff was with him.

"Where are you going?" She tried to keep the disappointment out of her voice.

"There's a couple hours of daylight left. We've got work to do to get ready for branding next week," Nick said, shouldering a well-worn saddle. "See you in the morning. I'll be late tonight. Jerri Beyer's bringing the girls back around nine." He swatted her on the rear end as he walked past.

"Hey!" Dacy jumped, hands flying to cover her backside. Nick was out the door and gone before she could say anything else. She stared after him, a slow smile playing its way to her lips.

Damn, he looked good. With that saddle over his shoulder, in jeans and boots and a red cotton shirt, he was so sexy she could hardly breathe. He was still avoiding her, even though the swat on the butt was a good sign. It wasn't exactly a kiss on the cheek, but she took it as progress.

Since he was gone, Dacy made herself a salad and took it into her office. She pulled the phone book to her and looked up Mildred Chamberlain's number. Mildred was the youngest of the Country Culture Club members at age seventy-six and she had the best hearing of any of them. Putting down her fork, she dialed.

"Hello, Mildred?" Dacy began. "Do you have a few minutes to talk? I'd like your advice about something...."

The next week was chaotic. Jessica and Amy finished the school year, including a few made-up snow days, and branding was under way. By the weekend, Dacy could only imagine what she had been thinking to assume she might find some time alone with Nick. Between shuttling back and forth to town and the ranches of people Mildred Chamberlain had told her to talk to, to the girls' friends' places, to the Reynolds home place where the branding was going on, to the grocery store in Belle Fourche, plus keeping tabs on the renovations at the house, and taking her turn at listening in on the Tallys, Dacy didn't have time for a good long shower, much less a seduction. In odd moments, she fretted about not having shaved her legs in two weeks, just in case she did manage to corner Nick. It was futile, though. The only times she saw him, one or both of them was dusty, dirty and tired, and there were always at least three other people present.

Finally, on Thursday afternoon, on her way home from picking up Jessica and Amy for a sleepover, Dacy gave up. The girls would be leaving next Tuesday morning to spend a month in Denver with their mother. Maybe after that things would settle down a little. In the meantime, she would have to tolerate her heightened awareness around Nick, and the restless impatience she struggled with every night.

Tuesday morning, Nick was getting ready to drive Jessica and Amy to the Rapid City airport. The sun was barely peeking above the horizon as they loaded the girls' suitcases into the back of Nick's pickup, and the smell of clover and sage was as heavy as the dew that soaked Dacy's tennis shoes.

"Come here, you two," Dacy invited, holding her arms open for Jessica's and Amy's hugs. Clasping both girls to her at once, she closed her eyes against the lump in her throat. "I'm going to miss you guys."

"We'll miss you, too." Amy squeezed her hard.

Dacy glanced up at Nick. He wore what was by now a familiar expression of mingled dread and desire, as if she were a rattlesnake carrying ropes of rubies and pearls in her jaws. He wanted the jewels, but he was afraid to take them. Closing her eyes, she shut him out and concentrated on Jessica and Amy.

"You call me if you need anything. If you forgot something, or if you just want to say 'hi,' I'll be right here," she assured them.

Jessica pulled back and kissed her cheek. "I know you will."

Dacy wished Nick would take a lesson from his daughter.

"And watch the makeup." Dacy didn't know where the admonition came from. She glanced self-consciously away.

Jessica and Amy laughed, and in a flurry of final hugs and calls of goodbye, Nick herded them into his pickup. As they pulled away, raising a low cloud of gravel dust along the drive, Dacy fought back tears. In that moment, she understood Nick a little better. The girls would be gone a month. They would grow in that time, and when they returned, they wouldn't be the same. Dacy worried about all the different ways Tammy might hurt them, and she knew better why Nick was so wary of letting her into his life. She didn't want to see Jessica and Amy hurt, and the protective impulses she felt were not as strong as Nick's, she knew.

All things considered, though, it was a little late to be worrying. She was already part of his life. All that remained was negotiating exactly what that meant.

Nick arrived home late that afternoon, determined to move over to the bunkhouse with Jeff and Cobie, their ranch hand, now that Jess and Amy were gone for a while. He needed a break from the hot, taunting looks Dacy kept sending his way, and from the sweet smiles she lured him with. With his control stretched as taut as it could go without breaking, Nick wanted to put some physical distance between them. He was starting to think things he didn't want to think. This morning, after he'd watched

Jess and Amy's plane disappear into the clouds, Dacy was all he'd thought about.

Before loading up two coolers at the grocery store she insisted had the freshest produce, he'd walked along Main and St. Joseph streets, doing a little window-shopping. He'd replaced a book on rock art in the cave hills area for Jeff, and he'd picked up some sausage that Cobie liked. He'd debated what to get Dacy. She hadn't asked for anything, and she could buy anything she wanted and afford to have it delivered the next day. Still, he'd wanted to get her something. When he caught himself in front of a jewelry store checking out the engagement rings, he'd panicked.

But he took a deep breath and went inside, anyway. Stalwartly refusing to ask the clerks about the rings, he picked out a pretty pendant in Black Hills gold, a cluster of grapes and leaves in rose and green gold to hang on a long golden chain—over her heart. It was still too personal. It wasn't a gift for a business partner.

Hell, who was he kidding? he thought, hoisting one of the coolers off the bed of the pickup. She was more than a business partner, and he damn well knew it, even if he wouldn't admit it.

And he wasn't going to admit it, because then he would feel honor-bound to do something about it. Right now, he thought, picking his way along a plank path over the dug-up ditches in the yard, he was going to retreat. He called himself a coward, and he didn't much care.

Shouldering his way through the back door, Nick heard Dacy laugh. Unconsciously, he smiled. Then he heard Rafe's deep laughter join hers, and he sobered. No doubt that slick detective was flirting with her again.

"I've got a pickup full of salad, if anyone wants to help haul it in here," he called out, putting the cooler down with a loud thump.

Dacy met him with a smile. "Hi, Nick." She made a move toward him, as if to hug him, then checked herself. He was relieved...and disappointed. "Jessica called from Tammy's. They arrived on time and with no problems."

"Good." He gave her a long look. In worn jeans and a green pocket T-shirt, with her hair tucked into a bedraggled ponytail, she didn't look like the investment banker who'd blown in on a cold spring storm a few months ago. More and more, lately, Dacy looked to Nick as if she belonged—here in this house, here with him.

The sooner he got out of here tonight, the better.

"I'll come help carry in the groceries," Dacy said, brushing a loose strand of hair back from her face. It made him want to pull that twistie thing out of her hair and brush it all back as he kissed her. His eyes roamed her face, from her hair to her lips. He fixed on her lips.

Rafe, who was sitting on the counter near the sink, jumped down. Casually, he dropped a hand on Dacy's shoulder. "No, you don't. I'll help Nick. You were in the middle of making those brownies." He pointed to a saucepan on the stove. "I don't want to interrupt anything chocolate."

Dacy laughed at him, and Nick felt fire boil right up out of his gut at the sight of Rafe's hand on Dacy's shoulder. His fingers were almost touching her breast, for Pete's sake. Who did he think he was? Why did he have to be so all fired good-looking and sure of himself? Why did Dacy have to look so happy around him?

Nick decided in that instant. He was staying here. Forget the bunkhouse. He wasn't going to leave Dacy alone with Rafe. Rafe might be in love with Dani, and Dacy might think she was in love with him, but all that casual flirting might light a spark. Without pausing to sort out what this possessive attitude augured, Nick turned on his heel to retrieve more groceries.

Rafe followed him out to the pickup. A thought occurred to Nick as he reached into the bed to grab some bags.

"She's making brownies?"

"She said you liked them." Rafe's tone was wry and a little challenging. "I also happened to mention that I'm partial to brownies myself."

Nick chuckled all the way back to the house. It was a good thing he was staying, he decided.

Chapter Fourteen

A week later, Dacy sat in Rafe's snooper van, as they'd taken to calling it, listening to rain pelt the roof. She was beginning to think their efforts to catch Earl were as pointless as her attempts to seduce Nick.

Since Jessica and Amy had left, there had been a few opportunities when she'd found Nick alone, but he had patiently rebuffed her advances. Twice she had surprised him into kisses in the dark, once on the porch, and once when she'd stumbled across him on her way back from a twilight walk along the creek. Each time Nick had quickly ended the interludes, walking away from her.

When Rafe was around, however, Nick was attentive. He sat closer to her at dinner, and he touched her in the little ways lovers have of staking their claims. He would lean into her when he'd reach across her for something at the table. He would lay a hand on her arm, sometimes even her thigh. That usually raised her body temperature a few degrees. He would run one finger quickly along the curve of her ear, or nudge her cheek lightly with his thumb. That ran shivers down her neck. These were lover's caresses, and he offered them with affection. Despite the fact that he was pushing Rafe to flirt more blatantly, Nick wouldn't be forced into anything more. That annoyed Dacy no end.

Not that he was around all that much in the first place, though. Dacy was rediscovering that ranchers were busy in the summer. Nick worked long days, often going out to work after supper in the evenings. Dacy wished she could spend some time with him and Jeff working the cattle, but between the renovations and the surveillance watches, that wasn't possible.

Next year, she told herself. She never doubted for a minute that she would be here next year. She did, however, wonder whether she would be with Nick.

The phone line crackled in Dacy's ear and she focused her attention on an incoming call. From eavesdropping so far today, she knew that Earl was home, working in his office because of the weather, and that Cliff had stayed out all night, apparently in possession of a bulldozer that Earl had spent half the morning trying to retrieve. What Cliff had been doing all night with a bulldozer, Dacy couldn't begin to imagine, but she doubted he was up to anything good.

Earl answered the phone, still using the cordless. Before he spoke, Dacy heard the swish-swish she'd come to identify as an exercise machine in the background.

"Tally here," Earl panted.

"Dad?"

It was Cliff. This should be interesting. Dacy checked all the gages and made sure the tape was running smoothly.

"Where the hell are you?" Earl roared. "And what the hell have you done with my bulldozer? Tom Cochrane called this morning, telling me it's wrong side up at the bottom of a gully out at Freeman Willey's place." Cochrane was one of the county's two deputy sheriffs.

"I know, Dad. Calm down, for Pete's sake. I'm in town at the shop, and me and Kootch are heading out there with String Kidder to haul it out."

"Are you sober?" Earl barked like a drill sergeant.

"I am now," Cliff grumbled.

"What were you doing with that dozer, boy?"

There was silence for a moment. "It's a long story."

"I want to hear it now!" Earl shouted.

Earl waited as Cliff recounted the prank he had played on his buddy Ricky, who had been parking with his girlfriend near the edge of a hill. The upshot was, the bulldozer was now out of commission at the bottom of that hill.

"You're a jackass, Clifford! How the hell old are you?"

"Old enough to do a good part of your dirty work for you!" Cliff shot back.

Dacy sat up straight. "Come on, Cliffie," she mouthed. "Blurt it out for the tape recorder. Come on, baby."

Earl's voice grew suddenly quieter and, if anything, more laden with anger than before. "Now you listen to me, you little punk. I support you and your shenanigans handsomely, and you don't do squat around this ranch except cause trouble. We need that bulldozer in less than two weeks, do you hear me?"

That would mean he needed it by the Fourth of July. Dacy made a victory fist and punched the air.

"Yeah, I know! I know what we need it for, all right? I want to get those stinkin' Reynolds brothers out of our hair as much as you do, Dad. I didn't do this on purpose!" Cliff was angry now and had thrown caution to the wind. Earl sputtered, but couldn't stop him. "The dozer will be fixed, and we'll tear up that pasture before the feds get out to look out at it. I won't screw it up! All right?"

"You stupid little cuss," Earl muttered before closing his connection.

"Good boy, Cliffie," Dacy whispered, rapidly rewinding the tape to duplicate it. "We got you now, Earl."

As soon as she'd made two duplicate cassettes of the incriminating phone call, Dacy stepped out of the van, even though her shift wasn't over yet. She left the tape running to catch any further calls and slipped down the gully and over a rise to where she'd parked the beatup old pickup they drove to and from the van. The rain had stopped and the clouds were breaking up.

It took twenty minutes to reach the house. When she got there, Dacy grabbed the copies of the phone call she'd made and hurried into the house. Rafe was there, playing computer games in her office.

"I got it!" Dacy waved the tape in the air.

Instantly, Rafe gave her his full attention. "Put it in the machine," he said, reaching for the boom box on the floor by her desk.

They listened carefully. Rafe nodded in satisfaction. When the tape ended, he ejected it and dropped it into his pocket. "Now that we have something, I'm going to call a friend of mine who's an attorney in Denver. Then we should find Nick and Jeff and talk about how to proceed."

"Do you know where Nick is?" Dacy was disappointed he hadn't been at the house.

"Over at the Reynoldses' home place," Rafe said, reaching for the phone. "Jeff went into town for some tractor part, and Nick's trying to fix it, I think. I'll call around to find Jeff. Do you want me to call Nick?"

"No, that's okay. I'll go get him. I want to tell him in person. 'Bye." Dacy was back out the door in a flash.

On the way down the valley to the Reynoldses' place, Dacy saw lightning, but she registered it automatically, not paying close attention to it. She'd taken her red Suburban with the four-wheel-drive. Even so, she had to concentrate on driving to make it cleanly through the gravel turns. She wanted to see Nick's face when he heard the news. She didn't want to wait. This was too important.

Dacy turned into the Reynoldses' drive, lined by an old lilac hedge, the blossoms now well past their prime. The barn was hidden from view by tall cottonwoods, but as soon as Dacy rounded the last bend in the drive, she saw Nick's blue pickup in front of one of the equipment sheds. Pulling up alongside it, she patted her pocket to make sure she had the tape.

After sidestepping a number of puddles, Dacy found Nick inside the shed, bent over at the waist, tinkering with a tractor engine. He had a smudge of grease on his cheek, and his hair fell forward onto his forehead.

Dacy practically ran to him. "Nick," she said, placing one hand on his back. He straightened immediately, looking at her with wide eyes. With her other hand, Dacy brandished the tape.

"We got Earl. Right here on this tape," she said, meeting his startled gaze with her own excitement.

It took Nick a moment to process what she'd said. Then the confusion cleared from his gray eyes. He dropped the rag in his hand and reached for the cassette.

"What did he say?" His voice was deep and excited.

Dacy tugged at his arm. "Come on. You can listen to it in the car. Rafe wants to talk to you and Jeff right away."

"Jeff's in town," Nick told her.

"Rafe's trying to get hold of him."

Thunder rumbled near at hand as Nick grabbed his denim jacket and followed her to the car. Climbing into the passenger seat, he shoved the tape into the cassette player even before Dacy had the car started. Motioning for her to get going, he waited for the tape to play.

Dacy drove while Nick stared at the dashboard as Earl's and Cliff's voices filled the car. He didn't say a word.

When thunder drowned out something Earl said, he punched the rewind button impatiently. At the end, he turned it off and rewound the tape. Then he looked at Dacy.

"I don't understand why Earl wants to ruin us" was all he said. "It still doesn't make any sense to me. Rivalry among neighbors is one thing. This is crazy."

"It's a power thing. Some people are just like that." Dacy glanced at Nick but kept her eyes on the road. It was raining again and the wind was blowing hard. At times she couldn't see the road clearly. "I dealt with several like him working for the bank."

"Dacy! Stop!" Nick shouted just as she rounded a sharp turn that descended a steep, narrow draw.

Dacy slammed on the brakes, rocking the heavy vehicle to a sudden stop. In front of her, the road had washed out. What was normally little more than a narrow crease in the hills had filled with a swirling torrent of water. Red and muddy, it churned past, carrying branches and other debris.

"Where did that come from?" She took a deep breath to steady herself. "I didn't even see it."

Bright light flashed, and at the same time, an earsplitting crack of thunder boomed, drowning out her words. Glancing back at the water, she saw that it was rising rapidly. She looked to Nick for direction.

"Back up," he told her, looking over his shoulder out the rear window. "Slowly. The road may be undercut by water."

The rain was falling so heavily that Dacy couldn't see anything out the windows, even with the windshield washers going full speed. She put the car in reverse, anyway, and gently gave it some gas. The wheels slid for a second, causing Dacy's heart to leap into her throat. Then they found traction and the car moved back up the slope.

"That's good," Nick urged as the car inched backward. "Easy does it."

As she eased the car back up toward the top of the hill, Nick kept up his gentle coaxing. When a crashing bolt of lightning hit and she jumped, he put one hand on her thigh. "Shhh. It's okay. Keep going. We need to get back farther out of this draw. The storm must have dumped a lot of rain west of here, in the buttes. The water's still rising."

Long seconds later and after another close strike of lightning, Nick squeezed her thigh. "That's good. Stop here. We don't want to sit right up on the crest of the hill where the lightning will be drawn to us. We should be fine here."

Dacy took a shuddering breath and looked at him. She looked back out at the solid wall of water falling from the sky, took the car out of gear and set the emergency brake. Lightning struck again close at hand, and she cringed at the clap of thunder that accompanied it.

"Where's it hitting?" Her voice was shaky.

"Too close." Nick's eyes looked as dark and stormy as the weather outside. He held his arms open. "Come here."

Dacy didn't need a second invitation. She released her seat belt and lunged across the seat.

Perhaps he was just offering comfort, but as soon as she felt his arms wrap around her, she lifted her face, asking without words for more.

He obliged. Firm and soft, his lips closed over hers, and the storm's crescendo of lightning and frightful thunder blended in her body with the hammering of her pulse. She needed him now, and there was no denying that need. Vaguely, she remembered that she had wanted to seduce him. This was no seduction. This was need, pure and driven, the need to possess and be possessed, to meet in as much intimacy as they could bear.

His kiss demanded all her concentration then, and she ceased to think about where it would lead them. She knew. He knew. She could feel his knowledge in the tension knotting his arms. She could feel it in her belly, deep and yearning.

Flexing her fingers, she dug her nails into his coat, wanting it gone, wanting to feel his skin beneath her hands. Nick groaned and shuddered, his lips never leaving hers. His tongue was hot and wild, sparking fires everywhere it touched—her lips, her cheeks, her chin, her throat. He drank greedily from her mouth, nipping now and then, needing her far too much to worry about the little hurts his loving might inflict. She understood. And he didn't hurt her. His fire found its match in her, and she met him nip for nip and kiss for kiss.

Somehow, she found the lever that released the seat back, and down it went. Nick rolled her atop him. Instinctively, she ground her hips into his groin, feeling how hard he was inside his jeans. She knew he wanted her. She wanted him. She let her hot eyes tell him so as she rocked her hips into him once more.

Between the wild kisses, they pushed and pulled at each other's jackets, until they were gone. Then their shirts followed, tossed over the back seat, and bare female breasts met hard, warm male chest. Panting now, unable to get quite enough air in a single breath, Dacy arched her back and drew away from Nick, displaying her breasts for him, full and soft, her nipples tight and swollen like pink rosebuds.

Greedy after so many weeks of denial, he cupped her breasts and lifted them to his mouth, first one and then the other, moving back and forth with suckling kisses. Sharp and ripe, satisfaction slithered into her belly as his warm, wet mouth shafted bolts of pleasure through her.

Nick's arms were strong with well-used muscle under her hands and she held him to her, loathe for him to stop. She had wanted this for so long. Nothing would stop this passion now. Nothing could.

While his mouth plundered her breasts, his hands dropped to her waist, undoing the button at the top of her jeans with easy skill, then sliding the zipper down. Shifting this way and that, tantalizing him by pulling her breasts away from him, just out of reach, she helped him push her jeans down. They caught on her tennis shoes. She laughed and squirmed, trying to reach the laces, bumping her elbows against the cold, steamed-over window and the sharp dashboard knobs.

"This is crazy." Nick's voice was deeper than she'd ever heard it, and rough with need. "Come with me."

He gathered her close and hauled them both into and then over the back seat. In the nearly empty back of the Suburban, he found a sleeping bag.

He grinned at her. "Were you plotting?"

Heat flushed across her already warmed cheeks. "No. I mean, maybe I was, but the sleeping bag is for emergencies."

He untied the bag while she untied her shoes. "This is an emergency."

"It feels like one." Her shoes came off, and her jeans followed. Clad only in black silk panties, she helped him spread the sleeping bag out. Then she sat back and gestured to his feet.

Bracing himself against the tailgate, he lifted one foot and then the other. Dacy pulled his boots off, tossing them forward. When her fingers sought his belt buckle, Nick sat back and let her work it. He wasn't as patient with his jeans. In one shove, his jeans and briefs followed his boots over the seat.

Dacy looked at him. He was beautiful, more beautiful than he had been at seventeen. His chest was fuller and sprinkled with a little more hair. His thighs were strong, his legs well formed. And he wanted her. Of that there was no doubt.

Dacy slipped her panties down her legs. She was ready for this. She was ready for him, to love him with her body and her soul. Leaning forward, she placed one hand flat upon his chest and kissed him—lightly, gently, and with love.

Nick sighed against her mouth. Then he came alive beneath her touch. Cradling her face, he took the kiss over, and it became a heated thing. Just like the kiss in the motel in Brookings, fire flashed so fast and hot, Dacy had difficulty breathing. This time, she let confusion take her. Her mind drifted, tethered tightly to sensation and nothing else. It was thought without words, liquid, heated, head and heart at one with belly, breasts and sex. There was only the moment. There was only Nick. There was only their love and their desire.

Their hands and mouths roamed each other's bodies, reclaiming terrain long left behind, yet long remembered. He kissed her behind the knee and she nearly fainted for the exquisite joy of it. She licked his shoulder, savoring the salty rime their heat produced, relishing his shiver when she blew across the wet line her tongue had made.

They were not so young as they had been the first time they had loved, but they were still impatient. When his fingers delved deeply into the folds of her sex, she parted her legs wide for him. With the next breath, she found his sex and took him in her hand. He was so soft, yet so full and hard—and hot. He warmed her hand and excited her heart. It thumped against her chest so hard she thought she might explode. Could she last? Would this fire between them burn her beyond life itself?

She would risk it. Because she loved him, she would risk it. Flushed all over, so hot, fire running in her veins, she tugged him closer.

"Take me now, Nick. Love me, now."

He met her gaze and his gray eyes were knowing. Then smoothly, and with strength, he came into her.

Her breath froze in her chest. Tears flooded her eyes, unbidden, and she could only let them flow. They dampened his shoulders, and when he felt them, he kissed them from her face.

"Are you all right?" His words were taut, a whisper only.

Nodding, she moved beneath him. Her mind could not form words to answer.

"Then love me now, Dacy. Love me now."

They moved together, man and woman, dark and bright, intent upon their pleasure. Tension built and fed upon fine touches and sweet kisses. Higher and higher, they spun into the firestorm, embracing the west wind, until it carried them clear of everything but the feel of their bodies, one upon the other, and the glory in their hearts.

And when their passions had played out, Dacy felt tears upon her breast. She treasured the knowledge that they were not her own.

Chapter Fifteen

Dacy spent long moments coming back to earth. Wrapped in Nick's arms, she felt safe and whole for the first time in a long, long time. Things were going to work out. Nick couldn't deny the love between them now. She knew he loved her as surely as she knew that she loved him.

Gradually, she became aware of the sound of the rain on the roof of the car, and thunder rumbling in the distance now. Feeling strong and content, she nestled her head in the hollow of Nick's shoulder, listening to his heart resume a steady rhythm.

After a few minutes, she leaned up on one elbow and smiled down at him. He smiled back, almost shyly. With tousled hair and eyelids half-closed, he looked divine, a storm god sated and replete.

Laughter bubbled up from her very toes and she dropped a laughing kiss on his nose.

"Oh, Nick. Now you've gone and done it," she teased. "You *have* to marry me now."

Before the last word was uttered, Dacy knew she'd said the wrong thing. Nick closed his eyes and pulled into himself without moving a muscle.

When he finally opened his eyes, all she saw was pain. Years of hurt and pain moved him beyond her reach.

He shook his head ever so slightly. "Oh, Dace." There were worlds of sorrow in his words. "We shouldn't have done this."

"Yes, we should have," she whispered fiercely. "Look at me, Nick Reynolds, and tell me you don't love me."

He looked at her. No words came. He only shook his head again.

Anger burned a bitter path where passion had so recently flowed. "Nick, don't do this," she pleaded.

"I'm sorry. Dacy, it's no good. I can't give you what you want. It just isn't in me. You know I want you. You know I care. But I can't make a commitment."

She pushed away from him, needing space for her anger. "You don't trust me."

He closed his eyes again. "I don't trust that you'll stay."

"It's the same thing." Her heart had gone cold. "Why do you resist me so, Nick? Isn't what we feel worth fighting for instead of against?"

Sitting up, he pulled the edge of the sleeping bag over Dacy's shoulders and tucked it under her side. "You're shivering."

"Answer me."

"I couldn't bear to lose you again."

"You won't."

"You can't promise me that." He raised his knees and propped his elbows on them, dropping his head onto his forearms. It was a defeated pose. When he spoke, his voice was flat, listless.

"Do you know what it felt like to hold my newborn daughter and my two-year-old in my arms and watch their mother walk away from us? Whatever her faults, I loved

Tammy. I made a commitment to her, and I would have stayed by that. Instead, she left because she was bored. She left her children, *our* children, because she didn't want to change diapers anymore or look at Antelope County for the rest of her life. She left me. She hated me and everything I cared about. I had nothing left emotionally.

"I'm not strong the way you are, Dacy. Without Jeff and my folks, I don't know what would have become of us. More than anything, I wanted a family, a whole family, and I wanted to work the ranch." He raised his chin and stared at the condensation sliding down the inside of the window. "But there isn't anything left for me to give in a marriage. Everything I have I put into Jess and Amy and the ranch."

Dacy was so mad at him, she wanted to hit him. "I know what it feels like to be left. Charlie left me."

Nick's response was swift. "He didn't want to, though. He didn't reject you. He didn't choose to leave."

"No." He was right. "But it still feels awful. That doesn't mean I can't love again."

"Maybe I can't, though."

"I don't believe that."

"Dacy, not everyone is as strong or as courageous as you are. I've tried every way I know how to tell you that I can't be the hero in your life."

"I don't want a hero. I want you as you are." Her eyes flashed with the anger she tried to keep out of her voice. "I don't think it's that you *can't* love me. I think it's that you *won't.*"

"It feels to me like I can't. Like there's a block in my heart. There's a place where I want to be able to tell you what you want to hear. There's part of me that wants what you want. But the words won't come, Dacy. I wish they would. But they won't. I can't do it. I can't live it."

"Nick, I love you. I think you love me, too." She placed one hand on top of his crossed forearms. "Please. For this love we share. Can't you try?"

His eyes were wild, like a cornered animal's, and his breathing grew shallow and fast.

"I can't," he gasped in an agonized whisper. "Don't make me tell you no again. Don't ask me again. You don't know how I'd feel if you said you'd stay and then you left. I won't do it."

"I know how I feel now." Dacy brought her hand back and curled tighter into the sleeping bag. The cold was seeping deep into her bones now and she was shivering. She was trying hard not to cry, and not doing a very good job of it. How could he come so close to heaven and turn away?

In silence, then, they sat, preoccupied with their own pain. At some point, Dacy gathered her clothes and dressed. The rain had stopped. She got out of the car and looked down into the draw. Only a trickle of water sluiced through the bottom, but the sides were littered with debris. The road had washed clean away.

The knowledge in Dacy's heart was awful in that moment, as awful as the knowledge of Charlie's death had been. Without a doubt in her mind, she knew she loved Nick and that she would until she died. Without doubt, she knew he loved her, too.

And without doubt, she knew that if he refused to give himself, she couldn't take him.

Nick collected his clothes and gear that night and left with Jeff after the strategy session with Rafe. He was staying at the bunkhouse until the girls came back. He didn't even tell Dacy he was leaving.

Earlier, as a group, Nick, Jeff, Dacy, Dani and Rafe had decided to work with one of the federal marshals assigned to the region, instead of the local sheriff, since part of the pasture Earl planned to bulldoze was forest service land. Rafe thought there was less chance of Earl finding out that they knew what he was up to that way. The marshal Rafe contacted, Cy Chekpa, would fill the local authorities in later.

After Nick and Jeff and Dani left, Dacy sat on the porch, watching heat lightning flicker in the east. The solitude was, for once, a relief.

The next morning, Dacy rose late to the music of meadowlarks trilling in the fields beyond the yard and the less than musical arrival of the work crew, slamming car doors and clattering tools. The sun was bright, the air fresh, but her heart was heavy. This morning, she should have awakened with Nick at her side, warm with sleep, smiling affectionately at her, drawing her into his arms. Life, however, wasn't a fantasy, and Dacy didn't spend time lingering over what might have been. Instead she rose and dressed. She had a lot of work to do.

Rafe and Dani were in the kitchen drinking coffee when she went in.

"Nobody's manning the snooper van this morning?" She opened a makeshift cupboard door to find a mug. The kitchen renovations still hadn't begun.

"I stopped on my way over to replace the tape with a blank one," Dani told her.

Something in her cousin's tone made Dacy look more carefully at her. Dani looked exhausted. There were dark circles under her eyes and she was pale.

"Are you all right?" Dacy asked.

"I've got some calls to make." Rafe refilled his mug and grabbed an apple from a basket on the counter on his way into the office.

After he'd left, Dani said, "I think when he goes back to New York, I'm going with him." Dani's voice cracked and her face crumpled. One tear leaked artfully down her cheek.

Dacy put down her cup, her own tears too close to the surface. "What happened?"

"Jeff and I had an argument last night after we left." She paused. "He told me, once and for all, there's nothing between us as far as he's concerned. He told me to marry Rafe and be happy."

When Dani's tears stopped, she drew back and looked at Dacy. "I could tell something had happened between you and Nick last night, too. Want to tell me?"

It probably wouldn't help, but neither would it hurt. "We made love. We got stuck in the storm where the road washed out." She paused, remembering. "It was incredible. I've never felt like that. Then he was horrible."

"They're both so scared."

"I don't think I can outwait Nick's fears."

"I know." Dani turned to look out the screen door. The work crews were gathering on the trampled grass in the backyard. "I think I've waited long enough for Jeff. I've been back here a year, and he isn't any more ready to face what we feel for each other than he was last summer. I don't want to do this anymore."

Dacy followed her cousin's gaze and looked farther, toward the trees along the creek. Tall cottonwoods shivered in the light breeze. She looked at the apple trees her great-grandfather had planted when he was an old man, almost eighty years ago. She looked around the kitchen and saw it as it had looked when she was a girl. There, next to the stove, on what was now a makeshift plywood countertop, was where she would put her crock of watermelon pickles. Next summer. Maybe this August, if Harley got the kitchen done.

"I want to stay," she said firmly. "I don't want to leave."

"What about Nick?" Dani asked.

"It may not work out with Nick." Dacy spoke slowly. "I want to live here, anyway. I'm going to do one thing for him, though, whether he wants it or not. I'm going to get him some support for that visit from the BLM people next week."

"It won't change his mind if he's set against you, Dacy," Dani cautioned.

Was that her motive? In all honesty, it was part of it. There was more, though. She wanted to support Nick's ideas about ranching because she thought they were right, because she thought they would help preserve and protect this land that she loved. And, because whether he wanted her to or not, she loved him. She wanted the best for him.

"I know. I want to do it, anyway." She picked up an apple and her car keys. "I've got some people to talk to this morning. Want to come?"

"Sure. I'll tell Rafe where we're going. Meet you at the car."

Dacy left the house feeling as if she were on a sinking ship, but determined to keep her head above water to the bitter end.

The weather turned hot, with scorching days over a hundred degrees. Without air conditioning installed in the house yet, and with doors and windows opened to flies and millers, Dacy was glad of the diversion of visiting with her neighbors in Antelope County. She invited people over for dessert and coffee, and she invited people to come see the renovations in progress. Most especially, she urged them to come out to the Reynolds place on the Fourth to meet the legislators and bureaucrats from Washington and show their support.

The Willeys and the Tabors came for dessert. The Beyers came to see the renovations. Mildred Chamberlain had her son Clyde and his wife, Bernice, drive her out with a batch of rhubarb sauce. To somebody, however, they hedged about the Fourth.

"I don't know," Carol Jean had said. "We always go to the fairgrounds for the picnic. It's such a long ways out here."

Clyde Chamberlain, who ran three hundred and forty head of Herefords on three thousand acres of short-grass prairie, was more blunt. "I'm not sure I like what those Reynolds boys are doin'," he'd said. "It's hard enough to make a living without worrying about native plants and three-toed lizards and peachy-pie butterflies or whatever the environmentalists want to save."

So Dacy talked about what she saw Nick and Jeff doing. She told the stories Nick had told at the conference in Brookings. She did her best to allay fears. She told Clyde Chamberlain what the going price for organic beef was. She talked about marketing cooperatives. Clyde began to argue less. Dacy didn't think she'd changed his mind, or too many other people's, but she was getting their attention.

By the end of the week, Dacy was tired and she hadn't seen Nick more than the three times she'd dropped groceries off for him, Jeff, Cobie and the other hands. He'd told her how Jessica and Amy were doing, and that had been the extent of their conversation. Rafe had left rather mysteriously in his van, saying he'd be back on Friday.

Early Friday afternoon, Rafe returned and found Dacy discussing flooring with Harley. He waved a file at her.

"When you're finished, I'll be in your office," he said, stepping around her and a stack of wall board.

Dacy chose one of the samples Harley had in his hand, then followed Rafe inside.

"I have good news," he began. "I found out where the letters to Nick and Jeff's clients came from."

"And?"

"As you all suspected, Earl Tally is behind them. Marielle Orbach, the woman who signed them, is, as it turns out, the daughter of one of Earl's cousins. She worked as a temporary clerical in the agriculture department last summer. Marielle is not the brightest woman in the world, and when Earl asked her to sign some letters while her boss was out, she did it. It wasn't hard to convince her to talk to Cy Chekpa about what happened."

"Will she tell Earl what happened? That could ruin everything."

Rafe smiled broadly. "I've done this a time or two, Dacy. By the time Cy had taken her statement, I had a ticket to Cancún and reservations at a resort hotel in Ms. Orbach's name waiting for her. By now, she should be sipping tropical drinks on the beach, watched over by my charming and attentive cousin Renato."

Dacy applauded. "A masterful stroke, I concede."

He held out an envelope, which she accepted. "The bill, madame."

Dacy laughed. "I wish all life's little troubles were as easily solved as sending a secretary to Cancún."

"So do I," Rafe agreed. "Do you want to tell the cowboys?"

Her laughter died. "No. I don't think so."

Rafe walked out of the room, muttering something in Spanish and a few words of English, at least a few of which included something that sounded suspiciously like "stubborn bastards."

Dacy couldn't have agreed more.

Nick saw Rafe approaching across the open meadow. He was riding the horse Dani kept stabled at their place for Jess's barrel-racing lessons, a long-legged palomino gelding named Summer. Rafe waved and Nick raised a hand in response. He wasn't glad to see the man, though. Nick had the uncomfortable feeling that Rafe was going to talk about Dacy. There just wasn't any point.

Dismounting, Nick led his chestnut toward a small prairie dog colony and made a show of studying the burrows. He dug up a prickly pear with the toe of his boot and kicked it into one of the holes. Maybe there were rattlesnakes in some of the dens. Now there was a thought. Maybe he would get bit and put himself out of his misery.

Miserable he certainly was. Cobie had told him he was exhibiting classic symptoms of lovesickness. He didn't want to eat. He mooned around worse than ever. He sighed too much, and he was distracted to beat the band. Yesterday, he'd run the breeder bull herd into a field they'd already grazed and left them there all morning before he realized what he'd done. Luckily, they weren't there long enough to muck up the streambed that he and Jeff had so painstakingly restored.

The only thing that stayed clear and ever present in his mind was that afternoon in Dacy's Suburban. He had felt so alive, so true to himself, when they had made love. He had forgotten for a while that he was afraid she would leave, and it had set his heart free. In his mind's eye, he saw her red hair and green eyes, her skin, pale in the dim light. He remembered how it felt to receive her love. He remembered how it felt to lose himself to the feel of her small hand curling around his sex while she kissed him. He ached for remembering.

"Fascinating creatures." Rafe spoke dryly, looking down at Nick and the prairie dog burrows.

"Jeff's Lakota friend Joe Two Eagle says they have ceremonies down in those burrows," Nick said. "Try as I might, though, I don't hear 'em singing." Lowering his hat to shield his eyes from the sun, Nick looked up at Rafe. "Come out to play cowboy with us?"

Rafe chuckled as he dismounted. "No, not today. I brought you some information from Pierre." Quickly, he relayed what he had learned from Marielle Orbach.

Privately, Nick was so relieved Rafe wasn't talking about Dacy, he almost missed the significance of what he was telling him. It took a moment to sink in.

"Hold on a second," Nick interrupted. "You're saying, with this evidence, Cy wants to press for a conspiracy charge?"

"That's right," Rafe affirmed. "Even if he doesn't follow through on the Fourth, we've got him. Of course, there are never any guarantees how long the whole process will take, or how much time he'll get in prison, if any."

Nick scowled. "Some judicial system we've got, huh?"

"I just help catch the crooks. After that, they're out of my hands." Rafe spread his hands before him.

"Heck of a job," Nick commented, shaking his head.

"Speaking of a heck of a job, there's something I want to talk to you about. You aren't going to like it."

"Dacy." Nick knew it had been coming.

"Yeah."

Rafe dropped Summer's reins and decked Nick with a solid right to the jaw.

Nick landed with a thud in the dirt surrounding a prairie dog burrow.

"What the hell!" He glared at Rafe.

"That was to knock some sense into you. I'm sick to death of watching you and your idiot brother make Dacy and Dani miserable."

He held out a hand to Nick, who was gingerly exploring his jaw with his fingertips. "Sorry. I don't normally resort to violence. But, man, don't you ever think about what you're doing?"

With that, Rafe shook his head and walked off after his horse.

Nick thought about "what he was doing" while he chased his horse down, and he thought about it while he rode across the meadow toward the cattle.

The biggest problem with thinking about Dacy, he decided, was that she got him all tied up in knots. Any logic he normally possessed evaporated when he conjured her image in his mind. His groin tightened up, and his heart seemed to surge in his chest.

Then there were the images that followed, the fantasies of waking in the morning with her head next to his on the pillows, her red hair trapped between them as they snuggled together. There were the images of Dacy holding a baby—his baby—cradled in her arms, with Jess and Amy crowded close around. There was an image where he and Dacy helped Jess, and then Amy, pack to go away to college, and the comfort and joy of knowing they had each other, even when the girls had left them. There were images of Dacy in flannel nightgowns and black silk panties. There were images of soft, yielding flesh and whispered cries, of gifts given and received, of love glowing in sea green eyes.

No, those were memories.

There were other images, too, powerful images of loss and pain. He could envision Jess and Amy crying, asking why it had happened again, why had another mother left them. He saw himself, alone again, the bed seeming larger and more empty than it had before she came. These images made him feel hollow, as if a bull had run right through his middle. They made him feel frozen, too. There were the images and feelings he couldn't get past.

In his heart, Nick knew he wanted more than memories and fantasies. He just wasn't sure how to get there.

Chapter Sixteen

Dacy spent the next day visiting her neighbors. There were only a few days left before the Fourth, and she tried mightily to interest them in coming out to Nick's to talk to the lawmakers and Bureau of Land Management officials. The delegation was scheduled to arrive by helicopter at ten o'clock on Tuesday. Earl's bulldozer was supposed to be fixed by Monday, the day before the Fourth.

That night she slept restlessly. The house was too quiet without Jessica and Amy—and without Nick. Rafe had slept in the girls' room since they'd left, but he was so quiet she hardly knew he was there. By five o'clock, the first gray light of dawn had filtered through the grapevines at the window, and she was wide-awake.

Mostly, her body was restless for wanting Nick. The taste of passion they'd shared wasn't enough. She wanted so much more. Staring at the chipped plaster on the ceiling, Dacy knew exactly what she wanted. She wondered morosely if she would be lying in this same house in fifty years, pining after Nick. It seemed fairly likely.

The phone rang, jarring in the early-morning quiet. Dacy leapt out of bed and got it before the second ring.

"Hello?" Her heart was thumping, anticipating bad news.

"Hi!" A woman's voice, bright and vaguely familiar, greeted her. "You must be Dacy. Is Nick there?"

"No."

"This is Tammy."

"Oh! Hi." Dacy placed the familiar nuance in her voice. It reminded her of Jessica. The recognition was unsettling.

"Where's Nick? I need to ask a favor of him." Tammy giggled and a man's deep voice rumbled in the background.

"I think he's camping out with the cattle. Or he might be at the bunkhouse." So Tammy was calling from bed and she had company.

"No, I tried there. They said to call you." There was a tiny pause and another giggle.

"Are the girls okay?"

"Yeah, they're doing great. But I have a tiny problem that's come up." Tammy gasped. "Darrel, stop. I'm on the phone!" Another pause. "Oh! Sorry!"

"What's the problem, Tammy?" Dacy was growing impatient.

"Well, see, I have this great new boyfriend—" She interrupted herself with a small shriek.

"Darrel, right?"

"Yes! How did you kno—oh, that's right, I said his name. Okay, right. Well, anyway, Darrel is leaving at six-thirty for a business trip to Hong Kong, and he just said, 'Tammy, come with me!'" She sighed dramatically. "Isn't that romantic?"

Dacy rolled her eyes. Tammy didn't seem to require an answer, so Dacy let her continue.

"So I said I'd love to, but then I remembered I have the girls for the next two weeks. See my dilemma?"

Dacy tried hard to control her temper. "I think so. Tammy, where are the girls now?"

"They're at my house with Yolanda, my housekeeper. She's great, and she speaks English and everything so Jessica and Amy are fine."

Dacy wasn't sure what the connection was between speaking English and being fine. "So you want to send them home today?"

"Yes! That's exactly what I want to do. That's why I need to talk to Nick. I don't have time to get them out on a plane if I'm going to get packed myself, so I wondered if Nick could just drive down here and pick them up."

If Dacy recalled Rafe's account of his trip up from Denver, Tammy was proposing a nine- or ten-hour drive. Each way. "Tammy, I don't know where Nick is, and this isn't a good time to pull him away from the ranch. He's awfully busy."

"Oh, that stupid ranch! Look, can't you find him for me? I don't want to miss this opportunity. Darrel's really special, you know what I mean?" Tammy pleaded in a whining tone.

Dacy's control faltered. *Aren't your daughters special?* she thought angrily. She wanted to tell Tammy exactly what she could do with Darrel and his trip to Hong Kong. Then she thought of Jessica and Amy. It wasn't fair to leave them caught in a mess created by their selfish mother. She had no idea where on the ranch Nick might be, and she didn't want the girls to have to wait a minute longer than necessary.

"I'll tell you what," Dacy finally offered, looking at her watch. "I'll come get them. I won't be able to get there before four this afternoon. Will they be all right until then?''

''Oh, sure! Great! Now I know why Jess and Amy talk about you like you're some kind of wonderwoman. Okay, I'll tell you what. I'll have Yolanda pack their things and take them to one of my salons. That way they won't get bored while they wait. All my stores are in malls,'' Tammy told her proudly.

Dacy wrote down the information Tammy gave her before hanging up. She was so angry she was shaking as she threw on a pair of shorts and a T-shirt, grabbed a sweater, a bottle of water and tossed her toothbrush in her purse. On second thought, she stuffed her nightgown and a pair of panties in, as well. She didn't know if she'd make it back tomorrow or not.

On the way out the door, she looked for Rafe. He wasn't anywhere. His bed didn't appear to have been slept in, and when she looked outside, his van was gone. She snatched up a notebook and scribbled a note to Nick. Stuffing it into an envelope, she scrawled his name across it in bold letters. She dropped it off for him at the bunkhouse on her way out to the highway.

Anxious not to leave Jessica and Amy waiting, Dacy drove like a demon. The gas tanks were nearly full, and she was too angry to be hungry. Racing south toward the Black Hills, Dacy understood more and more why Nick was so frightened of commitment. If his only experience had been with Tammy, it was no wonder he was wary. The woman had to be in a league of her own when it came to selfish self-absorption. A commitment shared with someone like Tammy probably was synonymous with pain.

Why couldn't Nick trust that she was different, though? He had the evidence before him constantly.

She stopped for gas in Torrington, Wyoming, and called the house. Rafe answered, and she explained what was going on. She asked him to tell Nick if he saw him.

"Where were you this morning, anyway?" she asked him.

Rafe laughed. "That's a long story. I'll tell you when you get back. Take care and don't drive too fast."

She didn't take his driving advice.

She did, however, have plenty of time to reflect. As Nick had implied, she saw more clearly that it wasn't a simple matter of logical analysis for him to separate the present from his past experiences. There were blocks in his heart that he had to get past if he was ever going to trust her.

With each mile south, she prayed he'd be able to move past them.

The moment in which Nick made his decision was much like any other. One instant he was waving his rope at the backside of a stubborn bull calf, trying to chase it back to its mama. The new brand, a double bar *R*, stood out clearly against the calf's black Angus coat. Dust and flies rose toward the late-afternoon sun as the animal hopped along ahead of him, frisky despite the heat.

Then he decided he'd had enough. He wanted Dacy, and he wanted to believe she wouldn't leave him. If he tried, he could make himself believe it. It was worth the risk.

"Cobie!" Nick bellowed, startling the calf, who bawled in protest.

From across the wooded pasture on the butte, a slim figure waved from horseback. "Hey, boss," Cobie Haas called back. In his late forties, of average height and slight build, Cobie sat on his mount as if he were part of the horse's back.

Nick abandoned the calf at the edge of the herd and picked his way through the cattle. Richie, his horse, seemed to have sensed his mood. He moved quickly.

"I've got to go over to the Fallon place," he told a surprised Cobie. "Can you handle these critters alone?"

"You know I can or you wouldn't 'a hired me." Cobie sent a stream of tobacco juice flying. "Finally decide to work things out with Dacy?"

Nick gave him a startled glance.

Cobie continued without a pause. "Well, you been mopin' around like a calf that's lost its cow. It's easy enough to see you made up your mind about something. Everybody in the county knows what's eatin' ya, so it was a pretty safe guess." He grinned and tipped his battered leather hat. "Go on, then. I can get these cattle over the next hill on my own."

Nick was already turning Richie around. "Thanks," he called over his shoulder.

Nick rode straight to the Fallon place. He approached the house from the creek bottom, and it wasn't until he cleared the trees that he saw that Dacy's red Suburban wasn't there.

He had a moment of panic. She'd gone!

No, he told himself, forcing himself to breath evenly, she was just out for a while. It was Sunday afternoon. She was probably visiting after church. She'd been going to church lately, he knew.

Disappointed, he rode up to the house and dismounted, tying Richie to one of the lilac bushes. He found Rafe nursing a beer on the front porch.

"Hi." Nick thought Rafe looked rather the worse for wear. "Do you know where Dacy went?"

Rafe shook his head slowly. "Didn't you know?"

The panic lurched in Nick's chest again. "Know what?"

"I thought you must have talked to her." Rafe sipped his beer. "I'm sorry, Nick."

There was a rushing in his ears so loud he could barely hear his own voice. "Sorry about what?"

"She's gone. Her toothbrush, her nightgown. Gone."

Gone.

One simple word. It was the word he dreaded most in the world.

Dacy was gone.

Backing off the porch, he stumbled across the yard. The tan pickup was there, one of the ranch vehicles, with the keys inside. He never looked at Richie, tethered to the lilac with his saddle still on. Instead, he jabbed the key into the ignition and hit the gas hard. Gravel flew in an arc as he took the curving drive too fast.

He didn't care. All he knew was that Dacy was gone. It had happened again.

Dani stepped out onto the porch and sat down in the rickety old porch swing beside Rafe. "Why did you do that?"

"He has to face it." Rafe scooted to one side to give her room. Then he gave the swing a push with one booted foot. "You saw how readily he believed me. Anyone else would have at least gone inside and looked around. He didn't ask me a single question. Nick has to face this demon of his and see how pointless it is. Otherwise, it will poison his love for Dacy." He tipped his beer bottle back and drank. "He would always be waiting for the inevitable, as he sees it, and it would destroy their love. So I gave him a little push."

"Playing God, are you?"

"Cupid."

"He won't appreciate it." Dani looked at him and shook her head.

"He might." The porch swing creaked under their weight.

"Dacy will appreciate it," Dani decided. "If it works." She looked across at Nick's horse. "He left poor Richie with his saddle still on. Since it's your fault, you'd better take care of him."

* * *

Nick didn't stop at the bunkhouse. He drove straight past and on toward Kenyon. There was no coherent plan in his mind. He simply had to move. The pain in his heart wouldn't let him stay still.

Maybe he would find Dacy in town.

At the junction with the highway, he pulled out without looking and cut off Jerri Beyer, who laid on the horn of her Subaru hard. He heard her, but he didn't look back.

Dacy was gone.

He drove past Char's, where he scanned the cars in the lot. There was no red Suburban. He drove through town, looking everywhere for Dacy. She wasn't anywhere.

On the north end of town, he saw Cliff Tally's black pickup parked next to Kootch Koehler's Camaro in front of the Lazy A Bar and Grill. With a screech, he turned sharply into the lot. He parked, got out of the truck, slammed the door as hard as he could and marched to the entrance.

He sent the door flying so hard it snapped back on the hinges. Taking one step forward, he stopped in the doorway.

It was dark inside. Nick glared around the room, waiting for his eyes to adjust to the gloom. There weren't more than half a dozen people there, including Gif Boom, who owned the place and tended the bar, and whose rotund silhouette was unmistakable. There were a couple of girls at a table in the corner. Nick thought they might be Roy Holloway's grown daughters, but he didn't really care.

His gaze fixed on the two young men leaning against the bar, beer bottles in hand. Cliff and Kootch had turned when Nick threw the door open. For an instant, Cliff had looked alarmed. Then he settled into a casual pose, one elbow propped on the bar behind him, his beer bottle dangling from a crooked finger.

Nick took a step in and slammed the door shut behind him. The muscles in his hands twitched as he took in Cliff's smug expression. *Come on, Cliffie,* Nick thought as he walked toward the bar. *Give me an excuse to nail your butt to the floor.*

Cliff didn't need the invitation. "Well, lookee who the wind just blew in. If it ain't Mr. Eco-rancher himself." He raised his beer and took a long pull. "We were just talkin' about you, Reynolds."

"Is that so?" Nick stopped at the bar to Cliff's left and nodded to Gif. "I'll have a beer."

Gif looked him straight in the eye. "I don't want no trouble between you boys."

Nick gave Gif a smile that didn't reach his eyes. He wanted trouble, and he knew Cliff was going to give it to him.

Gif set a beer on the bar in front of Nick, then backed up.

"Ready for your little Fourth of July sideshow, Reynolds?" Cliff chuckled with knowing glee. "Got all your prize organic calves gussied up with ribbons and bows?"

Kootch found this amusing and guffawed.

"Got all your little native plants blooming for the bigwigs?" Both of them snickered.

It appeared Kootch was in on things, too.

Nick made a show of ignoring Cliff. He drew on his beer and ran his thumb over the condensation on the shoulders of the bottle.

As he expected, Cliff didn't like being ignored.

"Reynolds, I asked you a question." Cliff's tone was belligerent.

Kootch had a comment. "He's probably more concerned with drowning his sorrows, Cliffie. Give the guy a break. His ranch is about to go under."

"You know, Kootch, I forgot about that. That's right. His house burned down and he didn't have no insurance.

He lost most of his beef contracts. Marv Petersen let it drop awhile back that the Reynolds boys were having trouble making their loan payments. Now he's got that bossy Fallon chick telling him what to do all the time. It's a wonder he ain't in here all the time sucking up beer like the sorry bastard he is."

Nick's mouth curved back in a grin that was not a smile. Taking another pull on his beer, he looked at Gif.

"My hand's on the phone to call the sheriff. If you boys want to fight, take it outside," the bartender warned.

"I bet he likes that redhead bossing him around, Cliffie," Kootch continued, not missing a beat. "Maybe when he's a good boy, she rewards him real nice."

Nick's blood roared in his head. Kootch's insulting remark roused his defenses to the ready and made his heart ache all the more with the knowledge that Dacy was gone.

"Yeah, I'll bet she does," Cliff concurred. "I wonder how long she's gonna stick around before she gets bored with old Eco-rancher here. A woman like that, she needs more fire than a stick in the mud like Reynolds can give her. She ought to wander over to my place some day. A real man could keep her satisfied enough to stay put. Send her over when she's ready to leave you, Reynolds."

Nick straightened and pushed his beer bottle back. Gif rolled his eyes in resignation and picked up the phone.

Before Cliff realized what was happening, preoccupied as he was with chortling over his juvenile insults, Nick stepped in front of him.

Grabbing Cliff's shirtfront, Nick hauled him upright. "This is going to feel real good, Cliffie. For me."

Nick threw a punch that landed squarely on Cliff's jaw, dropped him and neatly clipped him on the other side before his head had snapped back from the first blow. Tossing him against the bar, Nick stepped back and beckoned to both men. In the background he heard the chiming tones of the phone being dialed.

"Come on, boys. Take a shot. Show me what you got, seeing as you're 'real men' and all."

Cliff and Kootch came at him together and for the next few minutes, Nick ceased to feel the pain in his heart. All he felt were the fists that connected with his body. His head snapped back and he bit his lip hard. It felt good. It was physical pain. He smashed his fist into Kootch Koehler's face and the ache in his knuckles was real, more real than the emptiness in his soul. Cliff landed a blow to his stomach, and the air whistled out of his lungs. Dragging hard for air, he felt adrenaline racing in his blood and he grabbed Cliff around the middle, smashing him against the bar.

"That's enough!" Gif shouted, grabbing them both by the collar. He used his bulk to propel them through the door. Kootch followed, and they continued in the parking lot, where the sheriff found them a few minutes later.

Lester Grimm, the county sheriff, left his lights flashing and got out of the car, shouting. He tried to pull Nick away from Cliff, but Nick hadn't yet succeeded in numbing out the agony in his gut over Dacy's leaving.

Dropping Cliff and spinning on his heel, Nick threw a swing at Lester. Blood spurted from the sheriff's nose, and Nick lowered his head, stepping toward him, fists at the ready.

"I said," Lester bellowed, "that's enough." He pulled his gun and leveled it at Nick's midsection. "And I meant—" he waited for Nick to drop his hands "—that's enough."

Nick stood panting while Lester glared at him.

"I expect this from these punks, Nick, but not from you," Lester barked. "What the hell got into you?" He dabbed his nose with his sleeve. When it came away bright red, he holstered his gun and swore. "I'm puttin' the three of you in jail for the night. Koehler, Tally. You two get in the back. Reynolds in the front." He tapped the handcuffs dangling from his belt. "Am I gonna have to use these?"

Nick shook his head, as did Cliff and Kootch.

"All right, then, I'm gonna read you your damned rights, you brawling sons of bitches." Lester herded them toward the county squad car, reciting the Miranda lines.

Nick flopped into the front seat. His hands were sore and swollen. One eye was swelling and he would no doubt be sporting quite a shiner on Tuesday when the delegation from Washington arrived. His lip was bleeding and his diaphragm was sore. The worst of the pain, however, was still the deep ache that more physical ills couldn't eradicate.

Dacy was gone.

Chapter Seventeen

Dacy found Jessica and Amy reading fashion magazines in the back of their mother's nail salon. Elegantly dressed in two-piece pastel knit suits and faultlessly coiffed, each of them looked like a child model. Nick hadn't been far off when he said Tammy treated them like lap dogs.

"Dacy!" Amy jumped up and ran to her, throwing her arms around Dacy's waist. "You're early! Can we go? I'm soooo bored."

It was three-thirty, and Dacy considered it proof there was a merciful God that she hadn't gotten any speeding tickets.

She squeezed Amy tight and then Jessica, who followed her sister across the salon. There were no customers. A woman in a white coat was busy painting her own nails, oblivious to them, and there was an older woman napping in one of the loungers in the back of the salon.

"Hi, Dacy." Jessica's smile was warm and she hugged

Dacy tightly. "Tammy was really glad you could come. So are we."

"Yeah," Amy seconded, pulling back. "I never thought it could have happened, but I'm all shopped out." She blew a gust of air upward that ruffled her bangs.

Dacy smiled, running an affectionate hand over her head, smoothing her bangs. "I'm glad you're okay." Struggling to keep the knot in her throat from strangling her, she coughed. "You both look nice."

"Thanks. Tammy picked out these clothes. She has a suit just like them, only hers is cream colored." Jessica's was shell pink, Amy's pale mauve. "We aren't wearing any makeup," she said, pointedly.

"I noticed." They exchanged grins.

"Can we go?" Amy yawned. "We had to get up early and we've been here since nine."

"Sure. Where's your stuff?"

Jessica pointed to the back of the store. "By Yolanda back there."

Next to the sleeping woman sat a pile of luggage, boxes and shopping bags that might possibly fit in the spacious cargo area of the car.

"Wow" was all Dacy could say. No wonder Amy was shopped out.

"How's Dad?" Amy asked. "Have you slept together yet?"

"Amy!" Jessica squealed. "You aren't supposed to ask that. I told you not to."

"You're not my boss," Amy shot back, "and I want to know. I want to know if they're going to get married."

"Amy," Dacy began, acutely aware of the now interested gaze of the woman painting her nails. "I don't want you to get your hopes up that your dad and I will get married. It might not happen."

Amy looked distraught. "Why not? Don't you love him?"

Dacy crouched down and took Amy's hands in hers. "Yes, Tiger, I love him." Unconsciously, she used Nick's pet name for her.

"I want a real mom." Amy's face crumpled, and Dacy brought her into a hug. "I want you to be my mom."

"Me, too," Jessica added quietly. In the face of Tammy's actions that day, Dacy's heart went out to them. They had a mother, but not a "real mom" as Amy had said.

She reached one hand out to Jessica, pulling her closer. She set Amy back a bit, wiping a tear away with one thumb. "Even if your dad and I don't get married, I'm not going anywhere. I'll always be there for you. I love you guys."

"But I want a real mom," Amy persisted. She could be as stubborn as Nick was.

Dacy didn't know what to say. "Do you think we can talk about this later? I'd like to get something to eat and maybe take a nap before we drive home."

Amy looked inclined to fuss, but Jessica took charge. "There's a really good hamburger place across the street. Right, Amy?"

"Can I have a strawberry shake?" Amy brightened.

"Sure." It must be nice to be nine, Dacy thought, when the prospect of a strawberry milkshake could distract you from more troublesome worries. "Let's wake up Yolanda and get your stuff in the car."

An hour later, Amy and Jessica were nodding off even before their milkshakes, hamburgers and fries were finished. Dacy's eyelids were heavy, as well. She decided to look for a motel and get a room so they could sleep for a few hours before driving back. Tomorrow would be the third of July already, and she still wasn't sure how many people were going to come out to Nick's for the Washington delegation's visit. It would be a busy couple of days. She'd best rest while she could.

* * *

At nine o'clock, Dacy woke up and knew she wouldn't be able to get back to sleep. Jessica was still asleep, but Amy was reading in the chair in the corner.

"I guess we might as well drive all night. What do you think?" Dacy asked her.

"I want to go home," Amy said. "Jess can sleep in the car."

They woke Jessica and the girls changed into more comfortable car clothes while she called the house to let Nick know they were on their way back.

Rafe answered the phone again.

"Hi," Dacy said. "I'm in Denver, and we're about to leave. I wanted to let Nick know everything's fine and we should be there in the morning."

"He isn't here, but I'll let him know."

"Okay." There was something odd in Rafe's voice. Dacy couldn't put her finger on it. "Is everything all right there?"

"Yeah. I have some good news when you get back, too."

"About . . . ?"

"I'll tell you when you get here. Oh, and Dacy?"

"What?"

"Can you stop by the courthouse on your way in? There's something there you need to pick up. Drive safely." He hung up.

Dacy put the phone down. "What was that all about?" she wondered aloud.

"What?" Amy gave her a worried look.

"I don't know. Just my imagination, I suppose. Your dad wasn't there. He must be out with the cattle again." She looked at the girls. Jessica was rubbing her eyes sleepily. "Are you ready?"

They both nodded.

"Then let's go home."

Home, she thought. It wasn't the perfect place she had once thought it to be. It wasn't a magical cure for grief, and it wasn't a place where everything settled into an easy, familiar pattern. It was, however, the place she belonged. Even with all its problems, it sounded good.

The cell consisted of three cement block walls and one of bars, a pair of bunked cots covered with scratchy army blankets and a rust-stained sink and toilet. Dim light filtered in from a high, barred window. Facing the wall, Nick lay on the cot, studying the profane graffiti written in the grouting between the cement blocks. It was a bleak place, and it suited his mood just fine.

Dacy was gone.

Cliff and Kootch had been in a cell across from him. They'd blabbed drunken insults at him until they'd fallen into noisy, alcoholic sleep, replete with snorts and gasps and coughing. He couldn't remember what they'd said, and he hadn't even cared if they shut up or not.

Dacy was gone.

Finally, Earl and Fred Koehler had come in around dawn to pick up Cliff and Kootch, and he was alone. He hadn't called anyone to come get him, and he didn't know if Lester had his truck here or not. He didn't care.

Dacy was gone.

The outside door opened again and he heard sharp boot heels marching down the granite corridor. Recognizing Jeff's step, he didn't bother to turn.

The footsteps stopped outside his cell. "What the hell got into you?" Jeff yelled.

Nick rolled onto his back and stared at the unpainted cement ceiling with the single bare bulb screwed into a fixture too high to reach.

"She left. I lost it."

"What's wrong with you? Dacy went to Denver to pick up Jess and Amy. Tammy called, asking someone to come get them, and you were out with the cattle. For God's sake, Nick, get a grip on yourself!'' Jeff flipped something through the bars at him.

''What's that?'' He looked at the envelope lying on the floor.

''She left a note for you, you jackass. It was at the bunkhouse.''

Nick sat up, wincing when his back muscles pulled painfully. ''Rafe told me she left.''

''Read the damn note.''

Nick reached for the envelope. Holding it in his hand, he looked blankly at Jeff.

''You got one hell of a black eye, there. You deserve it for being such a moron.''

''Cliff looks worse,'' Nick bit out. His lip was still swollen and sore.

''You better read that.''

He tore the envelope open.

Jeff sighed angrily. ''Prepare to feel like a blue ribbon idiot.''

Nick didn't think he was going to need much preparation.

The summer sun was well up in a sky already dancing with puffy clouds. The warm air carried the scents of grass, sage and clover, and Dacy heard meadowlarks and blackbirds calling in the roadside pastures as they drove into Kenyon. Char's parking lot was full of eighteen-wheelers and pickups as Dacy drove past, slowing down as they came into the town proper. In front of the park and beside the school, she turned left onto Crook Street and followed it back to the old courthouse. Both the old tan pickup and Jeff's newer gray one were parked alongside the county sheriff's Bronco.

''Whoa.'' Jessica's gaze flew to Dacy. ''What's going on?''

"I don't know. Rafe told me to stop here. Maybe you two should stay in the car."

"No way," Amy announced, pushing open the door.

Jessica followed and Dacy had to hurry to catch up with them. "Wait a minute!" Dacy stopped them at the door. "Let me go in first. We don't know what's going on."

The foyer of the WPA era stone courthouse was impressive with its black-and-gray granite floor and walls, but it was cold. Their footsteps squeaked on the shiny floors as they crossed to the stairway that led downstairs to the sheriff's office. Somehow, Dacy knew that was where she should go.

Sheriff Grimm was at the desk in the front office, pecking at a typewriter when they approached, looking as if his big frame was going to topple the oak straight chair upon which he was perched. Without looking at them, he held up a finger, signaling them to wait. When he finished the line, he pulled the form from the typewriter with a flourish and signed it.

"Done." He looked up at them. "Ah. Dacy, girls." He nodded politely, then reached into his pocket and pulled out a five-dollar bill. "Jess, would you and Amy walk down to the feed store and get me a cup of coffee? Our machine's on the fritz here."

Jessica frowned, but she leaned across the desk to take the money. "We'll find out what's going on eventually, anyway," she told him. "Come on, Amy." They flounced out.

Dacy was quiet until they left. "What is going on?"

"Oh, nothing serious." Lester rose and started sorting through a ring of keys. "Nick started a fight with Cliff Tally and Kootch Koehler out at the Lazy A yesterday and I locked them all up. I wouldn't have done it if Nick hadn't bloodied my nose."

"Is Nick hurt?" Dacy couldn't mask her alarm.

"Nah." Lester waved a hand in dismissal. "He's got a bad shiner, and some bruises, that's all. But I want him out of here so I can go home. Everyone else is off for the holiday weekend, and if I can get Nick out of here, I can lock up and skedaddle. Earl and Kootch's daddies were here at dawn to collect their overgrown brats, and Jeff just got here. I called him to talk Nick into leaving. He's back there now. Damn fool says he doesn't feel like leaving. Door's unlocked and everything." Lester made a face. "I've never seen Nick act like that in his life. I don't know what got into him."

Had Nick confronted Cliff about his and Earl's attempts to destroy the Reynolds ranch? Dacy's heart sped up. She hoped he hadn't ruined any of their plans to stop the Tallys.

"Can I see him?"

"Yeah. Go on back. I'll keep the kids occupied until he's ready to go."

"Thanks." Dacy pushed open the heavy oak door that led to the small cells, then walked down a long corridor to Jeff's side. She searched the cell for Nick, gasping when she saw how swollen and bruised his face was.

"What happened? You look awful, Nick! Are you hurt?" She reached one hand through the bars toward him, then drew it back self-consciously. "Did something happen with Earl?"

Jeff answered tersely. "No."

"Then what's going on?" She looked from Jeff back to Nick. "The sheriff said you were in a fight."

"He thought you'd left. For good," Jeff offered. "He came tearing into town like a maniac and vented his feelings on Cliff Tally and Kootch Koehler."

Nick looked daggers at his brother.

Dacy was shocked. "Why did you think I'd left for good?"

"I guess I just flipped." He sounded exhausted. Dacy had seen him discouraged, but she'd never seen him like this. "I had expected you to leave for so long, and I didn't see the note you'd left me." Nick looked a little flushed under all his bruises.

Dacy felt as if she'd been hit in the chest with a bowling ball. She realized his reaction had come from his lack of trust.

Jeff coughed. "I'm going to wait outside."

Dacy's gaze remained on Nick, but she spoke to Jeff. "Jessica and Amy are getting coffee for Sheriff Grimm."

"I'll take them home with me." Jeff gave his brother a last pitiful look. "See you both later."

As Jeff walked away, Nick read through Dacy's note. When he finished, he raked his hand through his hair and turned away from her.

He spoke softly, with shame and regret in his voice. "I came to the house straight from the field to tell you that I'd decided to try. To work things out between us. I thought and I thought, Dace, for days. I finally decided that I would risk losing you because...I love you. With you I feel so...happy." He laughed ironically. "When I'm not afraid of losing you, I feel so good with you. I got to thinking I could move past the fear."

"I guess you were wrong."

"It looks that way."

"You were so afraid I'd leave that you manufactured an abandonment out of whole cloth."

"Rafe misled me. On purpose, I think."

"You didn't stop to think for even a second, Nick. You didn't bother to walk into my office, or check anywhere else. How many times have I told you that I wouldn't leave? This is my home now. How could you trust me so little as to think that I wouldn't talk to you if I was thinking about leaving? I love you, Nick! I know how you feel about this. I would never deliberately hurt you this way!"

He turned to face her. "I know that."

"You know that now. But what would happen the next time I had to leave unexpectedly? Would you react the same way?"

"Dacy, I know this isn't logical or reasonable in any way. I've been a fool. You're right. Everyone's right." Once more, his hand raked hard into his hair.

"Nick, I know better now what you had to deal with in Tammy. She's selfish, self-absorbed and careless. I would have torn her hair out for what she did to Jessica and Amy yesterday if she hadn't already been halfway to Hong Kong. But I'm not her." Tears of anger and regret filled her eyes. "Why can't you see that?"

"I do." His breath shuddered as he reached a hand to cradle her jaw. "That's what I realized up in the pasture. I know you aren't her."

She pulled away from his touch. "You reacted as if I were. You didn't trust me."

Fingers curling around the bars, he looked into her eyes, showing his pain, his fallibility. "I want to, Dacy. I want to learn to trust you. I can see how stupid I've been, but I think it's going to be different now."

"I wish I could be so sure. Because if you truly can't, as you told me before, we have no place left to go together. I love you. I believe you when you say you love me. But love is more than chemistry. It's more than affection and respect. There has to be trust, Nick, and commitment." She turned to look down the corridor toward the door. It seemed a long way off. "If you don't trust me, all we have left is a business partnership."

She left him without a backward glance.

Dacy went straight to Char's. Most of the morning rush had thinned, and Dacy took a cup of coffee to the back table and sat down. Lowering her head onto her folded arms, she wished she didn't have to deal with this. It hurt so much.

As soon as the last of the truckers had left, Char made her way back. "Come from the courthouse, didn't you?" she said, sliding into the opposite seat.

Dacy looked up. "How did you know?" She noted Char's bright red nails. Tammy would have a field day with those talons.

"Word gets around. Duane Tabor saw your car there, and everybody knows about the fight last night." Char laughed. "This is a small town. That was big news. What people don't know was why Nick picked a fight with Cliffie after years of paying him no mind."

Dacy figured she might as well tell Char to make sure everybody got the story straight.

Char shook her head in disapproval when Dacy told her about Tammy's early-morning phone call yesterday.

"That woman is a pestilence upon that family," she declared, tapping one nail firmly on the pressed-wood tabletop. "Yet Nick has never poisoned those girls of his against her, or kept them from seeing her. That's to his credit."

It was as if Char had radar that alerted her to Dacy's growing concern over Nick's ability to hold up his end of a relationship.

"I'm afraid he isn't always so noble." Dacy sighed. She told Char the rest of the story.

When she was finished, Char gave her an ironic smile. "Men are impossible, honey. Don't take it to heart."

"How can I not?" Dacy asked. "You know, I think I've been as big a fool as Nick. You told me yourself, the day after I came, when I was so fired up to get the renovations going and bully my way into Grandpa and Grandma's old house. You asked me if I thought I was being wise." She shook her head. "I wasn't wise at all."

"No, honey, but you love him. Love isn't always wise."

"I don't think love is going to be enough with Nick. I just don't know if I can live here, working with him, living in the same house until he gets a new one built, taking care of Jess and Amy. Not when he closes me out of his heart."

"Where else do you want to be?" Char challenged.

There was only one answer to that. "Nowhere else."

"Then you better give him another shot."

"I don't know. Do you think so?" She sounded doubtful to her own ears.

"Yes, I think so."

"What if another shot doesn't work?"

"You'll have to cross that bridge when you come to it. So what's your last shot going to be?"

Dacy looked out the window at the highway, thinking. "It's something I've been working on for the past month. I've been trying to talk people into coming out to the Reynolds place tomorrow to show their support for what Nick and Jeff are doing. Like a rally. I wanted to give that to Nick. But I also want him to see that I care enough about this place to get to know people and get involved. You told me to do that."

"I remember." Char's eyes twinkled.

"Unfortunately, I haven't had real good luck. Not too many people are interested in coming."

Char pulled a small notepad and a stubby pencil out of the pocket of the orange apron she wore. "You write down the names of everyone you've talked to for me. Then I want you to go tell Mildred Chamberlain everything you just told me about what happened with Tammy and you leaving and Nick going crazy and all."

"He's going to hate my gossiping," Dacy protested.

"Do you want to bring him around?"

Dacy nodded and began writing.

"You go talk to Mildred. We'll take it from there."

When she'd finished her list, Dacy gathered up her cup and her purse and rose. "I think you're a fairy godmother, Char."

Char cackled merrily. "And here I've been thinking I was just an old witch all these years. I'll have to tell my husband you said so. Maybe he'll be a little nicer to a fairy godmother. Now go on! There's a lot to do by tomorrow."

Dacy went.

Chapter Eighteen

When Dacy arrived at the house, it was barely midmorning. The alfalfa was blooming in the fields, and the air vibrated with the drone of bees working the tiny purple flowers. Rafe's van was parked beside the lilacs. Eyeing it with no little irritation, she intended to find out what exactly he'd said to Nick yesterday.

The house was oddly quiet. There was no sound of hammers and nail guns, country music or conversation. Last week Rafe had argued that it was best to not have the work crews there the day before the Fourth. Cy Chekpa was coming in that afternoon, and possibly some other law enforcement types. They had all agreed it would be better if there was no talk in the community about their presence, so Dacy had called a two-day holiday, preferring to avoid the risk of alerting Earl and Cliff. It hadn't been hard to convince Harley and his workers to take the day off, as hard as they'd been working.

Dacy found Rafe in her office, looking over some files. Dropping her purse on the floor beside the sofa bed, she confronted him, hands on her hips, and eyes snapping.

"What did you tell Nick yesterday?"

The man had the nerve to grin at her.

"I'm not laughing, Rafe. You told him I'd left him. Permanently."

"No. I told him you'd left. I let him believe you'd gone for good."

"Don't split hairs with me, Rafe. You did it on purpose. I want to know why."

"To give you both a chance to get past his asinine fear of you abandoning him and the girls."

"Great tactics," she snorted.

"He's faced it now, Dacy. He's seen what a fool he's been. Maybe he'll be able to leave it behind him." His dark gaze was steady.

Dacy wasn't at all sure about that. "I hope to heaven you're right, Rafael Saavedra."

"So do I," he admitted with a self-deprecating grimace. The flash of modesty didn't last long. "But then, I rarely make mistakes."

"It takes a lot to daunt your confidence, doesn't it?"

Inclining his head, he accepted her point. "I'm a lot like you."

She flopped onto the sofa and thought about that. "I suppose you are." Propping her feet on a cardboard box of files, she closed her eyes. "Which means you probably have the next twenty-four hours planned like clockwork."

"Of course. But you can take a nap now."

"Thank you, sir." She yawned.

"This afternoon I've asked everyone to be here at four to go over our plans."

"What was the good news you mentioned on the phone?"

"It'll hold until this afternoon."

She was so tired she didn't mind waiting. "Fine. Where are Jessica and Amy? They slept in the car, so I can't imagine they're napping now, but it's too quiet for them to be here."

"Dani took them for a barrel-racing lesson. I'm surprised you didn't see her car there when you drove past the Reynolds place."

"I was preoccupied." Pulling a pillow from behind the sofa, she tucked her feet beneath her and snuggled into a corner of the couch.

Rafe clucked his tongue. "You should be more alert."

Dacy's only answer was a delicate snore.

Dacy awoke disoriented. The phone was ringing. A quick lunge enabled her to reach the receiver before the answering machine picked up the call.

"Hello."

"Hello? Dacy, dear, is that you? You sound breathless." It was Mildred Chamberlain.

"I was asleep, Mildred."

"Well, I hope you got a good rest because I have some things I want you to do this afternoon. How are your baking supplies?"

What on earth? "Fine."

"Good. Then I want you to start baking. Cookies, brownies, cakes, that sort of thing. Make as much as you can, and bring it to the Reynoldses' place in the morning. What time is that group of people coming?"

"Ten."

"Get there early and bring the goodies," Mildred ordered before the connection went abruptly dead.

Dacy blinked at the receiver in her hand. She had her orders. How cookies and cakes were going to get Nick to trust her, she wasn't quite certain, but she was game to try anything. If Mildred said bake, then bake she would.

After, she amended to herself, a good hot shower.

* * *

Nick pulled into the drive at the Fallon place a little after noon. Still feeling like a prize fool, he'd figured out that Lester was itching for him to go home, so he'd gone. A shower and a change of clothes hadn't sweetened his mood much, but he had a lot of work to do yet for the visit tomorrow. The officials who were coming were also speaking at a big environmental rally in the Black Hills in the afternoon, before participating in a fireworks program at Mount Rushmore in the evening. Nick wasn't sure what that said about their commitments to the environment, but he was a realist. Politicians were necessary participants in any efforts to forge a better future for both the land and the people who made their living off it.

Dacy's car was the only one parked beside the lilac hedge. Nick parked beside it and sat for a while. He was unwilling to face her again. She was probably still mad, and he didn't blame her a bit.

Worse, he wasn't sure what he thought about where they'd left things. He knew he'd pushed Dacy so far that he wasn't sure she would be able to trust him, even if he thought he could live with the possibility of her leaving some day. It was a sobering thought.

She would have seen him drive in, though, so he might as well go on in and get to work.

He found her in the kitchen, lifting a ten-pound sack of flour onto the counter. Bent at the waist as she was, the material of her khaki shorts molded to her backside, drawing his attention. He saw that her hair was damp and curling around her shoulders. It was longer than it had been when she came. He liked it better. Swallowing hard, he squelched the desire to go to her and wrap her in his arms.

But what would he say? He'd thought he was ready to begin a relationship on fair and equal terms, but he hadn't been.

Dacy turned and saw him. The flour landed with a thud on the counter.

For the first time since she'd come back, Nick saw wariness in her eyes when she looked at him. She didn't smile at him, and she didn't speak.

"I have some calls to make. I thought I'd do it here in the office." He pointed toward the door.

Without expression, she nodded once, then turned away from him.

Icy dread weighted his gut like a millstone as Nick realized that, finally, after months of his wishing she would, she believed what he had been telling her. At long last, it was clear that Dacy believed that he couldn't give what she wanted in a relationship. She had given up.

It wasn't a satisfying victory.

The meeting that afternoon went smoothly. Cy Chekpa, the tall, barrel-chested Lakota federal marshal arrived with another marshal, Jed Groton, equally tall but lankier. Both of them looked like ranchers in jeans and denim jackets, driving a Bronco with Montana plates instead of the requisite dark sedan the feds were known for.

"We're undercover," Cy joked to Dacy when he shook her hand gently. Dacy laughed, liking him instantly.

They quickly got down to business. Cy and Jed outlined their plans for Jed to man a surveillance camera, positioned in the forest near the pasture Earl planned to destroy. Jed wanted to get out to the site before dark to look around, then come back to set the video cameras up under the cover of nightfall.

"I'll ride out with you, if you'd like," Dani volunteered. "We could make it look like a trail ride. If we leave from the corral over at the other place, it's about an hour's ride away."

Jed, who was proverbially tall, dark and handsome with a silky moustache to boot, nodded his approval. "That sounds good," he said.

"Rafe," Dacy reminded him, "you said you had some news. What is it?"

"That's right. After talking to Roy Holloway, I got suspicious about what happened to Nick and Jeff's last insurance payment. Cy, you already know this, but for the rest of you, I have it on good authority that the envelopes containing Nick's payments are on top of one of Earl's file cabinets, right underneath a pile of South Dakota Historical Society Quarterlies."

Nick swore softly and Jeff muttered, "I knew Earl had to have something to do with that."

"How do you know that?" Dacy asked. Then she remembered that Rafe had been gone when Tammy called. "Oh. Do you mean that you—?"

Rafe cut her off. "Careful, Dacy." He cast a warning eye toward Cy and Jed, then grinned wickedly. "I can't reveal my sources. Suffice it to say they are reliable."

He had to have broken into Earl's office.

"Do you have the necessary warrants?" he asked Cy.

Cy tapped the file folder in front of him. "Right here."

Nick had been quiet up until that point, and Dacy had avoided looking at him. Even so, she was aware of his every movement. When he reached for a cookie, she noticed. When he jotted down a note or two in his file, she knew it. Now, without looking up, she knew he was getting ready to speak. His chest expanded, and he glanced around the table. His eyes lingered on her, and she felt it like the touch of the wind.

All this she was aware of, but she also felt defeated in a way she never had with Nick. She'd always been so sure they would be able to work things out. Now she didn't know at all.

She listened to his voice, deep and confident, as he outlined the schedule for the delegation visit tomorrow. Cy knew the men in charge of security and didn't anticipate any problems with them.

"We should have Tally out of the way before the congressmen and the BLM guys ever get here," Cy commented. "The biggest problem I see is that Tally will destroy part of that meadow before we can stop him. I hate to see that."

"Jeff and I have talked about that," Nick told him. "We don't feel good about it, but we want to stop this nonsense. We don't have as strong a case against Earl without catching him in the act."

"We can stop him without losing too much of the meadow," Rafe assured everyone. "Cy, Jed, Jeff and I will camp out in the forest near the meadow, and we'll radio you here at the house as soon as things start moving. We'll also let Lester Grimm know what's going on."

"I guess we're as ready as we're going to be," Nick said, glancing around. "Everything's under control. What does everyone say to a barbecue?"

"Sounds great." Cy stood and stretched. "Your beef?"

"Absolutely. Nothing but the best," Nick said, grinning. "Where's that charcoal?"

He looked different, Dacy thought—more relaxed and more confident. The mess with Earl had taken a toll on him, but it was almost over. Tomorrow at this time, barring any unforeseen consequences, Earl would be in custody and Nick would be able to get on with his life and his business, unhindered. She wanted that for him. She wanted the best for him.

She had been so convinced she would be part of that picture.

The possibility that she was mistaken weighed heavily in her thoughts.

* * *

More than Dacy's relationship with Nick had gone wrong by sunset. Dacy had just finished putting away the last of the dinner dishes after a joint cleanup effort, when the phone rang. It was for Cy. Dacy went back outside with another pot of coffee.

When Cy came back out to join the rest of the group at the picnic table, he looked serious.

"What's up?" Nick asked.

"Jed and I are going to have to leave as soon as he gets back. I'm sorry." Cy shook his head.

Dacy, Nick, Jeff and Rafe all looked at him expectantly.

"There's a potential situation at Mount Rushmore with a Native American rights group. I have to get down there tonight." He frowned. "Man, I hate it when I know the guys on both sides of the fence."

Nick spoke for all of them. "We can handle things here."

"Contact the sheriff," Cy advised. "You'll need him now."

The expression on Nick's face made Dacy's heart ache. They had to make this work. Earl had put Nick through enough. They had to stop him.

Dacy's eyes trailed after Nick as he slowly walked away from them. She was acutely aware of the fact that Nick had not looked at her once since hearing Cy's news.

By the time the federal marshals left, Dacy found everyone else gathered close around the picnic table, planning what to do. It amazed her that four such strong-willed people had managed to sort out the situation almost before she got there.

Nick appeared to have taken charge. "All right," he was saying as she approached. "Rafe and Dani will go back out to the meadow tonight and set up the video equipment Jed left. Dani knows where to put it."

"We'll stay there tonight," Rafe interjected. "I want to be there when Earl shows up."

Jeff scowled at Dani but didn't say anything.

"Okay," Nick concurred. "Dani, you're going to call your mother before you leave and ask her to keep Jess and Amy overnight?"

"Yeah. I'm sure it will be no problem."

"Jeff, you'll drive them out to Edna's?"

His brother nodded. "Right. Then I'm going to stop by Tally's and see if I can't slow down that dozer a little bit in the morning. That should give Lester time to get his butt out of bed and out to the meadow."

"That leaves me to pay Lester a visit, then," Nick said. "I hope he doesn't shoot me first."

"He may." Jeff cuffed Nick on the shoulder lightly. "He'll think you want to sit in his jail all night again."

Nick stalwartly avoided looking at Dacy, but his neck flushed a dull red.

"I'll go with you," she announced.

That got Nick's attention. "You don't have to."

"I want to. Besides, Lester will feel sorry for me, having to put up with you and your shenanigans, and he'll be more amenable to helping us."

Nick looked doubtful.

Jeff rose. "Take her, Nick. She's got a point. Lester was ready to spit and roast you this morning."

Nick's feelings were shuttered behind his enigmatic gray eyes when he finally looked at her. Dacy was used to his saying he didn't want her company, but tonight she would believe him if he refused her.

He didn't. "Let's go, then," he said, gathering up the files he needed to show Lester. "It's going to take a while for Lester to sort through all this. If we want to stop Earl, we'd better get moving."

* * *

It took Lester Grimm the better part of two hours to absorb all the information Nick and Dacy presented to him, including waiting for Cy Chekpa to call to confirm their story. After a brief conversation with the federal marshal, Lester was more cooperative, and he finally agreed to help them out.

"Any chance I can get a couple hours' shut-eye first? You kept me up most of last night, too." Lester leveled a baleful glare at Nick.

"I know, and I'm sorry for it," Nick said contritely.

"You two work things out yet?" It was a conversational question, as if he expected they had.

Their awkward silence was all the answer Lester needed.

"I see you haven't. Well, that makes me feel a little better. If I have to lose two nights' sleep because of you, Reynolds, you ought to suffer, too. Now get on out of here. I'll be out at your old place at six."

Was Nick suffering? Dacy looked over at him, but he refused to meet her eyes. His expression was unreadable.

Chapter Nineteen

At five o'clock in the morning on the Fourth of July, Dacy was dressed and ready to go. All the cookies and cakes she'd made the day before were loaded into the back of the car since she didn't know if she would have time to come back for them later. Despite having had far too little sleep over the past two days, Dacy hadn't been able to sleep at all.

On her way out the door, the phone rang and she charged back to the office to answer it.

"Hello, is this the Reynolds residence?" The woman on the line spoke with cool professionalism.

"Yes." Nick had had her drop him off at the bunkhouse last night, but she wasn't going to quibble details when she was in a hurry.

"Is Nick Reynolds available?"

"No," Dacy told the woman. "He's not in."

"Are you Mrs. Reynolds?"

"Yes," she lied without hesitation.

"My name is Deborah Childress from Congressman Green's office. I'm coordinating the congressman's visit to your ranch this morning, along with some of the administrators from the BLM. We've received a report of severe thunderstorms west of you in Montana that are supposed to pass through your area around noon. I'm sorry, but we're going to have to cancel the visit."

"No! You can't do that!" Dacy's mind raced, trying to think of ways to talk this calm, detached woman out of canceling the visit. It would break Nick's heart. "There must be something we can do."

"I'm sorry, but the congressman is scheduled to speak later in the afternoon at the rally in Spearfish, and then at Mount Rushmore this evening. We can't risk a delay, Mrs. Reynolds."

"Can you come earlier? Before the storms come through?"

"I don't think so, Mrs. Reynolds. The congressman has to sleep sometime."

"Nick has been preparing for this visit for months," Dacy pleaded. *So have I,* she thought. *And I need this chance.*

"I'm sorry." Ms. Childress was about to hang up.

"Wait! Where can I reach you?"

Ms. Childress paused, clearly reluctant to give her a phone number.

"Nick will want to talk to you himself, I'm sure," she coaxed. "Please, Ms. Childress, we've put a lot of effort into this visit."

"All right." She rattled off two numbers—one at a hotel, the other a car phone—then hung up.

Dacy punched the number at the bunkhouse as soon as she got a dial tone. "Nick? Something's come up. I have to make a few phone calls. I'll be there in twenty minutes." She hung up without waiting for an answer.

Dacy hoped Jeff had succeeded in slowing down the bulldozer. They were going to need every minute he could give them. She flipped through Nick's card file quickly.

Crossing her fingers for luck, Dacy pulled Mitch Avery's card from the rings and prayed he was at one of the four different numbers Nick had for him at homes across the country. She tried the Montana ranch first.

A sleepy voice answered. "Hello, Annamaria?" She was in luck. They were there. "This is Dacy Fallon. I'm sorry to call so early, but we have an emergency. Is Mitch there?"

After six more calls to powerful politicians and business people, four of whom she reached, and all of whom she had awakened far too early to ask for favors on a holiday morning, Dacy ran to the car. Praying for strings effectively pulled in high places, she drove like a demon into the rising sun.

Pulling into the yard at the Reynoldses' home place, Dacy saw the Antelope County sheriff's car was parked in front of the bunkhouse. Lester Grimm and one of his deputies, Fred Gruen, were leaning against the back of it. Fred, as tall as Lester but outweighing him by fifty pounds, was a welcome sight. In their reflector sunglasses, with their guns tucked into holsters at their sides, Lester and Fred looked up to any challenge Earl and Cliff might pose.

Dacy hopped out of the car just as Nick came jogging over with the cell phone in hand. "Let's go," he hollered. "Rafe said Earl, Cliff and Kootch Koehler are out there, and they've just about got that bulldozer running." He yanked open the car door, jumping in and sliding the key into the ignition in one movement. Dacy barely made it in before he gunned the engine.

"What the hell kept you, anyway?" Nick spoke sharply.

The cell phone on the seat between them rang. Nick swore as he groped for it, but Dacy made a quick lunge and retrieved it.

"Hello?"

"Mrs. Reynolds? This is Deborah Childress again."

"Is it Rafe?" Nick asked impatiently. "Give it to me."

She mouthed, "No," and shook her head at him. "Yes, Ms. Childress. What can I do for you?"

The woman laughed. "Congressman Green has decided to include the visit to your ranch in this morning's itinerary, after all. He wasn't able to get the entire delegation together, but he and Robert Tobias from the BLM and a few others are on their way out there right now. They should arrive by helicopter in about twenty minutes. I trust you'll be able to accommodate the change in plans?"

"Yes! Of course we will! We'll be there."

"Good luck, then."

"Ms. Childress?" Dacy caught her before she hung up. "Thank you. This means more to me than you know."

The congressman's aide laughed once more. "Mrs. Reynolds, I doubt there's anything you want that you don't know how to get." She hung up, leaving Dacy to face the one thing in the world she didn't know how to get—Nick.

"Well?" he asked, eyes flashing with impatience as they flew over the bumps and ruts in the road. "What was that all about?"

"We have a big problem, Nick." She punched a number into the phone. "We have to turn around right now. We've got to be back at your barns and corrals to meet Congressman Green and Robert Tobias in twenty minutes." The phone rang in her ear, but no one answered. She cut the connection. "There's been a change in plans."

"What?" Nick roared.

"Watch out!" she cried as the car started to slide during the sharp turn onto the dirt road that led back to the meadow.

"Everything's under control," Nick insisted, neatly pulling the big car through the turn.

"No, it isn't." She began explaining about Ms. Childress's earlier call and the thunderstorms.

Nick swore fluently.

"Nick, we have to go back. Stop the car so we can tell the sheriff what's going on. The others can handle it."

If anything, he accelerated.

"Nick! You've worked for years to support the kind of legislation Congressman Green is interested in. Let Jeff get Earl. We have to go back. Stop the car!"

Abruptly, Nick pulled off the track, slowing and making a wide loop in the unfenced pasture. Lester slowed and stopped, then backed up along the track to meet Nick.

Nick came to a stop and explained the situation to the sheriff through his open window. Then he hit the gas pedal and they were off.

A few minutes later, they drove back into the deserted yard in front of the bunkhouse and barn.

"This is great." Nick turned off the engine. "There's no one here to meet these guys, who are going to want to make speeches and politic. We're in the middle of trying to stop Earl from destroying our showpiece meadow, and these guys are going to be itching to get out of here." He flung the door open and jumped out, scanning the sky.

Dacy grabbed the cell phone. "I have to make a few calls. I'll be back in a minute." She hurried away from him toward the bunkhouse, punching Char's number into the phone. She answered on the first ring.

"Hello? Char? This is Dacy. We have a small problem with the delegation visit," she began.

A few quick words were all it took. Char didn't ask any questions, accepting Dacy's request with characteristic equanimity. By the time she got off the phone, the helicopter was in sight.

Nick lifted his hat and raked a hand back through his hair. Dacy knew he was worried.

"I need to get out to that meadow, Dacy. I want the congressman and Bob Tobias to see what we're up against, and how important it is that we have more public support for new ranching. As soon as they're down, we'll head out there," he said, raising a hand against the glare of the morning sun.

"Are you sure that's wise?" Dacy asked, but the roar from the helicopter's motor drowned her out.

The big military helicopter flew overhead, then hovered for a moment before it gently dropped toward the ground. Nick took off his hat to keep it from blowing away in the wash from the blades. Dacy plastered a smile on her face and prayed for the best.

As the delegation members exited the craft, Dacy saw in a glance that less than half the number they had expected had come. She recognized Congressman Tony Green as the balding but square-jawed former football hero dressed in perfectly pressed khakis and shirtsleeves. The shorter man next to him was probably Bob Tobias, from the Bureau of Land Management. He was also a Colorado rancher, according to Nick. There were three other men she didn't know.

Nick ushered the men away from the helicopter, performing hasty introductions at the edge of the field.

"This is a desolate area," Congressman Green commented, looking around. "How far are you from the nearest town?"

"Kenyon is twenty miles northeast of here," Nick answered, shepherding the group toward the barn, where the cars were parked.

"And it's not much of a town, even in South Dakota," Jim Fredericks, a state legislator, added. He scanned the empty ranch yard. "I guess our change in plans left you unprepared for our visit."

"Not at all," Dacy interjected quickly.

Nick kept everyone moving and shot her a grateful look. "First, gentlemen, I'd like to begin your visit with a tour of the ranch, including a two-hundred-acre meadow at the base of the butte that my brother and I have restored to its natural state." He opened the car doors and got everyone in the Suburban, even though Ed, the security guy, ended up in the back with the cookies and cakes.

Nick didn't seem to notice the looks of astonishment the congressman and his cronies were giving them. Dacy did, and she sought to divert them with information about the ranch's operations.

Dacy kept talking and pointing, refusing to let herself so much as glance at the speedometer. Every bend and sway in the road sent her rocking into Nick, wedged as she was into the front seat between him and the congressman. His body was solid and warm when she was tossed up against him, and she gripped to his thigh hard to keep herself from toppling over onto Tony Green when the turns threw her in that direction. Aware of him as she was, and of his taut muscles vibrating with his impatience to reach the field to confront Early Tally directly, she also sensed that he was pleased with her performance. She thought she had surprised him.

To their credit, the visitors seemed genuinely interested. As they approached the butte, she segued into talking about how Nick and Jeff had restored the meadow they were nearing. The high trill of the cell phone interrupted her.

"Excuse me," she said, flipping open the phone. "Hello?"

Nick reached across her and peremptorily took the phone. "What's going on?" he asked, not slowing a whit.

Then he swore, dropped the phone in Dacy's lap and speeded up.

"Gentlemen," he announced as they hit a deep rut that sent everyone scrambling for purchase, "we're heading into an unfortunate situation at the meadow." Briefly, he explained what was going on. Then he stepped on the gas.

"What kind of insanity is this, Reynolds?" Congressman Green glared over Dacy's head at Nick. "Slow down, for Pete's sake!"

Nick concentrated on rounding the rocky spur of the butte that separated them now from the restored meadow. A moment later, the sound of a noisy engine and the scent of diesel fuel reached Dacy's ears and nose. As the trees on their left thinned, the meadow came into view.

Cliff Tally sat behind the wheel of the small bulldozer, scraping away the precious top layer of soil with all it's carefully nurtured plants, and the countless insects and small animals that comprised the fragile prairie ecosystem. Horrified, Dacy saw that he had cleared at least three acres.

Nick shouted over the combined noise of their jostling ride and the car and bulldozer engines. "Right now, Cliff Tally is vandalizing federal property. He just crossed the line from my land to forest service land, and what's more, he knows it."

Nick slammed on the brakes and hurled himself out of the car, running across the meadow toward Cliff. Dacy scrambled after him. Behind them, Lester flashed his lights and let the siren wail, driving past them into the meadow.

Chaos erupted around them. Jeff, Dani and Rafe raced out of the pine forest that bordered the north edge of the meadow, while Earl, who had been standing alongside the fence that separated the meadow from the pasture beyond it, turned to flee. Kootch Koehler ran for the flatbed they'd hauled the bulldozer in on. Lester pulled his revolver on Cliff, shouting that he was under arrest. Behind her, Dacy heard the delegation members hustling to catch up with the action.

Nick saw Earl take off and gave chase. Jeff singled out Kootch. Dacy raced after Nick, her sides heaving by the time she got close enough to see him make the flying tackle that knocked Earl's legs out from under him.

Earl landed facedown at the edge of the trees, but flipped over quickly, trying to gain his feet again. He kicked viciously at Nick, who dodged aside, defraying the main force of the blow that landed on his thigh.

Nick reached for Earl's shirtfront and hauled him up so that their faces were scant inches apart. Hatred blazed in Earl's eyes, and the veins in his neck looked as though they would pop.

Nick was ice cold, his gray eyes narrowed and almost without expression. For a moment, they looked at each other, absorbing the change in roles, where the hunted became the hunter, the hunter the prey.

Nick shook Earl once, hard, the way he'd shaken Cliff that night in April when he'd shot at the calf. Neither man spoke.

Fred Gruen brushed past her, handcuffs dangling. While Nick held Earl, he secured Earl's hands behind his back.

"Let him go, Reynolds," Fred ordered. "Earl Tally, you're being arrested on charges of..."

Fred's voice droned on, reciting the charges. Dacy didn't attend him carefully. Her attention was fixed on Nick. Flinging Earl away from him like an unsavory rodent, Nick turned on his heel and marched back across the meadow.

Dacy followed, unsure that he was aware of her presence. He stopped beside the long, violent gash that tore the meadow's fragile surface, and crouched down, laying one hand flat on the wounded earth.

The bulldozer engine died. Suddenly, the sound of the wind sighing through the pines was the only sound in the meadow. Nick closed his eyes and his lips moved, forming silent words. In his face, she saw his regret and his pain for the hurts inflicted on the meadow by Earl and Cliff's malicious actions. She also saw profound respect, and she saw love.

Dacy longed to touch him, but something held her back. It was a private moment, between Nick and the land he loved. He was in conversation. Quietly, she eased away from him, aware as she had never been of the depth of his attachment and commitment to this land, this way of life. He had been right when he'd told her that his connection here differed from hers. She was in awe of what she saw in him.

Dacy knew that she wanted something more than a house, a family and a place in a community. She wanted what he had, the connection she saw in him, the sense of relation he had to this meadow, the buttes, the creek, the prairies and all that shared these spaces with him. She hoped with all her heart, that he would understand that she would gladly spend a lifetime, if that was what it took, to build the grace she saw in him right now, because as surely as the blackbirds sang in May, Dacy knew that she would live in Antelope County the rest of her life—with Nick or without him.

Chapter Twenty

All at once, Dacy found herself surrounded by people, Congressman Green leading the pack.

"Why are these people destroying this meadow?" he demanded of Dacy.

"The Tallys oppose new ranching because they are afraid it threatens their right to make a living using traditional ranching practices," she told him quietly. "Earl was trying to make a point to you, as an elected official."

Rafe and Dani joined them. "Tally has been systematically trying to put the Reynolds Ranch out of business," Rafe added. "Part of his actions were based on opposition to the Reynoldses' ideas about ranching, but a good part of his motivation was greed, plain and simple. He wanted control of the lease lands from the Reynolds and Fallon places so he could expand his operations."

The congressman's gaze followed Lester as he led Cliff toward the Bronco. "If this degree of opposition to new ranching is widespread, I have to rethink my intention to support a bill that would make federal money available for your projects," he said.

Dacy felt a warm presence behind her and knew that Nick had joined them. "Changes always incur opposition," he said.

Bob Tobias shook his head. "I don't know, Nick. This is pretty extreme." He gestured toward the spoiled part of the meadow.

"Earl Tally is one man." Dacy was adamant. "You can't base your decisions about new ranching on one incident."

"She's right," Dani said. "Most people in Antelope County would be shocked by what's gone on here."

"Look," Tony Green interrupted "when we arrived at your ranch, there were only two people here to meet us. There was no show of community support, no opportunity to hear what people think about what you're doing out here. Don't get me wrong—I support you in principle. But based on what I've seen this morning, I can't lend my support to substantive changes in federal lease land policies or to legislation funding money for pilot programs. Maybe this new ranching isn't an idea whose time has come, folks." Like the politician that he was, the congressman offered his hand to Nick. Nick accepted it without enthusiasm. "I'm sorry, Reynolds."

The blank expression on Nick's face made Dacy's heart sink. More than anything, she wanted to redeem this visit for him, to give him the opportunity to show Tony Green and the others the support they wanted to see. She knew Nick didn't think it was there.

"Congressman Green, we haven't finished with the tour of the ranch. Perhaps you'll reconsider before you leave," she suggested with more confidence than she felt.

Nick put his hand on her shoulder. "It's all right, Dacy." He addressed the delegation members. "I appreciate the effort you all made to come out here this morning. If you'll excuse me, Rafe and I need to talk to Sheriff Grimm, and then we can take you back to the helicopter."

Dacy watched him walk away, his shoulders straight, his head high, his gait measured. The love she felt for him coursed through her as she admired his grace and strength in the face of bitter disappointment. Rafe followed him, and the delegation members drifted off.

Feeling a touch on her arm, she turned. Dani was beside her. For the first time, Dacy noticed that her cousin's hair was falling loose from its clip, her clothes were littered with pine needles and smudges of dirt, and there were shadows under her eyes. Dani certainly bore the marks of a night spent hidden in the trees, waiting for Earl.

"I'm sorry," she said. "At least we got Earl and Cliff. Jeff got Kootch before he could take off, too."

Dacy couldn't muster even a small smile. Grasping Dani's hand, she gave it a squeeze. "This visit isn't over yet. Dani, can you ask Jeff to surreptitiously loosen a spark plug on my car, or something? And don't let the congressman know you have the 4-Runner out here. I have a plan."

Dacy got hold of Char at the bunkhouse. The older woman tsk-tsked at yet another change in plans. "You're lucky I'm a resourceful fairy godmother, young lady," she clucked at Dacy after getting directions. "Not too many others would be able to deliver on this one, but I'll do my best."

Hanging up, Dacy forced herself to walk at a sedate pace over to the sheriff's Bronco where Nick and Rafe were talking to Lester. Earl and Cliff sat silently in the back seat behind the bulletproof panel, hands still cuffed behind their backs. Fred had Kootch Koehler secured and sitting on the ground a short distance away. She signaled to Rafe that she wanted to talk to him.

He excused himself and they walked just out of hearing distance. Dacy explained what was happening. "Can you delay things here so that we don't have to go right back to the ranch? Don't ask why. Just trust me."

Rafe looked at her speculatively and nodded.

Dacy prayed she was doing the right thing.

Twenty-five minutes later, Tony Green was pacing up and down in front of the Suburban with Bob Tobias as his shadow. "We have a tight schedule, Reynolds," he shouted as he stomped past Nick. Jeff had the hood up on the Suburban and was gazing at the engine with a baleful eye. "What the hell is wrong with this car?"

Jeff cast a patient look at Dacy. "Dacy, have you got a can of oil in the back?"

She did. Jeff made a production of puncturing the top of the can and pouring it slowly into the engine.

Bob Tobias finally came over and stood at Jeff's side, looking down at the engine. "Why don't you screw that spark plug back in?" he asked softly. Tobias recognized stalling when he saw it.

Jeff cast Dacy an apologetic look. "Oh. What do you know. That's got to be the problem. I wonder how that happened."

Tobias gave him a warning look.

Dacy shrugged, then looked out toward the plains. There was no sign of Char or anyone else. Lester was anxious to get his prisoners back to the courthouse, and Nick was scowling at them.

"I hope the rest of today is more productive than this morning's been," the congressman grumbled.

Was that a trail of dust rising along the road? Dacy shielded her eyes again and squinted. Yes, she thought it was. Her spirits rose a bit.

"Just a few more minutes, Jeff," Dacy whispered.

"Ouch!" He snatched his hand back, shaking it, then applying his handkerchief to his thumb. "Damn thing's jammed. I need a sprocket wrench. Maybe Lester's got one." He ambled off.

Tobias looked at Dacy. "How'd he get that thing loosened without any of us seeing him?"

Nick heard him. "What's going on here?"

Dacy prided herself on possessing an inscrutable expression that rivaled a champion poker player's. She gave it to Nick.

"Don't give me that look, Dace. What's going on?"

The sound of a pickup engine shifting gears reached them, then the vibration of the motor buzzing in Dacy's ears.

"I think we have some company." Dacy took Nick's hand in hers and pulled him with her to watch.

Char's big blue club cab pickup rounded the outcropping of rock that separated the meadow from the plain beyond. Char's husband Bill was behind the wheel. As soon as they saw Dacy, Char leaned across the cab and hit the horn a couple of times.

Behind them, Dacy heard more horns answer in response—a lot of horns. Excitement flashed through her as another pickup and then another followed the Potters through the gap at the bottom of the meadow.

She looked at Nick. He was staring at the vehicles, frowning.

"What are these people doing out here?" he asked.

"I think they came out to show their support," Dacy told him, tightening her grip on his hand.

He gripped hers back hard. "Did you do this?"

"With a *lot* of help."

Nick watched the growing line of cars and pickups driving into the meadow. Lining up along the east edge, they formed a semicircle, like at a local rodeo where the cars parked in a ring around the arena.

Char and Bill hopped out of the cab and came forward. Others followed. Edna got out of the next car, along with Jessica and Amy. The girls raced across the thick meadow to their father's side, wedging themselves between Nick and Dacy, but not breaking their joined hands. Jeff joined them, and the delegation members gathered slightly to one side.

Within a minute, they stood at the center of a large group of their Antelope County neighbors. For a long moment, they looked at one another appraisingly.

Dacy looked at Nick. His gray eyes were opened wide, and a muscle in his jaw ticked, betraying more emotion than simple surprise. He glanced at her. She smiled and rubbed her thumb over the back of his hand. If he squeezed any harder, she was going to have nerve damage, she was certain, but she didn't care.

Clyde Chamberlain took off his feed cap and stepped forward. He addressed Jim Fredericks. "Hello, Jim. We're pleased you could come out here today to visit us in Antelope County. We don't get a lot of attention, as a rule, from you east river politicians, so we're happy you've come. I'd like to welcome the rest of you folks from Washington, as well. I'm here this morning, though, to hear Nick Reynolds talk about his ideas about ranching." He nodded to Nick.

"Nick, I hear you got trout in Badger Creek again. My granddaddy used to fish for trout up here in the buttes. I want to hear what you boys have done to make this a good fishing stream again." He replaced his cap and stepped back.

Ross Kincaid stepped forward next. "I was looking at your pasture as we drove back here," he said. "It looks good, and things have been on the dry side this year. I'd like to hear more about your range programs."

And so it went. One after another, the residents of surrounding ranches and from town offered Nick and Jeff their support and questions. Several of them expressed dismay over Earl's actions. As the last person was finishing, Char stepped to Dacy's side and whispered in her ear.

Dacy nodded. When the last speaker was through, she introduced Congressman Green and the other members of the delegation. "If you don't mind, I'm sure the congressman would like to say a few words to all of you."

There was polite applause, and Tony Green took the floor. Dacy pried her fingers loose from Nick's and slipped away when Char signaled to her.

"I thought you said there were only a few people," Dacy chided as they unloaded a long folding table from the back of Char's pickup.

"I didn't want you to be disappointed," Char explained.

When they had the table up, Dacy gave Char a hug. "Thank you."

"Well, I hope it works. That boy needs you, plain as eyes on potatoes. Now let's get this food set out. We want to make a good impression, after all."

By the time Congressman Green, Bob Tobias and Jim Fredericks had given their speeches, some of the others drifted back to help. In no time, they had set out tables draped in red, white and blue bunting, lawn chairs, picnic blankets and had a couple of portable barbecues firing up. There were two washtubs filled with ice and soft drinks, and the main table held an assortment of salads, casseroles, chips, beans and desserts. Char and Mildred Chamberlain had organized everything, and supervised with careful eyes. Leaving Dacy free to circulate once the speeches were finished. Gratefully, she made her way from group to group, thanking each and every one of the people there for coming.

* * *

Nick watched the crowd disperse in the direction of the food and drinks when Jim Fredericks finished talking. Tony Green came over to meet Jess and Amy.

"I'm going to find Dacy," Jessica announced, pulling Amy along with her.

"You have a wonderful family," the congressman told Nick.

"Yeah, they're great kids." Nick looked after them fondly.

"Your wife is something else, too. I was ready to throttle her for the delay, but she knew what she was doing. She's very impressive."

"She's not my wife," Nick corrected.

"You'd better rectify that soon, then, hadn't you?" He laughed. "As she hoped, I've reconsidered my support for new ranching projects in congress. I misjudged the situation. You have a great deal more support, albeit cautious support, than it appeared." Congressman Green clapped Nick on the shoulder. "I'm going to work the crowd a little. I'd like to leave in about twenty minutes. Can you get that car running?"

"Sure." Nick grinned.

Left alone, he watched the crowd, nodding when he caught Carol Jean's eye, tipping his hat to Mrs. Chamberlain. Roy Holloway, the insurance man, approached him, offering a hand.

"You know, Nick, I had no idea Earl had tampered with your payments. That New York detective you hired told me Earl must have swiped them right off my desk, out from under my very nose. Now he says Tom Cochrane found the unopened payments in Earl's office this morning. First thing tomorrow, I'll get in touch with headquarters. We'll get you started on a new house in no time."

"Thanks, Roy. I appreciate it." Nick hadn't thought far enough ahead to realize that getting his house rebuilt was one of the results of unmasking Earl's crimes. Now that he did, he wasn't sure he wanted it. He'd been getting used to Dacy's house. He'd been getting used to Dacy.

Dacy. She had done this for him. Now she stood talking with Jerri Beyer, laughing at something the other woman said. Watching her, he saw how comfortable she was. She liked Jerri; he could tell by the way she smiled. By the easy greetings she shared with the men, women and children who walked by her, he could tell that they liked her, too.

Despite her city attitudes and ways, Dacy was doing pretty well in Antelope County. People were making a place for her, giving her support. Look at what they'd done for her today.

It suddenly hit Nick that his neighbors hadn't just come for Dacy. They'd come for him and Jeff, too. They'd asked good questions and complimented his work, even though he knew full well that many of them were still leery of new ranching. And he had Dacy to thank for renewing his relationships with his neighbors.

He walked over to her, intending to steer her away from the group for a private conversation. "Excuse us," Nick said to Jerri, taking Dacy's arm.

Jerri excused herself to look for her son.

"Thank you." He smiled at Dacy. "Green changed his mind."

Dacy's eyes sparkled when she smiled. "Good. That's really good, Nick."

"How did you do this? How did you get everyone out here?"

"I've been talking to people. Most of them have a lot of questions about what you're doing, but they never got a chance to ask you. Earl used their natural distrust of new ideas to create a sense of overwhelming opposition to new ranching, but you can see that he was wrong. People need some time to adjust, to ask questions, to think about things. But I didn't do this alone. It took Char and Mildred's help to get them here. I couldn't have done it alone."

Her words made him realize that he was more like his neighbors than he'd thought. "Time to adjust," he repeated.

"Yeah." She stopped, uncertain what he was thinking, he could tell.

"Do you think," he asked, gazing into her sea green eyes, "that maybe I've been guilty of the same sort of foot dragging?"

Excitement flashed through her eyes, only to be quickly veiled. "What do you mean?"

He took both her hands in his. "If some of these folks have had a slow time coming around to the idea of new ranching, couldn't it be that maybe I've had a slow time coming around to some new ideas myself?"

"Maybe," she answered slowly. "Such as?"

"Such as the notion that a successful professional woman from New York might really prefer to live in Antelope County, South Dakota."

Her lips twitched, but she didn't smile. "There's that," she agreed.

"Or the idea that that same woman, as smart and as beautiful as she is, might really love a no-account rancher enough to stay with him for a good long time." He tugged her a little closer to him.

"Like maybe forever?"

He didn't answer right away. For one last time, he felt the cords that bound him to the past, to his failed marriage with Tammy, to the failures that had nearly cost him the ranch. He felt the tight constriction in his gut that had stopped him so many times before from accepting Dacy's love.

He let it go.

In that moment, it felt like a rod pierced him straight through the top of the head, zinging through his insides in a hot flash of certainty. Lodged in his gut like a glowing ball was the certain knowledge that he was willing to risk losing Dacy because he wanted to share his life with her more than he had ever wanted anything in his life.

He laughed. "Forever and a day, Dacy," he told her, claiming responsibility for his decision fully. "I've been a fool. I know it, and I know I've hurt you. I can't promise that I won't ever hurt you again, but I can promise to love you with the same commitment and care you've shown me these past few months. I love you, Dacy. I always have, and I always will. Yesterday you said love alone wasn't enough, without trust." He smiled down at her, drawing her into his arms, oblivious to the attention they were attracting. "I know you won't get bored and leave. I know." He tipped her chin up with one finger and found her eyes glowing. "Can you forgive me for not trusting what I know about you, for thinking that you'd gone?"

She nodded. "Yes."

He folded her into his embrace and closed his eyes, burying his nose in her hair. "Thank you." He breathed the words against her ear and felt a shudder ripple through her. "More than anything, Dacy, I want to live with you and love you, here in Antelope County—where I know you'll stay."

She pushed him back and looked him square in the eye. "Does this mean you'll marry me, now?"

"Yes, ma'am. I accept your proposal." He lifted her in one arm and swung her around, whooping like a bronc rider. Dacy squealed, too.

Holding Dacy tight in his arms, Nick gazed out at the crowd of his family, neighbors and friends.

"Hey, everyone, let me have your attention!" he called.

Dacy didn't let him finish. "I'm marrying this cowboy!" she shouted, snatching his hat off his head and tossing it into the air.

Applause and laughter erupted all around them. Jessica and Amy came rushing out of the crowd, whooping and hollering.

Nick ignored the hoopla to concentrate on kissing the laughing woman he had loved and wanted as his bride since he was seventeen. Some things, he thought as he kissed her quite thoroughly, were definitely worth waiting for.

Epilogue

As she often did, now that winter's hold on the land was loosening, Dacy stole away from the house toward the creek. This evening, the sky was streaked with fiery orange and yellows, the bare branches of the cottonwoods outlined starkly against the colored clouds.

She followed the creek for almost half a mile, then turned west to climb a rise from which she could watch the last light fade. It was cold, stinging cold on the exposed hill, with the west wind whipping her hair straight back. There would be a storm tonight, she thought, sinking her gloved hands deeper into the warm pockets of her down parka. She shouldn't have come out, but this was one night she had to.

As the light faded, she looked east, where the first faint stars peeked out in an indigo field. There, far away, under these very same stars, lay the life she had left behind. One year ago tonight, she had sat in an emergency room in a Manhattan hospital, listening to a doctor tell her that

Charlie had died. The doctor, a woman about her own age, had hugged her, saying she was sorry. She knew Dacy's life would never be the same, and she was so, so sorry.

Three weeks later Dacy had stepped out of her car into an evening much like this one, and indeed, her life had changed forever. She would always miss Charlie, she thought, but she was happy as she had never been in Manhattan.

"I've found it, Charlie," she whispered, praying that the wind would carry her words to wherever he was. "All the things I was missing and couldn't name. All the things we wanted for each other but couldn't give." She moved her buried hands close over her swollen belly while tears slid down her cheek, chilled to ice by the wind. "Goodbye, Charlie. I won't forget you. Not ever."

Turning back to the west, she let the wind scatter the last cold traces of her tears as the day faded. It was time to go back. She'd done what she had come for.

At the bottom of the hill, she met Nick coming toward her from the creek. He stopped and waited for her to join him.

"Are you ready to come in? I was worried." He glanced at her stomach, covered by the heavy coat.

Dacy laughed. "He won't get cold," she said, moving into his arms. She squeezed Nick tight.

He put his cheek to hers. "You're freezing."

"I have a warm heart," she told him, smiling.

His grin matched hers. "Let's go," he ordered, his arm around her, propelling her along with him. "Dani called. She and Rafe are in Miami, finishing a shoot, but they'll be here for Earl's trial in three weeks. Harley called, too. He's got his bids ready on the new house and Jeff wants to go over them with you before he gives him the go-ahead."

"I don't know why he doesn't stay here with us," Dacy said.

"He needs his own place. Maybe he'll decide to get married if he gets lonely enough."

They talked the rest of the brisk walk back. As they approached the house, Dacy slowed.

"What's wrong?"

"Nothing," she said. "I'm just admiring the house."

In the glow from the security lamp, it looked trim and tidy. All the siding had been repaired or replaced, the roof was new and tight, the porches straight and true. New white paint gleamed softly, and warm yellow light spilled from several windows.

"It looks even better from inside. Come on," Nick urged.

A sudden craving struck her. She was at her sixth month of pregnancy, and the cravings were getting worse. "Okay. I'm getting a craving again."

The glass rattled in the door when Nick pulled it shut behind them. Dacy stepped into the warm, bright kitchen that Harley had finally finished two weeks ago. Jess and Amy looked up at them from the round kitchen table where they were studying. A newborn calf nestled at their feet in a cardboard box filled with blanket scraps, and Snap, a tortoiseshell cat, lounged on a pile of schoolbooks.

Dacy's heart was so full she thought she might burst. Just a year ago, she hadn't even known she wanted this life.

"Hey, are there any of those watermelon pickles left?" Nick asked the girls.

Jessica jumped up and went to a cupboard. "There's only one jar left," she said.

"Break it out." Nick helped Dacy off with her coat. He placed one big hand over her belly. "Your baby brother's got a craving."

They all laughed. Jessica opened the pickle jar and poured them into a dish, which she brought straight over to Dacy.

Nick picked out a big chunk and held it to her lips. She accepted it eagerly. It was sweet and tangy with vinegar and cloves, crisp and tender. She closed her eyes and she might have been eight years old again, standing next to her Gran.

Opening her eyes, she met Nick's gray gaze, his eyes crinkling with a smile. No, she wasn't eight years old, she thought, as she watched his eyes fill with desire.

"I love you," she whispered. "I'm glad you finally married me."

"Later," he whispered back.

Dacy's toes curled in her boots thinking about the promise that one word offered.

* * * * *

This July, watch for the delivery of...

An exciting new miniseries that appears in a different Silhouette series each month. It's about love, marriage—and Daddy's unexpected need for a baby carriage!

Daddy Knows Last unites five of your favorite authors as they weave five connected stories about baby fever in New Hope, Texas.

- **THE BABY NOTION** by Dixie Browning
  (SD#1011, 7/96)
- **BABY IN A BASKET** by Helen R. Myers
  (SR#1169, 8/96)
- **MARRIED...WITH TWINS!**
  by Jennifer Mikels
  (SSE#1054, 9/96)
- **HOW TO HOOK A HUSBAND (AND A BABY)**
  by Carolyn Zane
  (YT#29, 10/96)
- **DISCOVERED: DADDY** by Marilyn Pappano
  (IM#746, 11/96)

Daddy Knows Last arrives in July...only from

DKLT